"THE DIFFICULTIES AND PLEASURES OF FAMILY
LIFE . . . PORTRAYED WITH INSIGHT AND LOVE."
—*New York Newsday*

"A persuasive, aware, abundant novel . . . peopled with characters I came to know the way one knows the cast that
animated Dickens. This book goes deep. There is wisdom
here, and family history, and a sense of perspective . . .
an exploration of how the world of our mothers and fathers
and theirs before them informs our habits and choices and
ways, and those of our children. I settled into *Years from
Now*, and was so comforted and convinced, I backed right
up to read it again."

—Mary Robison

GARY GLICKMAN is a graduate of Brown University.
The recipient of a 1986 New York Foundation for the Arts
grant, he has had work published in *Vanity Fair* and *The
Mississippi Review*, and has taught fiction writing at Vassar
College. He lives in East Hampton, New York, where he
is at work on a new novel.

YEARS
FROM
NOW

A NOVEL BY

Gary Glickman

A PLUME BOOK

NEW AMERICAN LIBRARY

NEW YORK AND SCARBOROUGH, ONTARIO

PUBLISHER'S NOTE

This book is a work of fiction. Names, characters, places, and incidents either are the product of the author's imagination or are used fictitiously, and any resemblance to actual persons, living or dead, events, or locales is entirely coincidental.

NAL BOOKS ARE AVAILABLE AT QUANTITY DISCOUNTS WHEN USED TO PROMOTE PRODUCTS OR SERVICES. FOR INFORMATION PLEASE WRITE TO PREMIUM MARKETING DIVISION, NEW AMERICAN LIBRARY, 1633 BROADWAY, NEW YORK, NEW YORK 10019.

PLUME TRADEMARK REG. U.S. PAT. OFF. AND FOREIGN COUNTRIES
REGISTERED TRADEMARK—MARCA REGISTRADA
HECHO EN CHICAGO, U.S.A.

SIGNET, SIGNET CLASSIC, MENTOR, ONYX, PLUME, MERIDIAN and NAL BOOKS are published *in the United States* by NAL PENGUIN INC., 1633 Broadway, New York, New York 10019, *in Canada* by The New American Library of Canada Limited, 81 Mack Avenue, Scarborough, Ontario M1L 1M8

Original hardcover designed by Julie Duquet.

Library of Congress Cataloging-in-Publication Data

Glickman, Gary, 1959–
    Years from now.

    I. Title.
[PS3557.L52Y4 1988]   813'.54   88-5184
ISBN 0-452-26142-2 (pbk.)

First Plume Printing, September, 1988

1 2 3 4 5 6 7 8 9

PRINTED IN THE UNITED STATES OF AMERICA

For my mother,
Babette Schlosser Bergner,
and in memory of my grandmother,
Esse Yawitz Schlosser

*Many thanks to the New York Foundation for the Arts;
the Virginia Center for the Creative Arts; the MacDowell Colony;
my agent, Andrew Wylie, for a thousand moments of insight,
discovery, and wise counsel; my editor, Adam Gopnik, for a
shared beginning; and Ann Close, for a gracious and helpful adoption.
To D.L. and M.W., gratitude and love.   G.G.*

YEARS

FROM

NOW

The Man Upstairs

It is not merely because of the horizon—mountains on one side, a city on the other—that for generations certain families of Lewiston have thought themselves very close to the center of the universe. The land itself seems to change right there, where glaciers, cutting mountains as they melted south, finally stopped, disappeared into lakes, and left the farmland in peace. Even on maps the town lies just in the middle of the state, halfway between the Palisades of the Hudson and the cliffs of the Delaware Water Gap, as if New Jersey itself were a great island, floating between two rivers. It was there that the first two highways of the colony long ago met and crossed each other, north-south and east-west, and a village sprang up. It was there that Thomas Paine came for refuge, that Alexander Hamilton found his bride, and that Samuel Morse first tapped out his amazing code. Washington stopped there two winters with his army, surveying the British in New York from the vantage of Lewiston's foothills, while still close enough to the safer wilderness of Pennsylvania. Valley Forge is more infamous, more celebrated a winter, but the blizzards of the two Lewiston years were the worst of the eighteenth century, troops shuddering through April in crude log cabins and flimsy tents, and locally, at least, those winters are considered the more important; developers still find mass graves in the woods, or the half-buried ruins of a fieldstone hearth. The streets and schools are named for those heroes of revolution, and the town itself, as well as the surrounding township, the hills, even the whole county are named for its native governor, a signer of nothing less than the Declaration of Independence. Even the quiet, shady street where Zellie was born had been named for Governor Lewis; hidden just behind the town hall, her narrow, dead-end block still seems to her, driving past it sometimes on the way to the cleaner's, as deep into the center as one can possibly get.

In that small town where she grew up, bordered on one side by farms, on the other by older, larger towns leading—or so it seemed—straight to the confusion and grandeur of New York City, life's purpose evaded her, even in her seventh year. Swirling on a stool at the counter of her parents' restaurant, or sipping an ice cream soda she had had to pump all by herself, life—as she saw it pass by, disguised as her tired, overworked parents, or as businessmen waiting for the train, or farmers coming in with eggs and milk, or vagrants just passing the time, sipping beer for a free lunch—seemed even then full of contradictions, unexpected emptiness, and visions as close but untouchable as those familiar horizons of city excitement and pastoral peace.

It was that year, the year of discovering loneliness in all its vast, imposing dimensions, that she also discovered what it was that made other, older people carry on with their lives, dressing for work every day and taking the train, driving old trucks or even horse carts into town full of cabbages and chickens, hugging children, cleaning dishes, wiping tabletops, sitting like Rose, her mother, every day and night at the restaurant cash register, ringing in nickels and dimes and pennies, all instead of just lying down on the sidewalk and closing their eyes. It was no abstract idea that saved her—it was love itself, large as loneliness, but whole and palpable and close, and furthermore embraceable, in the person of Harry Schwartz from New York, the man her cousin Gloria was about to marry.

It was the first wedding in the Keppler family, or, rather, in that part of the family which had migrated so many towns west, six of eleven daughters having upon marriage left Newark for cleaner air, larger houses, and the privacy to do with their lives what they wanted, keeping kosher or not, speaking Yiddish or not, going to *shul*, and *mikvah*, and family dinners—or not. Pioneers, they called themselves, still caught in the accents and shadows of New York, and it was true that not many people in Lewiston had ever seen a Jew before, except once or twice perhaps taking a wrong turn down a city street. Oscar, the old man, was a butcher all his life, an immigrant with the black hat, sidelocks, and long beard that made people stare and then turn their heads away. He would not talk of *shtetl* streets, or people left behind, or journeys across the world from old to new; he was American now, he said, the accent too thick ever to mistake. But the sons-in-law, eleven of them, were American born and bred—businessmen with short hair, bow ties, and mustaches, not so rich themselves but not so poor either. One was a rabbi. One had made a fortune in stocks and was retired already at forty-five. The others worked hard, in small businesses, brokerage firms, or as salesmen, and claimed to know the value of a dollar. For the occasion of the wedding, Zellie herself was given her first new dress—delicate lace on the hem and puffy shoulders—and so was excited in her own way, having little to do with the talk of fortunes, mortgages, and interest rates weaving back and forth over her head many weeks in advance.

"Seems nice enough," said Max Levin, her father, gentle-voiced, shrugging far away in the front seat of the car.

"He's good-looking," said Rose, good-looking herself, and

well schooled in the virtue of appearances. Among eleven daughters, she was the one people had called a beauty. "The father's rich," she said, "and he's a nice boy. But what's New York to this? Look, Max, what she's giving up!"

Riding with them out to the farms, for eggs, for milk, for a Sunday drive (one day there would be neighborhoods, houses —her own house), Zellie looked where her mother pointed, counted the cows in the fields, followed with her gaze the arrows of weathervanes; and then, standing by barnyard fences and chicken coops, tried to imagine gathering eggs every day, or squeezing milk from the veined and swollen underbellies of masticating cows. But in the squawk and rustle of chickens fleeing roosters, the rotting, wafting smell of manure, all the pleasures of open fields and quiet, sunny dirt roads escaped her. The earth was dusty dry to the touch, was gravel to the shuffle of feet; the grass was coarse and wet all day; and blue cornflowers, if you picked them, would fade in a minute. Sitting in the backseat again, the flowers in her lap already shriveled to weeds, she looked through the window in frustration but also with renewed longing, because once again the richness of that bucolic life had evaded her. Coming home again, she found the pavement and the sidewalks a comfort, at least: the swings in the playground squeaked at exactly the same place every time, while visible on clear days from the top of the hill there was always New York, drawing into its horizon every road, every bride, every morning businessman, a vanishing point into which Gloria too might disappear, drawn away by the irrepressible charms of New York's incarnate son, Harry Schwartz.

Still that distant place appeared far enough away that the town of Lewiston, and even more Zellie's own family, seemed as stable, as central and as long-standing as if one of her own uncles had been chiseled in profile up on the front of the Lewiston Trust, a cameo portrait in line with Washington, Hamilton, Thomas Paine, Samuel Morse, and Governor Lewis. On every corner, it seemed, behind every counter, in the driver's seat of every third car, were cousins, aunts, and uncles, grandparents, godparents, and family friends who were also, mysteriously and without explanation, aunt or uncle. Almost across the street was the gracious brick station where every morning hundreds of men—gray-coated, high-collared, and wide-brimmed—gathered into trains for the city and reappeared in the evening, dispersing all at once with their solemn, tired faces. Four of her uncles took that train, drinking free coffee every morning in her parents' restaurant—Washington's Kitchen—and waiting there at night for their wives. Through the dark winter afternoons, or at night, or even sometimes in the middle of school, Zellie could hear its warning and disillusioned whistle, still far off down the tracks, coming down from the hills or up from the city, then going away again. Next door, like a looking-glass version of her own family, the Schneebaums—Minnie and Irv—had two children as well, Danny and Margie, who would be waiting on the porch for Zellie on their way to school, or after school, when they had dropped off their books and changed their clothes. More than once, hearing a sound or expecting a visitor, Zellie had jumped out of bed and run onto the porch, where although there was nothing but a bicycle or an old broom, or Aunt Minnie sweeping the porch in her Japanese gown, there would be Danny also coming out at the same time from his own side of the house. Exactly the same age, both of them still in their pajamas, they were like two figures in a giant children's clock, emerging to strike the hour. Danny's hair was, except on special occasions, uncombed, and he carried at all times a large silver gun with an ivory handle. Once, both of them waking up to a mysterious whimpering beneath the window, they found a dog scratching at the milk box, floppy-eared and dirty, crying each time his claws would scrape against the metal. When the two doors opened the dog looked up, then went back to his scratching, as if neither child was worth worrying about, but also was no one who could help. Zellie bent down to pet him, and for a moment he stopped, scratching wildly again when she rubbed him behind his ear. Then he whimpered again and returned to work, trying to get into that box.

Danny stood before the dog, transfixed. "Whose is it?" he asked in a whisper.

"Ours," Zellie said, and looking up at Danny's face—embarrassed, blushing—saw that she had changed in a second the innocent course of their childhoods. Danny pulled up his loosening pajama pants and ran inside. They loved each other.

Margie, standing in the doorway, was a year older and would not play with them if she could help it, although sometimes, at the children's table at family suppers, or on afternoons when Greta Carp across the street was unavailable, she would lean longingly toward the whispers of her juniors, wishing that she too could have someone so close who was part of the family, in whom she might confide. When Danny ran past her at the door she looked for a moment toward Zellie, wondering what their new secret was, and then followed her brother inside. Letting the screen door slam behind her, Zellie went back to her own silent house and, looking back as the dog ran away, listened anxiously to the voices next door, hoping that somewhere under a bush that dog was only waiting until it was safe, and would come to her again.

Next door was not her own house but might have been— the furniture looked the same, the books were the same, the high arch of the radio, even the piano against the wall. But through that wall Zellie could sometimes hear the harsh words from which doors slammed and tears flowed. When her own parents fought, they would disappear for an hour or two in the car, coming back flushed but silent, Rose merely brushing her hair from the wind, Max humming a tune on the porch while he smoked a cigar. After working all day in the restaurant Rose could never bear to cook too much at home, sitting down heavily at the kitchen table and staring out silently, even angrily into the dark; but the air in Minnie's kitchen was always thick with onions in fat, or paprika sprinkled on brisket, or the charred bottoms of pots, as if it were only through that thin wall— through the mirror on that wall, jumping and wobbling with every slam and footstep—that real life was going on, with all its noises, tears, and small songs, while on Zellie's side, in the room she shared with Pearl, her sister, in her own family's house, her own life went on missing a dimension, like a pantomime or a radio play, and she must watch it all in silence or listen carefully with closed eyes.

Down the block her Aunt Flora and Uncle Sasha Berensky owned the Hamilton House Hotel, a rambling red building on a hill where every Friday the rabbi spent the night and every year gypsies gathered for the Lewis County Fair—dishonest, Flora complained, filthy-smelling and in rags, but popular among the children, who every year congregated on the lawn to watch them carry in their trunks.

"Greenies," said Rose under her breath, as she sat watching on the porch with her sister. Flora blew out a long stream of smoke above her head and laughed. Zellie, between them, didn't turn around, but listened carefully for the joke.

"That's not nice, Rosie," Flora said, but still she laughed again at the word, their own childhood name for the cousins and strangers who had come over steerage: greenhorns, immigrants, all the lonely, foul-smelling men who had stayed with them in Newark and then moved on.

"You were too old, Flora," said Rose. "You couldn't have known. But we knew. They slept in our bed. They tried every toothbrush."

Flora laughed again. "Oh, Rosie!" she said. "You girls were too little."

Rose stopped smiling and lowered her voice, but Zellie knew

her mother's whisper. "Listen—in the middle of the night, Flora, I felt something hard against my back."

"Rose!" Flora said. "For God's sake, the girls! Anyway, *feh*!" she said, imitating their mother, and seemed to be swatting away a swarm of gnats. "*Shayn vergessen*—forget it, Rose. It's over, let it go." Rose didn't answer, but prodded Zellie down the steps into the crowd of children.

Even more on her father's side—up the hill, beyond the town hall and the village green, where the houses still looked like museums of nineteenth-century life—Zellie's other family seemed to her a first family, welcome, long-standing, and important. Max's parents had a modest clapboard house and a garden; tall, light-eyed and square-jawed like their son, with brash American accents and straight teeth, Theo and Esther Levin looked as rooted and American on that street as any of their gentile neighbors—the Smiths, the Clarksons, the Coles. Theo himself spoke hardly a scrap of Yiddish, wore white Panama hats in summer, and played the harmonica. As a young man he had grown a long mustache—white now—to disguise a physiognomy his father had called Hebraic. No Irishman at work had a handlebar thicker, blonder, or longer curled. Esther in her late middle age had a grape arbor, a flower garden, and a quince tree, and baked cherry pies that every year won prizes at the local Women's Club, though with her last name she could not officially join. Still, she had marched in their ranks for women's suffrage, written letters to Congress, rolled bandages during the war, attended their concerts, and was friends with her neighbors—waving friends at least—with all except Mayor Cole next door, and his unmarried daughter.

One day, not long before the wedding, walking too fast for Zellie as they passed the Coles' sharp white picket fence, Esther found her nerve, at least with the daughter, who was head of the Women's Club itself. "Hello, Helen!" she called, screwing up her face as if to summon the grin which then appeared; from the street she waved, confirming a proximity too long unacknowledged. Helen Cole, a tall, immobile figure emerging from behind the wisteria, slowly raised her mousy head, as if she had heard something off at a great distance. Smiling then as if there were sun in her eyes, she nodded too far up and too far down to see really who it was. Afterwards Esther was irritable and distracted, still walking too fast and shaking her head. "Still," she said, without turning or slowing down, as if Zellie behind her could follow her thoughts or were standing three feet taller, "we still ought to wave, don't you think?" But already her voice was high and broken, and their walk had become almost a race.

"Stupid shiksa," she said to Theo, coming inside and tossing her hat onto the sofa. "And I'm a stupid fool." With her face red she turned to Zellie, her gray eyes glossy in the light. "And what is the girl going to think?"

Vehemently Zellie shook her head, as if somehow that small movement might convince her grandmother she was not a stupid fool, was not indeed anything bad or undesirable. Zellie was many years a mother herself before learning one day (it was her turn for the car pool; she was waiting after dance lessons at the Women's Club and reminiscing with a lanky old woman, Miss Cole) that Helen Cole had nodded for that rule against Jews—still did—just as she had nodded that warm autumn afternoon at Esther and her granddaughter, waving from outside the fence.

Although her mother had come from Germany—Karl Marx was a relative—Esther Levin was proud of her own and especially her husband's very American heritage. Her father's family had fought in the Civil War—there were graves in Newark to prove it—and Theo's father's family had come over not too long after the *Mayflower*, founding the first American synagogue up north in Rhode Island. "Zellie," she said, before they napped in the afternoon, lying on the long sofa, the venetian blinds drawn down, "do you know who this is?"—and she held up a thick tin picture of her father and mother, sepia brown and severe. All the shadows and sobriety of those faces had been preserved, all of the troubles and none of the light, no smiles, no gentleness. "Why didn't they smile?" Zellie asked, and Esther held out the round plate at arm's length to see, squinting but also raising her eyebrows. "Well," she said, "they used to tell them sad stories, so the children wouldn't fidget." She looked over and smiled. When Zellie pointed out that they were grown-ups there, no children, Esther quickly picked up the box and took out another.

On the wall above them were two large pictures next to each other in their frames, which together made up a village scene. In one half, an old woodcutter walked home through the forest at sunset, kindling on his back; in the other was the village itself, the cobbles of the street, the overhanging loft of a barn, the water trough in front of an inn. Some of the scene was painted, or drawn in ink, but most was a subtle collage of the real substances themselves: grass and tiny twigs for the forest and the basket of wood, real bark for the sides of the barn, and some animal's pelt for the flanks of a mule. Esther's mother had pasted, cut, and drawn the scene; it was the village she had left as a girl, somewhere in Germany. But even that, Esther was quick to point out, was before the new century, and her father, at least, had been in the war.

So, she explained, whenever Zellie would ask, she really was a DAR—Daughter of the American Revolution—and Zellie was too, and they both should have been allowed into the club. At the same time, she and Theo had sent their boys every Saturday to Hebrew school and kept the silver box nailed to the door, with its scroll of paper rolled up inside like a secret. "What does it say?" Zellie asked, coming in and going out, and once when Theo was away Esther pulled the paper out for her.

The Hebrew letters were mysterious and tiny, more like scratches than writing, but in her high formal voice she pretended to read the old prayer, as if before the congregation: "Hear, O Israel!" she recited. "The Lord our God, the Lord is One!"

"And the rest?" Zellie asked.

"The rest?" Esther looked down suspiciously at the slip of paper. She squinted, rubbed her eyebrows, and as she could not really read that language, merely rolled up the paper again, pushing it back into its box. "The rest," she said, "is a secret."

The ancient language was a mystery, but still they said the familiar prayers on Friday nights over candles, wine, and the bread Esther had braided and baked. Yiddish too was a foreign language, from Europe, from far-off ghettos, Vilna, Minsk, and Warsaw, falling from the tongues of immigrant friends as if Esther, Theo, and sometimes Zellie herself should have understood. But they were Americans; they could not. Sometimes the two grandmothers sat rocking on their children's front porch, Esther responding to Hannah Keppler's Yiddish from the pale of Russia with some rusty German from her own mother. "*Das ist wahr*," she would say, nodding, or shaking her head. And to Zellie, at least, standing between them shelling peas or squeezing the pits out of cherries, they seemed to understand each other and get along.

It was her tall, blue-eyed grandmother Esther, however, whom she herself could understand. Walking home from school, she would stop at Esther's house for milk, soft crackers and grape jelly; and while Esther stirred something steaming in a pot or peered down her nose peculiarly to sew a button, Zellie would tell her about school, Esther nodding patiently, drawing her lips down and her eyebrows up in appreciation, her glasses sliding down too low as Zellie watched. During the week, when Rose was working at the restaurant, Zellie stayed late at her grandparents' for supper, playing food games with Theo when

Esther had turned to the stove. With no girls of their own, Theo was glad to let her touch his still handsome face, smooth from shaving, while Esther was glad to sew the hems of her small skirts, comb her hair into braids, and talk with her while they weeded in the garden, her face hidden beneath the wide brim of a hat.

Much later, years later, when her grandmother was long dead, long before Zellie or anyone else expected—she should have lived to a hundred, everyone said, no one foreseeing the truck that would kill her—Zellie would still look back at those afternoons of just that respect and attention she had longed for ever since. Waking up alone before her children, still in her own, warm side of the bed, pouring out water for coffee, and walking the dog to the road and back, she would wonder what she and Esther might have done, given more years together, more time to grow up, grow old. Beside the calm surface of the new swimming pool she might wait for a ripple—suddenly there was time enough to sink down again and remember, time she didn't want. What might they have done? she would ask, almost aloud, addressing no one in particular but only silent, distant things: the cold, other side of the bed, the calm surface of the water, the early-morning clouds, a huge crow flapping down from a branch. Her husband having left her, everything would come back, powerfully but different. Now, in memory, Esther's voice seemed to be her own, asking that question— what might they have done?—as if those years might have been different from all the others; making oatmeal and cinnamon toast, lying quietly together on the sofa, listening to the radio. As if wishing could control what had been, what must be.

"Have you learned about our town yet?" Esther asked one autumn day, the second day of Rosh Hashanah, when everyone else was celebrating the new year but Zellie and Esther had stayed at home—to make dinner, Esther had said, winking theatrically.

"No, that's fourth grade," Zellie said, shaking her head, as they arranged apple slices on a plate. "I'm in second."

"But don't you know about the soldiers yet, and Tempe Wick?" Zellie shook her head, while Esther stood there looking at her, rubbing her square chin. She dumped the apple slices back into a pot of water, grabbed her pocketbook and her great black coat—rough wool on the outside but thick red velvet inside, gilt-embroidered like a cushion, a secret bed—and took Zellie's hand. Together they climbed into the car and, jerking and swerving, drove quickly out of town into the woods, finally up a steep hill to where the trees thinned out and the road stopped before a boulder with an iron plaque. Below them was the town, huddling and miniature, a scene from a different, serene century, with its white, spired church, its reddening maples, and its town green at the center—a picture postcard, only grayer somehow and more diffuse, as if the whole scene could not quite be contained and arranged. Beyond, down the hill would be the train station—steel and brick and sooty windows—the railroad bridge, the restaurant and the hotel, and all the real houses Zellie knew were hidden there behind town hall. Obscure in the distance was the skyline of New York City; and when she turned around, there were the mountains, swollen bands of purple at the edge of the world.

"This was Fort Nonsense," Esther announced, "which they built just for something to do. Read the dates, Zelda." Holding her coat closed at the throat, she climbed back into the car even before Zellie could find the numbers, and they continued. Esther's shoulders were wide, her wrinkled, spotted hand on the gear shaft was strong, and Zellie leaned back safe and content in the front seat, watching the world go by.

"And this," said Esther, when they had come out into open fields, where the ancient, twisted apple trees were already brown and gold and horses switched their tails in the shade, "this is the farm where Tempe Wick lived with her family. The soldiers camped out in these woods, but some were stealing horses to go home to their own families, because it was so cold. And Tempe was a girl just like you, Zellie, and she hid her horse in the bedroom. The soldiers came in, but they didn't look upstairs!"

At the end of the field was a dilapidated house, almost a shack, where they stopped the car. Zellie opened the door, but her grandmother stopped her. "Up there!" she whispered, pointing, and together, from the car, they looked. At the upper window, dark and dusty, a girl's face appeared from behind the curtain, then withdrew.

"Was that her?" Zellie asked, as Esther accelerated suddenly into the gravel and sped away. She had always answered Zellie's questions, but this time she merely shrugged her shoulders, smiling vaguely at the road.

One spring morning, pretending to hide under the covers with her beloved, endangered horse, it seemed to Zellie that everybody, suddenly, was gone. The light came down in rays through the curtains, the ring on the end of the shade was tapping quietly against the glass; but otherwise there was no movement, no sound. The other bed was already straightened and pulled tight, as if her sister had never slept there. The door was slightly open, as if someone were about to knock and come in or silently to go out. But nothing else, no one else, was alive in the house. It was Sunday, when Rose didn't usually walk down to the restaurant until noon, and Pearl, the elder, the first child, would study in the kitchen or conduct experiments in the backyard. Sometimes she lit fires with a magnifying glass, or filled every glass jar from the kitchen with water, each to a different level, arranging them in a row like a musical instrument, tapping one after another with a fork. Sometimes she climbed onto the garage, to jump like Amelia Earhart, or to drop feathers and tin cans and sweaters, testing for gravity. She had plans, she said mysteriously.

Now Zellie listened, tried not to breathe. Still, there was her heart, interrupting, interfering, beating outward as loudly as if she were frightened; occasionally a necessary breath rushed in, raising up her chest. But otherwise there was no sign of life: no scraping of kitchen chairs against the linoleum, no murmuring in the front room, no musical bottles ringing or tin cans dropping in the backyard, no dishes clattering into the sink. Everybody else, it seemed, everyone but Zellie, had things to do, people to see, problems to talk about, someone waiting with open arms, a place in a room somewhere that was waiting, expectant, empty. For years—thirty years, forty years—it would still seem to her that while other people's lives were comfortably bounded by definite desires and destinies, her own life was still secretly unbounded; that everything definite about her was false; that if she ceased to smile even once, or pulled over to the side of the road, or wandered out in just her nightgown through the fields, people would shake their heads as if they had known all along.

Her father was head of the temple, its first president, with his picture in the paper, leaning on the cornerstone, a handsome young man with thick brown hair and a square chin. Every Friday night he sat down in a special chair waiting for him behind the pulpit, just as an angelic soprano voice—unrelated to Mrs. Gruber, the piano teacher, who walked out afterwards from behind the screen—would sing the opening prayer while one of the mothers stood by the rabbi and lit the candles, reciting the Hebrew, covering her eyes with her fingertips. Sometimes it was one of the Keppler sisters, Flora or Minnie or Rose herself; each aunt had her turn, and even Esther Levin had said the prayers more than once, standing tall and self-conscious before so many people. Watching her grandmother, Zellie wondered if she too would stand up there one day in that place, holding her hands over the flames, reciting the prayer by heart before her own family and everyone she knew.

Her mother too had a place to go, a special chair high up at the restaurant behind the cash register, where customers coming in or going out knew her name, said "Hello, Rose" and "Good-bye, Rose"—knowing her in a way Zellie could not—and returned the change if Rose had miscounted. And now Cousin Gloria, the bride, would walk into the waiting arms of her lover and be carried off to the distant city. There would be no more celebrations to look forward to, nothing to dress up for, no more grooms waiting, blond and mustachioed, for a dark-haired bride. Even Pearl was always studying, or waiting tables at the restaurant, or dressing up to wait on the front porch, for the boy who would someday appear and take her away as well. Seven-thirty on Wednesday nights "The Lone Ranger" charged onto the radio, but if Pearl was around it had to be saxophones and clarinets until she was gone. Afterwards she would come home like a stranger, unwilling or unable to speak, looking into the mirror as if she could see into the other side, farther away than just her aunt's living room.

"How was it?" Zellie would ask, running into their room.

Pearl would look at her strangely, as if for a moment she didn't recognize her.

"What did you do?"

"Oh, nothing." Looking again into the mirror, Pearl would smile and then, as if Zellie were not there, open a thick book at her desk and pretend to be studying.

Now, as Zellie wondered if she could make any noise, if she could even raise her head from under the pillow, move through the air, take up space, she heard Pearl come briskly in, snapping up the window shades. Quickly, before Zellie was fully awake, Pearl had lowered the white dress down over her younger sister's raised arms. Pearl was ten years older, and already she wore high heels and lipstick, even when she worked in the restaurant. For the wedding she had bought a low-cut dress, but Rose had objected, and so this morning she wore her mother's white sweater as well, covering up the plunging neckline. "Should I wear a sweater, too?" Zellie asked, seeing her sister's, and worrying that Pearl had gotten something extra. When Rose wore that sweater, Zellie would button and then unbutton the round wooden beads from her neck and down to her lap; but now, seeing them on her sister, she was hesitant.

"No," said Pearl sharply, twisting Zellie's dress to the front. "Can you get your shoes on by yourself?" she asked, looking at herself in the mirror, and Zellie, comparing her own round face with her sister's sleek, critical gaze, wondered what Pearl was looking for in there. Next door, behind the mirror, they could hear Margie and Danny getting up, and Minnie and Irv yelling back and forth, about hot water, coal, the bathroom door—mysterious, vital questions, *"Gott in Himmel!"*—in loud, angry language. "What are they saying?" Zellie asked, holding her fingers in her ears and then her ear to the wall. Pearl listened against the wall herself, but shrugged and turned away.

"Well, it's hard to explain," she said, pleased to repeat at last what she had been told too often herself: "You'll understand when you're older."

In the sanctuary of the Jewish Center, high and cool and dark (once it had been the cafeteria of a school, but now, with a new wing and a prayer, was an edifice, a temple), Zellie stood in a crowd, holding her mother's hand, pressing her face against the warm silk of Rose's fancy dress, sniffing and luxuriating in the perfume she knew from Friday nights, splashed on quickly after the dishes were done. Zellie was eating the apple her mother had given her, just in case the lunch was late—you never know at weddings, Rose had said, defending herself against Max's shaking head. Behind Rose stood Minnie, a year older but glad to follow close in the shade of her younger sister. "I don't know, Rose," she said nervously. "She's not going to like it!" Their voices seemed to joke, though they never quite joked; and their eyes, dark, intelligent, almost Oriental eyes, were both laughing and secretly suspicious. Minnie, too, had a child in her skirts —Danny, also eating an apple and hiding his face.

"So?" said Rose. "She'll live. It's not so many, anyway."

"I mean," said Minnie, "about the mother—it's a curse for a family."

"Minnie!" said Rose angrily, and held up her hand.

"Hello, everybody!" called a voice from the hall, Flora bursting into the room with her arms spread out, announcing herself almost in a song: "Make way, make way! Flora Berensky's here! Mother of the bride!" From all around her people came up to Flora, opening their arms to hug her, kissing, laughing, exclaiming about her dress. Looking up at her quieter, younger mother, Zellie thought, But mine is the beautiful one.

"Rose, what do I do?" Flora asked.

Above Zellie's head her mother said, "What do you mean, 'What do you do?' You go out and buy more chickens." For emphasis, she shook Zellie's hand, rubbed nervously at the puffy shoulder of Zellie's new dress. The material scratched Zellie's skin as she was pushed from side to side, but even so she loved the pressure of her mother's hand, the confident voice of her advice—down there, in the unnoticed turbulence, she was held tight.

"Me!" said Flora. "*I* should go out and buy more chickens! My daughter's getting married and *I* should buy chickens! They should eat pigeons! They tell me thirty people and they bring ninety—what is that, Rose, a joke? They're so rich and fancy! I'll tell you something—it's plain rude, if you ask me."

"Of course not you, *mamela*," said Rose formally in her public, fancy, almost English accent, raising her eyebrows and smiling in case people were watching. Leaning close to her sister, she said, "Have Lenny run out, or the *schvartze*. I'll go tell Lenny right now."

Through the crowd Zellie was pulled along, passing along the way all the older cousins she knew, Cousin Bobby, Cousin Berny, Cousin Ceil with her new husband, and older people she recognized from town—parents of her friends, friends of her parents, even Mrs. Gruber, who had not—everyone knew it—been invited. Esther and Theo were standing with Max and George, their sons, stiff in their tuxedoes, and as close to the door as they could get.

"Hello, pretty," Esther said, still in her coat, winking as Zellie passed.

"Grandma!—" Zellie said, rushing up to tell her about her dress; but Rose pulled her along. There were friendly but frightening uncles from vague family dinners far away in Newark: Uncle Moe, who pinched her cheek; Uncle Milt, who kissed her quickly on the head; Uncle Sam, who didn't know how to touch her, shaking her hand as if she were a grown-up man. And all the other aunts who looked like her mother: Bertha, who was old; Betty, who laughed wildly; Ida, who was small and taught third grade; Etta, who had danced in a contest; Vera, who had left her husband; Lottie, who had married a rabbi—who beat her; Ruthie, who was a communist; and Rachel, who was not very sharp. Bertha Betty Ida Etta Vera Lottie Ruthie Rachel; then Flora, Minnie, and Rose. They were small and resembled each other, people said, though to Zellie each was older, older, and much older, like her small, round grandmother among them, hunching over a cane—Bubbah Hannah who hardly had to bend down to kiss her, at the same time murmuring to Rose, her own youngest.

"Oh, Mamma!" said Rose, squeezing Zellie's shoulder in her annoyance. "This is Zellie." And she pushed Zellie forward.

And Hannah Keppler—with her high, pinched nose, her dark eyes, and sunken cheeks—looked long into Zellie's own eyes, their faces close together, and grinned for a long moment as if really she had known all along, as if secretly Zellie were her favorite grandchild; but there were thirty others, it had to be a secret. "Zellie, *shaynala*," she said, and for an instant Zellie's own eyes were staring back at her from that old face.

"Ach, Rose!" she said, and though the rest was Yiddish, Zellie understood, and remembered. Had she once known that foreign language? Had her mother told her the story later, already translated and transformed? Such mysteries, later on, were unanswerable. "Don't tell anyone I forgot," Hannah said, shaking her head at her daughter, at her own old age. "That I forgot her name, Rosela—okay?" From her purse she handed Zellie a quarter.

Suddenly, they turned into a huge kitchen where, facing them with a long triangle of knife in his hand, stood Mr. Minkoff, the cook from the restaurant. His cheeks and bald head glistened in the harsh light; dark hairs grew out of his nose.

"Lenny," said Rose, "we have a problem."

"With that little girl, you have a problem! You want me to take care of it? How are you, Zeldala!" He bent down to kiss her, but she leaned away from his blooming lips, into her mother's dress.

"We need chicken for sixty more. They said thirty and meant ninety. Would you believe it?"

"It's a miracle."

"What's a miracle?" said Rose.

"It's a miracle! Where am I going to get enough chickens on Sunday? And kosher?"

"I don't know, Lenny. Otherwise, get meat."

"I tell you, it's a miracle, Rose. I just happen to have an order of chickens come in. I could do sixty, I could do ninety. I'll send the boy right over."

Although he was greasy and smelled like chicken fat, onions, and sweat, Rose leaned over Zellie and kissed his cheek. "Thank you, Lenny," she said.

"Don't thank me," he said. "Thank the man upstairs!" And he pointed, sharply, with his knife.

There, in a little bathroom crowded with suitcases and tiny bottles of rouge and mascara and perfume, Gloria sat on a high stool in her white dress. Zellie ran up to her, with her eyes and her mouth wide open. But she was too scared to touch. She looked at her cousin's dress, her fingers poised expectantly above it, and gently, as if petting some delicate, newborn creature, merely stroked with her fingertips her own white sleeve.

Gloria at twenty-one was just a cousin, Rose's niece, with Flora's wide, unpredictable face and loud voice. But she was also a college girl, with her father's blue eyes, a grown woman with boyfriends in cars; and now, as if by some hidden design meant for all of them, she was a bride. Pulling her youngest cousin into her arms, strong and perfumed and white with lace, she seemed for the first time beautiful, trustable, safe, and Zellie kissed her, loving to be held there: both were exactly where they should have been, as they should have been—transformed. But looking up after a moment, Zellie saw Cousin Margie as well, standing in a corner in Zellie's same dress, rubbing her sleeve also and—it seemed to Zellie—smirking mysteriously. She wasn't smart; her hair was wild, even clamped down with its large bow. And yet, as if they were the same, as if no one could notice the difference between them, or cared to notice, they were spoken of together—the girls, the children—in the same careless breath. There was the same dress, the same puffy shoulders, the same lace hem; only on Margie, a full year older, it looked like a little girl's dress, triangular and silly, and Zellie closed her eyes in shame.

Soon Flora came up between them and stroked Gloria's hair.

"It's all right," said Rose, sitting down on the closed cover of the toilet, arching her eyebrows cheerfully, though Zellie could see she was tired. "Lenny can get the extra chickens. It won't be a problem."

"What chickens?" said Gloria, releasing Zellie and looking up in the mirror, turning her head only slightly. "What problem?"

"Nothing," said Flora, seeming to grin, staring at Rose in the mirror with wide, dark eyes. "No problem."

"What problem, Mother?" said Gloria, spinning around, and Zellie thought she had never seen so beautiful a sight, the white dress flying out. "Tell me."

"All right," said her mother. "Guess who just arrived in a bus from New York?"

"Who? Harry's parents? Why did they take a bus?"

"They didn't take one bus, they took two. Two buses—can you believe it? Ninety people are here from New York."

Gloria jumped up, gasping and turning from her mother to her aunt, listened as they told the story, responsively, and in unison—". . . said thirty, come with ninety . . ."—then pushed out through the door, Zellie running after. Down the hall she saw a veil of white disappear into a doorway, and she followed.

There, in a small, crowded room of strangers, all very large and very old, Gloria stood, red-faced and stiff, holding her wrists in front of her, and nearby was Harry Schwartz himself, trapped in the arms of a large, frightening, gray-haired woman with dark red lips, who looked just like Harry only transformed, in a bright red dress, with wide shoulders puffed up like wings.

"Hello, everybody," said Harry, beneath his blond mustache, tall and blond in his shiny black coat with long tails; and Zellie thought she had never seen anyone so handsome, had never imagined that a man in real life could look like that. Her own father she knew from his unshaven kisses good night, and in the morning his uncovered belly while he shaved, wrapped only in a towel. All around were men with big noses, thick glasses and sparse, stiffly combed hair. But Harry Schwartz was perfect.

Gloria was strangely silent and red, and Zellie too was flushed, understanding suddenly what her cousin must feel, looking at Harry, her husband-to-be, Zellie's own cousin-to-be. Gloria, who had never been silenced by anyone before, was suddenly a blushing, beautiful bride; and Zellie saw in that moment why she would have to eat suppers alone in the restaurant and wait with only her sister, bored, angry, for their mother to get home from work, too tired even to play a game. This was what she had to wait for, to look for, this prize, this celebration, this beauty which made even her cousin Gloria look like the heroine of fairy tales; and remembering how the cook had pointed, thankfully, with his knife, Zellie too gave silent thanks to Harry Schwartz, her new cousin, who seemed to have brought with him such an abundance of good things, and so many chickens.

"Who's the little princess?" he asked, looking down at her, but no one answered. Zellie herself tried to speak but could not. Instead she closed her eyes, looking into that darkness for her mother's hand, or any hand to hold. Someone took her hand; they trampled out of the room and downstairs, where Rose pulled her into the gray metal seat next to her.

First came the rabbi, white-haired and somber, out of the double doors, and then came Lenny Minkoff, who wiped his bloody hands on his apron and sat down at the upright piano. He played "Here Comes the Bride," and then, just before Gloria herself swept past them down the aisle, Zellie was pushed out in front of her along with Margie on the other side, identical and mocking in her same white dress; and although Gloria gasped in surprise and almost tripped, the girls threw pink petals onto the carpet before them, just as they had been told, paving the way.

The Rewards of Charity

LONNIE SLAMS THE station-wagon door without saying goodbye and races inside to show her mother what she has made in Hebrew school: a seder plate cut out of red paper, pasted with all the special Passover symbols—an egg, a bitter root, a piece of matzoh—also cut out of paper and colored with Magic Markers. From the hall she can hear her mother far off behind the bedroom door, laughing quietly. Lonnie laughs too—already excited about staying up late, and drinking wine, and showing her laughing mother the replica of exactly what they will eat very soon. At the heavy door she stops, her hand already grasping the wide brass knob. She stands trying not to make a sound, not to breathe, not to turn the handle the rest of the way or even let it slip noisily back. Still, she is breathing heavily when her seder plate slips to the carpet, and her smile drops open-mouthed in surprise: her mother is crying.

By the time Zellie opens the door, she has brushed any tears from her eyes; she hugs her daughter cheerfully, tightly, so that her face is hidden by her hair, stiff from hair spray.

"What's that!" she says, picking up the red circle of paper from where it lies. "A seder plate! Lonnie, I love it!"

"It's for you," Lonnie says sullenly, and stomps away into the den, turning on "Kimba the White Lion" just at the commercials.

Zellie watches for a moment from the doorway, starts toward her daughter, then hurries back to the bathroom, where she was leaning across the sink to the mirror when her husband called. Now one eyelid is blue with powder while the other is still white. "Israel is on the line," said Joyce, his secretary. "Can you hold?" And Zellie held on, waiting impatiently on the bed, trying to pull on panty hose and still cradle the phone against her neck. "He's still on with a client, Zellie," Joyce said finally in her low, measured voice. There was a pause, a search for courage. "I'm afraid he can't make it tonight."

"What do you mean?" Zellie said, angry at first, then frightened, looking around her rich, spacious, threatened bedroom: the king-size bed with its velvet cover, the portraits of their children, their own wedding portrait, their parents. She had framed them all herself—even his parents—and remembering the care she had taken to find the blue velvet, to match frames to matting, matting to bedspread, and all for hardly a word of acknowledgment though the pictures had been hanging there ten years, her anger returned. But to Joyce she was always polite. "Why can't he make it?" she asked. "Why can't I speak to him myself?" She frowned, squinted dramatically, and shielded her eyes with her hand.

"Well, he's still on with Schlumberger."

"Then why did he call me now?"

"I don't know. I guess he wanted you to know in time to make plans. I'll tell him to call you, okay? And happy holidays!"

Upstairs in the attic, directly above the bedroom, Zellie's younger son had been going through old boxes with his cousin, looking for overlooked antiques and nostalgic souvenirs from before his time.

"Matthew," David said, "look at this," pulling up from a carton some tintype pictures of their ancestors: a severe lady in a bonnet, a man whose mustache curled at the tips.

"So?" said Matthew, trying with some trouble to light a joint rolled too loose and too thick.

Carefully David replaced the pictures in their box, and also a bag of photographs, creased and faded. "I don't think you should do that here, Matthew," he said, but the flame had just taken, and Matthew inhaled grandly.

"It's all right," Matthew said. "No one knows we're up here." He exhaled and sat down on the carton, collapsing into the pile of photographs and old skirts.

"Hey!" David said, and reaching in to pull him out he fell in himself onto Matthew's lap, and all the fragile pictures; and he was about to scream or strike out, anything to escape, when he heard his mother's voice, vehement at the phone; and then the tears.

Zellie cried, slamming down the phone, smothering her sobs in the pillow until it felt foolish—a picture of herself as a girl. Then she called Rose, a town away. "He's not coming," she told her.

"What do you mean, dolly? A family seder and he can't come?"

"I don't know. He won't. His secretary called."

"What is he, *meshugge* altogether?"

"I don't know, Ma. But I'm not going either. I can't."

"You're going!" said Rose, her voice, at least over the phone, sounding higher and more girlish than her daughter's. "You're going to call up your sister, and you'll go with them—there's plenty of room. We'll go with Gloria. Call her up right now."

"I can't."

"Of course you can."

"I can't."

"Don't say 'can't.' "
"I can't." ·

In the car, Zellie sits up front with Pearl and Mel Green, her
brother-in-law of almost twenty-seven years. She has dried her
tears, put on her best suit, and her long hair now curls formally
and perfectly down to her shoulders. Both women wear long
woolen skirts, and boots; Mel's suit is so old the wide lapel is
back in style. They speak in low voices, not using names, and
occasionally a Yiddish word comes up—"shtup," "shiksa," "shmuck"
—because the children are listening in the back, six of them in
the station wagon, hunched and crowded in their suits and ties,
Zellie's David and Warren entirely silent, their cousins Matthew and Stevey arguing between them. Lonnie, in her party
dress and Mary Janes, is trapped in the way-back with Teddy,
Pearl's youngest, who pinches her from time to time.

"Where's Daddy?" she asks, and although there is less noise
for a moment, no one answers. Neither of her brothers turns
around. "Where's Bratty?" she says, again to no one. "Where's
Fatty?"

From the villages of horse farms, tennis courts, and geese
crossings they travel east through the older, more crowded
towns, back along degraded main streets, past shabby delica-
tessens and dry cleaners and under railroad trestles, where every
face is dark and poor. To Zellie, driving so many years back
and forth, it seems that each town opens up, giving birth to
the next, so that going back toward Newark is like folding up
again into a womb and then again, like a Russian doll, womb
into womb. It is the path of her own family, raising their children and growing older. Her cousins, she tries to believe, older
in these older towns, were not after all thwarted but have stopped
by their own choice in smaller houses, smaller streets; and
where she herself has stopped, far west among the sloping fields
of former farms—gardens and a pool where the corn had been,

a Mercedes in the barn—is not after all the end, though it seems
to be: where else could they go? But her children *will* go beyond,
she believes, wherever that is. They will go to Paris, to London,
to Rome; they will be artists, professors, world travelers—all
that she was too ignorant, too poor, and then too busy to com-
plete (and she could have gone to Smith, perhaps, or to Welles-
ley; the application cost too much). In triumph, then, at least
her children will go back, to Europe, to the world. Until they
do, this once a year the family still collects to embrace itself,
traversing backwards that old migration of parents and grandparents: Europe, New York, Newark, and then beyond.

Now, in Newark they stop. Once it was the parents' house,
Hannah's and Oscar's, eleven daughters coming home for a
meal, and all of their children, each family with a different last
name. The table stretched into the kitchen and onto the porch,
and Hannah grew old cooking for all of them, sending home
extra soup, brisket, Passover cakes. Every week they came, the
older ones, with babies to be fed, hems to be sewn, long hair
to be washed and braided again. Then the daughters too were
grandmothers, and no table would have been long enough.
Oscar died, and Bertha, the eldest, and even Flora, before her
mother. Still, Zellie, the youngest grandchild, remembers her
grandfather as a white beard, and a thick gold watch before her
eyes, swinging from its chain.

"You couldn't," says Pearl. "You weren't old enough."

"I'm sorry," says Zellie through her teeth, "but I do."

As for Hannah, she was a little old lady stooped in pain.
"Hitler should feel like this," she said near the end, and when
she died they found half of every pill she took hidden under
the bed.

As the doors open, the children struggle out, racing up the
carpeted, awninged staircase of the restaurant to see their cousins, their aunts and their uncles, the coat room with its revolving
rack, and all the banquet halls as well. Lonnie races up the

stairs with the others but stops suddenly before the entrance, waiting for her mother.

"What'll I do?" says Zellie, still gripping the handle of the car door.

"He's a shit," says Pearl. "That's all I can say."

"Why don't you go in, honey?" Zellie says, grinning up to her daughter, but Lonnie runs back down and hides her face in her mother's blouse, turning away from the large buckle of her belt. "Come on," Zellie says, stroking Lonnie's hair, climbing the stairs, and she herself is ready to cry again, spotting her own cousins through the revolving doors.

"Come on, Lonnie!" says Pearl. "Let's go in. What are you, scared? A grown-up girl like you?" She speaks playfully, lovingly, but her grip on Lonnie's shoulder is firm. All her own children are boys.

Lonnie submits, and pushes through the doors in the same wedge of space as her mother. Inside, the red carpeting is faded in places almost to white, but the girl cousins play their old game with it anyway, shuffling to make the red plush turn pink, and then shuffling it back again to red.

"Hi," Lonnie says, forgetting the name of a girl she knows is her second cousin, and beginning the shuffling game along with the others. Soon Teddy comes up to her and punches her arm. He is a fat little boy, though behind buckteeth and glasses he has Pearl's pretty face and the first signs of Max's strong chin. "You want to steal candy again?" he asks.

"Okay," she says, and together they run from the lobby, disappearing into the passage between two heavy curtains.

When Zellie turns around, her daughter is gone, her only distraction and protection from glances she cannot yet bear to meet. But Minnie is coming up to her, frail and shaking, grinning with her arms opened wide.

"How are you, Zelda dear?" she says, quietly, intimately.

"I'm fine, Aunt Minnie. And how are you?"

"Oh, we're fine, we're fine. Irv and I are so happy to be here." Closely, they look into each other's eyes, smiling, and they continue to smile, protected, embraced. Zellie can go on smiling, she knows, for as long as anyone in her family. And here, with her aunt, she would rather stay embraced than turn and see a hundred others, who would also smile but would not be safe.

"Where's Israel?" says Minnie, still looking into Zellie's eyes.

"I don't know," Zellie tells her. "I don't know. He was supposed to come, but—"

"Maybe he'll come later," she says, nodding, and Zellie nods as well, kissing her.

"I've got to find Lonnie," she says, ducking for a moment into the coat room, where for fifty dollars more they could have hired a girl to check coats. Now no one is there, no children are playing, but Zellie sorts through the coats anyway, pretending to look for her own.

Halfway down, where the curtains divide, Teddy takes Lonnie's hand.

"Through here," he says, and pushes through the opening. They stand in a vast, dark room, ghostly white tables just visible beyond them, and white lilies jutting luminously into the air. "Look," Teddy says, reaching across one of the tables, under a flowerpot. In his hand are tiny eggs in silver foil, chocolate eggs for Easter. Stuffing them into his pocket he unwraps one, eats it, and reaches for more. Lonnie, too, stands on tiptoe and grabs a handful of eggs.

"Hey!" says a man's voice. "Get out of there!" Teddy runs back to the curtain and ducks under, but Lonnie is still crawling through when the lights go on. She screams, but Teddy pulls her through and holds her mouth closed, the salty sweat and chocolate mingling on his hand. A dark arm reaches through the curtain, but at the wrong place. Teddy ducks under again, on the other side, and Lonnie, terrified to be alone, follows him. The lights are bright, the room is filled with people and noise, and an old woman who looks like her grandmother but is not approaches her with wide-open arms.

"Lonnela!" she says. "I missed you!" And turning away in terror, Lonnie falls into her mother's arms.

"Hey!" Zellie says. "Hey, honey, come on now, what's wrong? Say hello to Aunt Gloria!"

"Hello," Lonnie says, but only Zellie can hear it.

Behind Gloria Zellie can see Margie approaching through the crowd. For too many years they were sent together to the same parties, shared the same clothes, and sat together at the children's table. At thirteen Margie stayed over weekends, forcing Zellie to dance and play records long into the night. Every year now at the seder they kiss each other's cheek, and for the rest of the year Zellie remembers and rubs that cheek in annoyance. Now Zellie must repeat to herself that her cousin is well intentioned; she is benign; she is her cousin; still, she is unbearable. This spring, for the first time in twenty years, she wrote to Zellie—a birthday card a foot long, saying, "SO NOW YOU ARE FORTY!"

"Did you get my card?" Margie says, kissing Zellie's cheek and holding her arm.

"Yes," Zellie says, looking away.

"Well? Did you like it? Have you ever seen such a card?"

"No," Zellie says, "I haven't."

"And where's Israel?" Margie asks. "I want to give him a big kiss."

Zellie nods and smiles, snorting at the same time as if in response. Sometimes, she knows, in noisy, crowded rooms people are embarrassed to ask the same question twice. As a child Margie didn't know better; now, Zellie knows, she has problems enough of her own: a daughter in jail, a son with a shaved head and a guru. Still, Zellie clamps her jaw and turns away.

"Zelda, didn't you hear me? We're all getting old, I guess, *kaynahora!* I asked you, where's Israel? My wonderful lawyer —that husband of yours."

"Margie, he couldn't come tonight," Zellie says, and walks quickly away. At being kind, to Margie at least, she knows she has failed again.

"I'm sorry to hear that!" Margie says, speaking loudly to cover the distance. "I'm sorry to hear he couldn't come tonight. He's so nice, Cousin Izzy."

Zellie finds her parents, already sitting down, and sits down beside them. Rose, with her bad knee, sits with her chair pulled out from the table, her swollen ankle propped on a little stool. "It's no good," she is saying to no one in particular at her table, all of them her children or grandchildren. Only David, Zellie's David, is listening. "It's a lie, what they say about age, let me tell you. There's nothing golden about it." Max, tanned from the Florida sun, distinguished and handsome even without hair, is shaking his head. "No one's listening to you," he says.

At forty, Zellie is ashamed still to need them. She kisses them both on the cheek, and holds her hands on the table rather than reach for her mother's hand, small and soft, freckled with age. Her own hands are long, bony, red from detergent and gnawed at the tips. When she twists her wedding ring on her finger, Rose notices and taps her daughter's hand, her eyebrows suddenly arched, her eyes lively, cheerful.

"Smile, dolly," she says. "No one'll say anything, I promise. This is family here. Why don't you eat something?" At each place is a fruit cup and a hard-boiled egg. Smiling, Zellie shakes her head and stares down into her lap. After a moment, she picks off a grape.

"Where's Daddy?" Lonnie says, sitting down next to her and

squeezing her hand. Zellie squeezes back, too hard, and Lonnie knows the squeeze is only a signal to let go. Still, she holds on.

"Daddy had to work late," Zellie says. "Maybe he'll come later."

"And will he sit next to me?"

"No!" says Zellie sharply, and Lonnie begins to eat her fruit cup. After a moment, Zellie says, "Your brother has to sit there."

"David or Warren?"

"Either one."

"And where will Daddy sit?"

"I don't know!" Zellie says, shouting by the vehemence of her syllables, but without the breath. "It doesn't matter," she says, to the flowers on the table.

All at once, as if by chance, the crowd has divided into eleven separate clusters, each encircling a round white table, each of those laden surfaces suddenly blooming, shuddering above white plates with a smiling face, a bright shirt, a nervous set of hands. The hum of welcomes, reminiscence, and laughing recognition falls all at once to whispers as the family arranges itself into order, ten, eleven, and twelve all around, as everyone takes his place.

A stooped but elegant old man rises from his seat at table number ten, which is marked with the number as well as the family name, Schneebaum, and walks to the nearby podium. In his hand he carries a briefcase, and on his bald head he wears a skull cap. Once, twice, he taps the microphone, blows into it, and says, "One, two, three, four; this is only a test. One, two, three, four; does anyone know what's next?"

"Five!" Lonnie shouts, twisting in her seat to see him, her old Uncle Irv, who is also her mother's uncle, leading the seder every year, every year asking the same question.

"Five!" repeats the old man, and laughs, clapping his hands lovingly as he looks around the room. "Thank you! Of course!

That must be Zellie's little girl, let's see—little Lonnie! Isn't she pretty! Well now, aunts, uncles, nephews, nieces, cousins, children: Welcome once again to the Keppler family Cousins' Club seder!"

Before the supper and the prayers comes the family news. Minnie stands up first, with the help of her daughter. Before a crowd she seems particularly frail and tiny, her hands shaking, her head nodding perpetually. But her grin is sincere, and her voice, though quavering, is still clear.

"Irv and I are very happy to be here tonight with our family, and very happy to be with my sisters once again and their families also for our family seder. As you all know, Danny's Sylvia was engaged in the winter to a wonderful boy, Michael Shapiro, who, I'm happy to say, is with us tonight."

Ushered up at both elbows, the young man—he is over thirty—stands for a moment and nods shyly as the family applauds, turns to look, and whispers its response among the tables. Over the whispering, Minnie continues:

"My daughter Margie's little Robert will be graduating this spring from high school and has been accepted, I am very happy and proud to be able to announce, to Princeton University. Margie and her Marty went on a cruise this past March, celebrating their twentieth anniversary. Margie looked very beautiful, I saw the pictures."

"Mother!" Margie says, reaching up but only holding her mother's hand.

"And last but not least, Irv and I are in good health, thank God, and came up from Florida again just to be here, with our wonderful family. Thank you, and I love everybody here."

Nodding, grinning, as if to encourage agreement and understanding from her audience, Minnie is helped down into her seat, and from table number nine Gloria stands up, holding a note card subtly in one hand.

"Hello, everybody!" she says, and begins to read the various events of her family's year: a bar mitzvah, a skating prize, a second engagement after divorce. . . . While Gloria speaks, across the room Zellie leans her elbows on the table, shielding her eyes with her hand, dreading the turn of table number eleven. On her left, Lonnie quietly eats fruit salad; her two sons politely listen to the family news. David, at twelve, is a sullen, distracted, secretive boy, too sensitive to criticism, smart in school, kindly to his grandparents, impatient only with his mother. Warren, almost seventeen, is handsome, slow-tempered, cheerful, and arrogant, though secretly threatened and offended, Zellie knows, by his younger brother; well liked by girls and by the baseball players on his team, he doesn't seem to take his family—at least his mother—seriously. For a moment Zellie forgets her absent husband, wondering how she might bring Warren back to her, remind him that she, and no one else, will be his best friend. Others, she knows, will claim all kinds of loyalty, all kinds of love, lovers, friends, fathers, but in the end—she doesn't know where they lead in the end, only that loyalties change, love changes. But a mother, she says silently to Warren, her firstborn, nodding when he glances over, a mother is always a mother. When Gloria sits down and Aunt Ida stands up, Zellie takes Rose's hand.

"What are you going to say?" she says.

"Say?" says Rose. "What are you worried about? I'm your mother." They both glance, irresistibly, at the empty seat next to Warren, where Israel should be. The place, like all the others, is set, untouched, with three forks, ice water, and a hard-boiled egg, although Warren has taken the metal dish of fruit salad for himself. "Elijah," says Rose, turning back to her daughter, and pointing with her hand held discreetly to her chest. Set an extra place, she always said, and open the door, in case Elijah comes, to save us all. And every time she told how once, in Newark, her father had opened the door and a dog walked in, a giant bear of a dog, right off the street.

Across from them, Pearl's boys are giggling, swearing, and jabbing their forks into their plates, into hard-boiled eggs, into each other. "Hey!" says Mel, loudly but very fast, and pulls Teddy's hands into his lap. Deep lines around his eyes and mouth preserve old worries in his face. "Matthew, cut it out! Hey, Big Steve," he whispers to his eldest son, "do something there with your brother, will you?" Matthew, next to him, quickly jabs Teddy one more time and runs from the table. "Hey!" says Mel. "Matthew, get back here! Matthew!" But Pearl leans over and shakes her head. "Let him go," she whispers. "For God's sake!"

Ida is the oldest living sister, well over eighty, and looks, from a distance of some tables away, like an old woman of a former age, from Europe, from the shtetls: red-haired, stooping, smallest of all the sisters. Rose, turning for a moment from her own table, can see not only Ida but also, perhaps, her own mother, standing there at the far table telling family news— the same high bosom, the same cheerful, ancient face, sunken and pale, the same girlish voice, mixing Yiddish into English like a joke. Why? she wonders, grimacing. All of them were born in America, every one, and still the older ones talked that way, as if to remember their parents by, keeping their mother a little bit with them.

"My mother," says Ida smiling and shaking her head. "Mamma had no mother of her own. At her fiftieth anniversary—do you remember it?—it was Gloria's wedding, and they got married all over again, like newlyweds."

"It wasn't my wedding!" Gloria calls to her. "It was Didi's."

"At her fiftieth anniversary," Ida continues, "with all of us children there, and husbands, and grandchildren, Gloria looking so beautiful—"

"Ida!" calls Cousin Marty. "It wasn't Gloria!"

"—what did I hear her say but, 'I wish my mother-in-law was here.' Her mother-in-law, who she hated! 'Mamma,' we said, 'why?' 'Because she said I'm too small to have children. And look at me now!' Well, I wish Mamma could be here to see us all, so many years later!" With her handkerchief she dabs an eye. But she is smiling.

Rose cannot bear to listen. All of them are old ladies now, infirm, cheerful, sharp or foolish, whatever they have always been. And Rose too, as she well knows, is old now herself; her own legs old ladies' legs—she is afraid to look. The eldest of the girls are dead—Bertha, Betty, Etta, Flora—their lives lived out, finished, like the turning of a wheel, their own daughters already grandmothers. Seven are left, Ida down to Rose, and Rose taps against the table, counting with her fingers each one who is gone. Bertha, Betty, Etta, Flora—and then perhaps Ida. Slowly the wheel has turned; subtly Rose bends her head, pretending to feel the turn and the gravity, the slow fall to the ground. Now Ida is the oldest, and in her face Rose can see each of her sisters, still alive, already dead. Quickly she turns back to see one of the children—David, the middle one—staring at her, his eyebrows low and furrowed. Smiling, she winks at him, and he smiles back.

"And now," says Irv from the podium, following some mysterious, troubling order no one understands, "Aunt Rose, will you tell us the Levin family news?"

"But of course!" says Rose, in her fancy British accent saved for happy occasions, pursing her lips into a rosebud and batting her eyes haughtily. Once, she likes to recount, a woman asked if she was Rose Kennedy.

"I'll be back," Zellie says, jumping from her seat, but Pearl across the table calls her name in a whisper, shaking her head. "Come on, Zellie," she says, and Zellie acquiesces, sits down, frowning, spreading her napkin out across her lap. A hundred people are watching.

"First," says Rose, "I would like to say that Max and I are very happy to be here with all our family—"

"Can't hear you, Aunt Rose!" yells one of the men—Uncle Marty. "Stand up!"

"She can't stand up, Marty!" says Pearl angrily. "Her bad leg!"

"We're very happy to be here," Rose continues. "Everyone is in good health—the children are fine. Of course, we'll be having a bar mitzvah next fall—both David Rosen and Matthew Green together—and we hope most of you will be there. This month Max and I will be celebrating our fiftieth wedding anniversary."

Rose nods to the tables, and to her family, indicating that she has finished, and all the cousins applaud, whistling, exclaiming "mazel tov!"

"Is that it?" shouts Cousin Marty, but no one responds, and Irv calls upon the next family on his secret list. The Levin family has taken its turn.

"Is it over?" Zellie asks, still looking down at her lap.

"Yes, dolly," says Rose, sipping a glass of water. "That's all."

"It's not over," says Lonnie, bending her head down to look, dark-eyed and smiling, up into her mother's face. "It hasn't started."

When finally Zellie looks up—at her parents, older than last she noticed; at her sister across the table, winking; at the empty seat (for Elijah, now); at her sons, one bored, one staring at her nervously; at her daughter in her lap—the last table has finished, and Uncle Irv is standing with his prayer book opened, waiting for quiet.

" 'On Passover,' " he reads, " 'we celebrate the exodus of the Jews out of slavery in Egypt, explaining to our children, so that their children will understand, and explain. . . . ' "

Everyone else has opened a blue book and reads along responsively, and Zellie too opens her book, sharing with her daughter. Over, she whispers quietly to herself, it's over . . . while at the same time voices all around her speak, young voices, old voices, old words in unison, an ancient prayer to remind her, and anyone else, that in this place at least, whatever once had been might begin again.

ZELLIE WAS PREGNANT the same time as Pearl, still a young mother while Pearl, with Matthew and then again with Teddy, laughed at the miracle and called herself Sarah in the wilderness. From the first, in the eyes of the world, David was the good cousin. Born eight days apart—one circumcised while the other emerged—and raised by sisters across a quiet neighborhood street, David and Matthew were each other's first friend, playing through quiet afternoons in mysterious basement corners, or through the backyards of the neighborhood, making friends who could never count as much, not being related, and later forgetting them. Their own bond, however, they understood: Matthew was the elder by a week; they were meant to be together—after school in the woods, during summers at the beach, in class at Hebrew school, on the porch at family dinners. For a while they would play at whatever game—sandbox, puppets, or war—until at last Matthew would smash the sand castle, kick over the puppet house, or throw rocks instead of imaginary bombs. In the rubble, in the mess of broken games, he would smile or laugh, and ask as if in triumph: "Now what?"

Before he died Matthew stole everything, as if he knew more than anyone that he would never get too much. Going into his parents' house today, it might seem that he took it all with him: all the sterling; the silver pots and trays and fancy serving spoons; Pearl's fur coat; all of her jewels; her diamond engagement ring; the brooch and earrings from her mother; even Mel's rare coin collection, books and books of antique silver dollars, sold for a dollar each to the coin dealer in town.

"Where is it!" Mel found himself yelling each time, storming up the stairs as Matthew drowsed in his bed until noon or sat watching TV with nervous friends whose names Pearl never knew. The house is a comfortable, affluent person's house in a wealthy Lewiston neighborhood, and although everything looks rich and comfortable still, there are no more treasured objects, and after all the yelling there is no more noise. All the broken windows have been replaced, the burned cushions reupholstered, the dents in the car hammered out; but the inside doors still have padlocks, the drawers have locks—obsolete now—and glass cabinets have had their keys hidden away.

When they ran away from home, David and Matthew planned the whole thing out together, Pearl packing them lunch and helping to carry over the tent, extra blankets, and flashlights to the woods between their houses. Teddy and Lonnie, as well as the older cousins, were eluded, excluded, and finally chased from the campsite. Matthew chopped down birch trees with his father's hatchet while David gathered pine needles, and together they built the tree house where they would live. In the soft earth under the leaves they found brick after brick, a buried pavement which seemed to mark a lost civilization, perfect blocks for a campfire. Pearl helped identify the bricks, deciphering the letters, even calling up the brick company to know their age and value. They were indeed artifacts, she knew, although she knew as well just what lost tribe had preceded them: Warren and Stevey, the firstborns, eldest boys of all the cousins, had abandoned them years before to the rotting leaves and fallen branches—their own failed, forgotten attempt at a brick swimming pool.

Soon education separated the slow from the fast. "Gifted" was the name for the top class, while "specially gifted" was the name for the bottom. Once promenaded together in a carriage, eventually they were bar mitzvahed together in a huge joint ceremony of all the relieved, amazed family; and every year

Matthew was more and more the darker, failed reflection of his cousin's evident success. Where Matthew disappointed, David fulfilled: a good student, bound for a really *good* college. (One day, he would fulfill even his aunt's dream to be a doctor; and his mother's, to be a musician, to know real artists and intellectuals.) Even when they were thirteen, the Hebrew ceremony seemed to be announcing the difference to them in its harsh, foreign syllables. David sang his portion by heart, squeaky-voiced but confident as he pretended to read from the huge Torah scroll before three hundred guests, a silver finger pointing to the words before him, though suddenly the vowels were gone as well as all the meaning. Matthew too had learned the Hebrew, but didn't dare sing. Afterwards came David's meditation on "The Rewards of Charity," a speech he had also memorized; while Matthew sat down behind him, waiting with impressive patience.

Patiently he went from school to special school, then, less patiently, from job to job, dishwashing, mowing lawns, guarding a store at night, selling drugs or stolen watches, stealing cars. Pearl and Mel pretended even to each other that it was all temporary, this picture that wasn't the right, happy picture—Matthew's failures, his petty crimes, his menial place in the world—that next month, next year, or the year after that, Matthew's life would be successful and easy, as would his brothers', as would all his cousins'; that without pretending, without other eyes lowering when he walked into a room, he would remember something to be proud of, something more than just having come that far, and all that time, having waited.

For the first years they all waited together—the daughters, their husbands, their parents, their children, and their pets—in a new, cozy, sunny neighborhood where the children could grow up safely, away from traffic, poverty, and the cramped, sunless neighborhood of their past, of their parents' past, where life, when they looked back on it, seemed never to have been so sweet a time. Now Rose and Max, just retired, lived at the corner in a brick house they had built, with Zellie, Pearl, and Gloria just down the block with their own families. Every morning at her pink table Rose had a full kitchen for breakfast: daughters, sons-in-law, Gloria, or even Danny from across town, and all the children on their way to school, who had pinched from beneath the fence a sprig of parsley or mint from Pearl's garden, proud and grateful for their aunt's or mother's mastery of nature, and for the intimacy and easy bounty of their world. "He's the lucky one," said Lenny Minkoff, long retired, sitting one day in Rose's kitchen. He was pointing to Warren in his high chair, shaking his old head regretfully. "That's the prince of America there. Everything's waiting on him. You bet you, I wish I was him."

Not only on Warren but on all the children of the neighborhood, America itself seemed to be waiting, bestowing new clothes for school every year, dance lessons, piano lessons, new bicycles and wagons on the street, new swings in the connecting backyards, camp every summer and weeks at the beach. Rose's grandchildren felt the privilege most of all, united underground and invisibly, welcome among the kitchens, bedrooms, bathrooms, and front doors of four houses on the street. For each of them Rose was knitting an afghan, pulling different-colored yarns from her paper shopping bag year after year, for cold nights, for lonely, future nights when she would be gone. It was all they knew, their special connection, reinforced in towns east and west by cousins and aunts and uncles whose front doors in far neighborhoods, or office doors all around the Lewiston green, would gladly open to smiles or handshakes or warm things cooking, if any child should find his way there. The whole world seemed open to them, respectful of the family's loyalty, their hard work, their final prominence and promise. They would all become prosperous and beloved.

Stevey, Pearl's firstborn, would be a doctor. Gloria had girls, but Big Steve (his father called him that), younger by a year, was the first boy. Big Steve, his father said, could throw a ball, run across the lawn, or drink a cup of milk like the best of them. Gloria's girls could sing a little song, but already Big Steve—a small child, after all—was learning to sit on the toilet, and loved hot dogs, and burped when he was done. Big Steve would be President, Mel said, proudly throwing him up in the air too soon after his meal. And Pearl would take him firmly in her arms, murmuring her reprimand: a doctor first.

Zellie's Warren, next in line, would do something with his hands—he liked to take things apart and try to fix them—and there was money in that. David would be a great musician, Zellie said, or else, like his cousin, a doctor. Let him be a doctor first, said Pearl, will you please? Then he can play the piano too, all he likes. Teddy would be a lawyer. Lonnie, the youngest, the little girl, would be whatever it was she wanted to be. And Matthew, too, Pearl always said, would do what he wanted.

Zellie's children, at first, had to bear the taunts of their cousins; "the children of Israel," Mel had named them, and the title stuck, screwed so tightly between humor and criticism. But Zellie and Israel only laughed and were proud. In the temple all the cousins were teased but had to be proud: their grandfather's portrait hung in the hall of presidents, in the place of honor as number one before their own fathers and uncles and cousins as well as the Sisterhood presidents across the hall, smiling back at the men only slightly. The later portraits were photographs—Mel, Israel, and Harry Schwartz among them, as well as Gloria and Pearl, just across—but the early ones were paintings in oil, as cheerful and modest as could be managed in that medium, though still somber and dignified enough to be mistaken for a hall of ancestors absconded from Europe, or else for the Puritan predecessors of some high but still local political official. On the memorial wall above the candles were plaques with the names of other aunts and uncles and cousins, names that were read out loud each year at the appropriate Friday-night anniversary—the mothers' aunts and uncles really, but the honor was extended to the cousins and to the men. The dead of other congregants had disappeared far away—they had no plaques, no dates of death, no anniversaries—but all the towns from Lewiston to Newark had Levins down among their dead, as far north as Newport and south to Philadelphia. Keppler's name had disappeared without violence, all the daughters having married.

Every year, every spring, the Hebrew school hosted its Purim festival in the auditorium, a family banquet as much as possible like the feast of Esther the queen when she had outwitted Haman the hateful prince and saved her people Israel once again from destruction. Every year, every spring, it was one Levin grandchild or another who won the costume prize as King Ahasuerus or Queen Esther or the banished Queen Vashti. And each time, resurrected from the attic, turned inside out and restitched at the fragile seams, it was Esther Levin's old coat that exalted them, transformed them, itself transformed into a royal cape in red velvet, gold-trimmed and still luxurious year after year.

Even on Lonnie, youngest of all, it seemed the heavy mantle would one day fall. Almost two years old and learning to walk alone, they had pointed her down to the end of the street where Rose was standing far off in the sun and waving her hands. "You see Ma Rose?" Zellie asked, encouraging her daughter, still holding her up by the arms. "Can you see her, Lonnie, way down there? Someday, you too'll walk up the street—all the way by yourself!"

At first, when she was old enough to walk, Lonnie was always Queen Esther, later on preferring Vashti, the subjugated queen. Warren was always Mordecai, the good uncle, or else the hangman. Stevey and later Teddy were always the Purim scroll itself, a costume Stevey had made with his father one spring, hammering and nailing, and used again and again until it crumbled in a pile. Only Matthew and David ever vied for the robe, taking turns some years but mostly leaving the contest to their mothers, who stood on the street arguing with the old coat between them, as if to pull it apart. Only one boy could be the king each year, and the other, it seemed—though the logic was unclear—must be Haman, the dark prince. "Haman!" the rabbi would shout as he recited the story year after year, and all the children would swirl their noisemakers, and the adults would hiss. No one wanted to be Haman.

THEY ARE LINED up in two rows facing each other, the boys on one side of the room and the girls on the other. Miss Cole drops the needle on the record and the boys must break ranks and wander across to bow from the waist, as if casually, and ask a girl to dance. "May I have this dance?" they are trained to say. They are dressed in black shoes and black bow ties; the girls are in knee-length ball gowns and white gloves— compulsory—without which the offender must sit against the wall and watch.

Like every other boy in the line, David has chosen his girl well in advance, tried to catch her eye before the music begins, so that she will watch David as he crosses, and not accept another boy first. She is not the prettiest girl, but perhaps she is not the homeliest, either; still, she is ungainly, tall for her age and yet still chubby with childhood—no breasts, and shoulders that could wrestle a boy down instead of curtseying as she must in grateful acceptance. The girls have been taught each to wait, to curtsey with a smile and to take her partner's arm. No girl is taught how to say no, although it must have happened, and no boy is taught how to recover gracefully and bow to someone else.

Debbie is his girl's name. They have sat in class together every year and never spoken a casual word, until now, in sixth grade, the others are bringing them unaccountably together: forging love notes; moving desks, winking as if there were a secret. Why? they both want to know. They do not like each other, but they have nodded across that gulf and made a pact; David will not leave her unasked, and she will not refuse him. In that they have absolute trust.

But though the waltz begins and they are safe within their box steps, repeated rigidly again and again around the room with the instructions called out in a hoarse voice by Miss Cole, it is not Debbie that David desires. They stare past each other's head, or study the shifting boxes made by their feet, as if they were shy with twelve-year-olds' passion. Their real passions, his own at least, have shot across the room in cold observation, cold itself because as soon as it rises up it has to flee or hide, so that David hardly knows it himself.

The other couples step and turn in their own boxes in a subtle but distinct spectrum of the most desirable to the very least. Tommy Burns, the sixth-grade star of musicals and base-ball, is dancing with Karen Deedles, whose early breasts have plunged her into intense popularity. David and Debbie are not the only couple staring at Tommy and Karen. They are not the only couple whose passions are far away from their own little box. Although catching Tommy's informal wink is David's real imperative for every clever step, every glance up from the progress of his feet, he does not know what he is looking for when, staring over Debbie's shoulder, he is instructed, vaguely, to "spot" before each turn.

All they know, Debbie and David, is that they are not the very last couple in the spectrum of desire. Certainly they are far from that privileged height where Tommy and Karen swirl in effortless beauty and grace. The evidence is hidden, to their brains if not their eyes, but they know that they are comfortably, gratefully obscure, somewhere two-thirds down near the bottom, perhaps, but no further. They could have danced with one or two others, they know; and they have escaped notice, so that even if they hate themselves they have not been sacrificed to derision.

Another couple has been chosen for that. Robin and Susan dance with extreme concentration, and as long as the music lasts they will not have to look up, either at each other or out at the rest of the world, which despises them. Robin is despised for his name, which is considered effeminate, affected, or merely ridiculous. He has other vices—wild, uncombable hair, an illegible scrawl, a messy desk, and the misfortune of having cleaned it out one June while everyone watched, so that the cupcake from January falling out was not only impossible to hide but became a class myth, pursuing him even into high school. Susan is despised for reasons less justifiable: early breasts, for her, made the girls laugh in gym class and tell all the boys. She wears thick glasses, cringes away from scorn, and generally has nothing to hide but her intelligence and shyness. When either one of them is absent from these Monday afternoons, the other is condemned to hope for a group dance, or an extra boy or girl with no alternative, or else to sit by Miss Cole and help with the changing of records.

At the end of the waltz the two sexes quickly divide, and while Miss Cole explains—slowly, and with her cane as partner—that the fox trot can also be imagined as a box step, critiques are rendered in whispers on both sides. "Did you see the dog David got?" someone whispers to Tommy, hoping for a nod of agreement. Even if the girl is perfectly pretty, a criticism to Tommy's ear, it must be supposed, is meant to strengthen the bond of friendship; there will be no romance that could not be his own, if he wanted it; there will be no loyalty that excludes him. Whatever the girls whisper—that certain boys smell bad, or step on feet—it is shared among them more intimately, lips whispering in ears, hands over mouths, giggles instead of guffaws.

During the next dance, David is with Debbie again. A bond of gratitude has sprung up between them, and as long as no one notices, they are relieved to have each other, though such repetition is strictly forbidden. The fox trot leaves them with more time to their private thoughts, and David is veering—in great, awkward leaps—around the perimeter, although he is not sure why. Debbie follows without complaint by now; it is her primary lesson to be learned, and also David does not step on her feet. He is trying to "spot," but with each turn they crash into another turning couple, or rather Debbie does, help-lessly trusting his lead. Where David is leading them, he does not know. Sometimes it is through a crowd, sometimes into a clearing; eventually, as they make their quarter-turn, they bump into Tommy and a second pretty girl. Or rather it is David, this time, bumping into them, pretending afterwards that he has something to whisper into Tommy's ear that cannot wait.

"Wait!" Tommy says with a calm smile, the smile he shows even to Robin when occasionally they are forced to speak.

"Okay!" David tells him, nodding too hard, as if it were Tommy coming for a favor and David were merely glad to comply.

All through the next dance he is excited and impatient for his moment, when Tommy will wrap his fingers around David's too soft arm, pull him through the crowd of all the envious other boys to a quiet corner, and ask, with his chin raised, what David wants. And David will take the liberty—like the girls —of leaning up to his ear for added intimacy, and whisper whatever he has to tell him.

At the end of the dance it is refreshment time, when they

line up for juice and cookies, receiving instruction in the ways of holding napkins and plates in one hand, and in eating at chairs without tables; you balance the plate between your legs when you sip your juice. Robin, having no partner for the last dance, is helping to pour and soon drops the juice bottle. Girls scream and jump away as the purple stain spreads down the paper cloth. In the sudden disturbance Tommy appears before David, his plate loaded with cookies.

"So what was it?" he asks, still two feet away. As his hands are full, he cannot lead David into a corner; and as David's mouth is full, David cannot answer. He swallows, too hard, looking around for the corner where they might still withdraw if Tommy would understand his glance.

"What?" Tommy asks again; and though David has swallowed now, still he is silent. Whatever he had to say is gone, and he is left only with a mute longing which distorts his face. "Okay, forget it!" Tommy says, and laughs, turning away. But David's mouth is still open, empty, as if words might somehow still flow out, beautiful, attractive and powerful, filling him with eloquence.

In a whisper, Irene, the maid, told Zellie she had had a dream.

"A dream!" Zellie whispered back, surprised as always by their intimacy.

"Yes," said Irene. "I had a dream that you gave me a raise."

Now she rustles onto the patio in her formal black serving dress, her hair done up in stiff loops for the occasion, carrying out a tray of blintzes, which will be cold, and also a silver bowl full of ice, which will have melted.

"Oh! Irene!" Zellie calls, waving. "Don't put that out yet!

It'll be—" and her last word is quiet, spoken only to herself, useless—"cold."

"What is it?" says Pearl, standing up quickly from her chair. "What can I do, Zel? You're not supposed to yell, you know, on your wedding—bad luck."

"The food will be cold," Zellie says. "Tell Irene to keep it in the oven." Pearl, Irene's employer the other half of the week, hurries down the aisle with the message.

Surrounded under the *huppah* by her children, her rabbi, and the large, sweating man she will marry, Zellie is waiting for the soon-to-be stepchildren she has never met, who are driving out for the wedding and have promised not to be late. With three sides of the canopy upheld by her own children, the fourth awaits a child of the groom, though for the moment Sol himself is holding up the short metal rod, all six-foot-four of him stooping slightly to fit inside. The wedding canopy is flimsy but portable, rolled up and carried in the rabbi's backseat for such weddings at homes or hotels, in parks or forests, on mountaintops, even at the beach. He will say the prayers almost anywhere—grateful, these days, for any wedding at all of a Jew to a Jew. Over the heads of her parents, her sister, and fifty guests on the lawn, most of them family from town, she watches the September clouds suspiciously for a storm, surveys five vulnerable tables of cake and wine, listens to the pool cleaner buzzing side to side, forsaken in the pool—someone should have thought to turn it off—and recalls other weddings she has celebrated, her own among them, in which the ritual, the romance, and the movement toward union and order still had a power over her, an authority to which she could submit. Not long ago, the lawn where they stand was a hay field, the town little more than a village. Skyscrapers now tower over the green, and the highway plows through what once were quiet lanes and wild meadows. Though grateful all around—for her children, her new husband, her parents (still alive), and her white house in the hills with its sloping lawn, its red barn, and a pool—she is also, secretly, ashamed; is a woman still a bride the second time around? Her round cheeks have been red all day. Her hair is penitentially short, her dress this time is dark brown and gray. Patient and wide-eyed she stands among them, trying to remember. Over their heads, over the tops of the trees, a dark cloud covers the sun, and a breeze quivers through the upper branches. But on the lawn it is almost hot, and the air is still.

Raising his hands for silence, the rabbi calls the guests to attention as inside the house the phone begins to ring.

"Let it ring," says Sol.

"It's probably them," Zellie says, wiping her neck.

"Let it ring, I said." His jaw is clenched, and a vein stands out on his forehead. Under each arm a large circle of sweat already darkens his suit. "They said they're coming and they're coming."

After a while the ringing stops, and the rabbi recites the opening prayer, the Hebrew words unknown to everyone else, but at least heartfelt and familiar—*Baruch Ata Adonai, Elohaynu Melech Ha-olam* . . .—so that almost at once Zellie begins to cry, silently, with her head bent. Rose and Pearl are crying also, but with their heads held up and their eyes open, not to miss anything. Even Sol himself is weeping, loudly, so that forgetting her own tears a moment Zellie looks up at them all, wondering why.

"Well," says the rabbi, in his deeper, public voice. "It's been a long time since I've had the chance—" already the family laughs, right through their crying, but for the sake of the others he continues—"the chance to marry one of Rose's daughters!" Now all the audience laughs. Rose in the front row is laughing most of all, shaking, in her excitement, the metal walker she hates people to see.

"You had your chance, Jerry!" calls Pearl, loudly enough to be all in fun. Once, during the war, they had been to a dance.

"Zelda?" he continues, his voice riding up with each phrase, then dropping back, as if, before he can finish, even his statements must become questions. "Sol? This time we're a little older, a little wiser even, but I can't promise anything. Maybe it means our promises are wiser promises, our dreams, our expectations are maybe not so fragile. I'd even say we've learned how to love. . . ."

As if in synchrony the car full of Sol's children accelerates up the driveway just as the sun emerges again over the trees. On all the rows of guests a giant shadow races past, the light making faces turn up and gold jewelry glint from bare necks, from ample earlobes, from rough or tender fingers.

"Okay!" says Sol, grinning for the first time, standing up as straight as he can. Awkward, embarrassed, and too slowly, the four Friedman children climb from the car and make their way to the back of the crowd, and then down the aisle to their father. "Hello there!" he shouts, letting the canopy droop as he embraces them. "Here!" he says, handing over the metal pole to his eldest son and kissing his cheek, though his son quickly turns his face away. "Am I glad to see you!"

The ceremony, abridged for modesty and uncertain weather, is quickly over. Zellie's children are tired of holding up their ends, each like the meager handle of a small umbrella—their arms are cramped, they feel embarrassed—so that the canopy disappears as soon as the glass has been broken, the benediction spoken over bowed heads, and the cries of "Mazel tov!" have echoed and re-echoed over the lawn. Looking up, Zellie can see the sky again, the sun quickly hot and welcome on her face, the wind, descending from the trees, blowing ripples across the pool. Where did it go? she wonders, disappointed to find, turning around, that already the canopy is rolled up and lying on the grass, more like a rustic Torah of canvas and metal than any roof, even one so symbolic and brief; she imagines unrolling it right there on the grass and finding black Hebrew letters inside, etched and ordered into columns, old Bible stories and long lists of commandments darkening the page instead of empty seams.

"So? Mazel tov!" calls Pearl, coming up and embracing her. Zellie kisses her sister first, then, grinning but still tearful, reaches to kiss in careful order first Lonnie, who waits for her impatiently; Warren, who looks away; David, who kisses her also; Lonnie again, pulling on her skirt, who does not kiss this time but merely holds out her own cheek like a grown woman; Sol again; and then, quickly, Rose, who has not stood up but is leaning over with a story to tell whoever will listen. ". . . I remember Viola came late to our wedding," she is saying, and Zellie waits until she finishes. "And because we didn't visit her—an old aunt, it was only right, she said, for an engagement—we had to wait three hours at the wedding—or more, was it, Max? It was to get even, I'm sure. Three hours we had to wait before she came, at that old *shul* on Prince Street. But we made it up to her, I'll tell you that much. When she died, I never went to her funeral."

"Hi, Ma," Zellie says, bending to kiss her.

"You look beautiful, dolly. Stand up and let everyone see you."

"Well, Daddy?" Zellie says, sitting down and kissing her father's cheek.

"Well!" says Max, well tanned on the top of his head, smiling while he holds Rose's hand. Already he has all the signs of age—the hairless forehead, the loosened flesh of his cheeks, earlobes longer than she remembered. And yet how old are they now? she wonders, squinting to see. How old can they be? Fifty? She herself is nearly forty-four. Sixty? They were sixty when David was born. Even then they were the same, sitting there in the bedroom, always vaguely older and mature, like a different race entirely, that older generation, watching with relief and longing the child at her breast. Now they are facing straight ahead, where Sol is introducing, in a loud, happy voice, his own children to the rabbi.

Finally Max nods and turns slightly away, as if that alone were his answer. "That's some guy you've got there," he says, leaning back toward her intimately, still alert when he cares to be. "But then," he says, straightening up, "you know all that, I suppose."

Zellie has lived all her life for their approval, always expecting, despite her better sense, that in the near but undetermined future her parents would again come near her own life, hover somehow above it, and take care of her once more. Trying to take her father's hand, he takes hers first, and after a squeeze, taps it twice to escape politely. Then he is standing, helping Rose to stand, a hand on her behind, pushing, and all the other guests are crowding around Zellie, waiting to kiss her, offer their good wishes, and see for themselves if her tears are tears of happiness. "Of course they are!" she says, in a girlish, untroubled voice, grinning, even laughing, with a wink to her sister. "What else?"

Fulfilling despite himself the brooding destiny of the middle child, dissenting with his back turned to them, David has been trying to escape the introduction of Sol's children. "David!" he hears, pretending not to hear. "Hey there, David!" All through the ceremony he has heard their whispers and voiceless laughter, their winks to each other, their glances to the ground. He has heard of their fights with their father, their name-calling, their mocking, in advance, of his mother. They are handsome, expensively dressed, tanned from California, and still they sneer, in the eyebrows, in the corners of the mouth.

"Hey, Poppy," David says, coming up to Zellie and her parents, taking Max's hand though at sixteen he knows the gesture is already suspicious. "Have you seen my garden?" With a vague smile Max nods slowly no, indicating yes, he will come. He himself has stood too many minutes humming without conversation.

"But David," Zellie says, "they're calling you."

"I know," he says, turning to show her his sneer, and she is frightened of pressing him further; embarrassed, right now, to risk an argument.

"Just go say hello," she says. "Then show Poppy the garden."

"All right," he says, and sulks away.

"It's wonderful this year, Dad," Zellie says, aware somehow that she has disappointed them both, a bitterness passed on, as if through her own blood. "Full of flowers," she says. "All these flowers came from David's garden." Flipping back her hand, she indicates the place, empty now, where the *huppah* had stood, still decorated with bouquets of autumn flowers; the double row of sunflower stalks forming the aisle; the huge piles of fruit and flowers heaped on all the tables by the house, chrysanthemums, zinnias, pyramids of grapes, cornucopias of nuts and gourds, each platter crowned with a pineapple.

"That so!" says Max, nodding. He stands with his hands at his sides, debonair but uncomfortable in a suit, biting his bottom lip. At least with the grandchildren, Zellie knows, he and Rose are slow to criticize, are as mild as can be; even Rose will seldom shed her smile, her winking eye, as if only good things have ever come to them.

Looking down at the barn, toward the garden, Max nods. "Looks like he's worked hard," he says, but clearly this is not what he wants to say. He reaches up to one of the sunflowers draped in vines, picks at one of the seeds. Next to that oversized flower he might still be a child himself, smooth-skinned and naive, lost in some garden of his youth. "Why doesn't he stick to his vegetables?" he says at last, searching in his breast pocket for a cigar. He bites off the tip, spits it out, and holds the open end up to his lighter. "What do you mean, Dad?" she wants to ask, defending her son already, already knowing the answer. But she doesn't dare. His flame has not caught; he flicks it up again, puffing.

"Mom!" calls Lonnie, somewhere far away. Zellie turns but cannot yet see her. "It's just a garden, Daddy," she says, still looking away.

Because her mother would not answer when she called, would not turn to her, Lonnie has decided to run away, and takes her piece of cake down to the barn. She is still afraid of things inside—the rats, the bats, and the ghosts of bogeymen her brothers long ago scared her into believing were true. She is scared, but she will not answer, she swears, when they call her. They will miss her but she will not come, she will not budge, until everyone has gone home and it is too late. Past the heavy sliding door of the barn the air is dank and dark, and seems always smoky up where the sun fans out in blades from the hayloft. From behind the car, from somewhere in the darkness, falls the sound of diabolical laughter. It is deep, it is devilish, but so low that she can hardly hear it. "Don't come in here!" threatens a voice, slowly and ponderously, and she screams, falling to the ground. Burlap bags have cushioned her, but her eyes are closed; her mouth is slack.

"Hey!" Warren says, coming out from behind the car, running to her. "Hey, Lon, I was just kidding. Hey there!"

Behind him, Matthew throws down a joint and leans against the car to watch. At sixteen he is already wild with his friends and secretive with his parents. A minute after the ceremony his tie was in his pocket. Warren, four years older and home from college, had even from under the canopy held up two pinching fingers to his mouth, signaling "smoke" to his delinquent but amusing cousin. "Hey, Lon," he says, standing her up, lifting her piece of cake from the dirt, picking out pebbles. "Sorry about that. We were just having a cigarette, there. Didn't mean to scare you. You won't tell anyone now, will you? Come on!" he says, winking, touching her head.

"Come on there, little rooner!" Matthew says, in the exaggerated cowboy accent he has invented, which now all the cousins affect when being bad, as well as his invented words —"rooner" this time, for any dog or small child. Picking up the joint again, he holds it to his lighter—gold-plated, stolen. "You're not gonna tell on us there, now, are you, little thing, you?"

"Of course not," she says, getting up quickly and brushing herself off—tough, she believes, as any boy cousin. "Course not, rooner," she says, in her high voice, and Warren winks. "I won't tell!" she says, running out, stopping at the door to wink back at them.

"He's a shit," says Pearl, shaking her head. "That's all I have to say."

David has come unexpectedly into the living room through the French doors, where Pearl is sitting with Rose. "Come here, David!" she says, tossing her head in a friendly way. "We'd like to know," she says. "Tell us, how could Israel have left all this?"

Rather than run away, he sits down with them on the velvet sofa. "I don't know," he says, shrugging, as if that were enough to dismiss such questions.

"Such a beautiful family!" says Rose, shaking her head. "A

beautiful wife, three beautiful children, a beautiful home like this. What did he want to run away for? I certainly don't know." Her forehead, her lips are wrinkled, pulled together like a pouch, as if she were withholding the answer. "Do you know?"

Again David shakes his head, shrugging, eating his cake.

"I always liked Izzy, you know," says Pearl, for David's sake. "He's still my brother-in-law, you know, as far as I'm concerned. It's been a lot of years. I don't know, maybe it was all too much for him, all the family."

"Tell me this," says Rose, leaning forward in her chair, pointing with her thumb as if she were holding a deck of cards close for protection. "You're a big boy—you don't mind if I speak frankly?"

David shakes his head.

"Did he have a girl?"

"I don't know, Ma Rose," he says. None of the questions are new; but his mother, David knows, will no longer listen to them, nor will his grandfather, who hums as soon as the questions begin.

"Here," says Rose, holding out her hand, in which her thumb is clenched. Reaching for it, David gets instead a slip of paper money, folded tightly into quarters. Suddenly the doors are pushed open, and Gloria comes in with her arms held out, plump already as any of her old aunts.

"Hello, Aunt Rosie!" she calls, walking up to them. "Hello, Cousin Pearl!" Outside, through the doorway, David can see his mother laughing on the patio, deep-voiced, indulgently, false, for the comfort of someone else, though he cannot yet see who it is. "Hello, Aunt Gloria," he says, standing up to kiss her. Even standing up, he cannot yet see.

"Oh!" Zellie calls, "Harry!"—seeing him come up the steps to the patio. Slowly, gracefully, slightly stooped, Harry walks up to her, brushing back his thick gray hair. At sixty he is still the best tennis player among their friends. "Harry—" she says, smiling, and Harry interrupts her with his slow, gracious manners.

"Zelda!" he says, eyes widening, head back, as if he has come upon her just now by accident. "Tell me, is this where we get to kiss the bride?"

"Oh, Harry," Zellie says, embarrassed, but kissing him. His cheek is rough with gray stubble; for years, being blond, he could get away with it.

"And who gets to dance the waltz with her?"

"No dancing, I'm afraid, Harry."

"No dancing!" he says. "Whoever heard of no dancing at a wedding? We'll have to do something about that. How about a radio? An old record player—"

"I was worried for Sol," Zellie says, lowering her voice, nodding to the tables nearby, where Sol is already sitting because of his hip, leaning back in his chair as he blows a smoke ring from his cigar. "Sit down, sit down!" Sol says, gesturing to a chair beside him. Danny, standing next to him, cannot squeeze past him and must acquiesce. Rather than intercede between them, Zellie turns her back, even on Harry; even, for a moment, closes her eyes. "Take a seat there, Dan," says Sol, "and tell me how you've been."

Still she is too close; she can hear everything and do nothing. Like a stray echo, his name brings back much more than just the brief, uttered syllable. Even now she can hear their pounded scales at the piano long ago, up and down the spinet. Faster and faster both hands would race, like clumsy crabs, and down again. Then, quietly, came the sound once more, muted by the wall, this time from Danny sitting at his own piano next door, also playing scales. Up both hands would go, treble and bass mostly together, and then they would return. Each time she raised the scale, from black note to white, from white again to black, Danny would follow.

He followed her as well on her journeys around town, to the school after hours, to the woods above the train tracks, to the duck pond across town. It was all, she said, in search of the dog, who had wandered in one day and often stayed. With the dog, Zellie believed, she had found at last that mutual devotion which makes life fast and rich, freed from its slow eddying back and forth from one mistake to the next. With Danny, at least, when the dog ran away, she would pack a lunch and set out after it. But even when they came back unsuccessful, there was a sharp though unspoken sweetness to the search, as if what they were looking for up in the woods and through the town was not just the dog but something elusive and quiet as well —a deer like a nymph through the trees, the stream gurgling almost articulately, a word whispered between them—that they alone had seen or heard.

"Wait!" Danny called, carrying the bag of food as well as the blanket. But Zellie was anxious to escape.

"*Regardez!*" called Margie, as they passed her on the steps. Greta Carp was with her, sitting on the railing. Her parents were German Catholics, had fled from Europe, and because no one else in school would talk to her, she and Margie were best friends, speaking only French in front of younger neighbors and siblings. "*Oui,*" Greta said. "*Les voilà*. But *je ne* care *pas*."

"Wait!" Margie called, glancing nervously at the blanket, the paper bag. "Where are you going?"

"Nowhere," Zellie said, ignoring them both. "I'll bet he's up at the pond, Danny, chasing ducks again. Don't you think?"

Margie walked into the street to watch them go off without her. "Are you looking for the dog?" she called, but they were too far away to answer. She kicked a pile of leaves, ran a few steps. After half a block Zellie turned around to look, but Margie had run back into the yard, out of sight.

Beside the water, Zellie remembered, under the greenish statue of Thomas Paine, they had spread out their woolen blanket and set out the sandwiches, bananas, a bottle of grape juice—waiting, watching the black geese circle the pond in formation like an arrow, pointing lower and lower in their spiral until they landed on the island in the middle, where people weren't allowed. It was summer, in memory always green and too humid. "Maybe this time he ran away for good," she said, looking into Danny's eyes. "Maybe he wasn't happy with us anymore." She was shaking her head, looking down at the blanket, and Danny touched her hand, as he had only once before, when she had seen what afterwards she could never forget—Esther's black coat in the middle of the street, the big pocketbook through the legs of the crowd, Margie crying loudest of all. Danny had touched her then, tried to hold her, but she had run away.

"Maybe he was kidnapped," Zellie said, "or run over by a truck."

"No," Danny said, no, it wasn't that, and though her face was hidden, he brushed back her hair and leaned his forehead against her. She turned, holding him suddenly in her own arms, and kissed him. He was scrawny, he was her cousin Danny, but she had wanted to try it out, see how it felt to be hugging somebody who was at least on his way to being a man. Thus engaged, neither of them noticed the swans, the geese, and even green ducks that had waddled up from the banks of the pond and were quietly, even secretly increasing their ranks. Looking up at last past Danny's smooth, disappointing, little boy's face, Zellie saw the swan running at them, hugely arching its wings and stretching out its long neck as it honked, waddling fiercely. Behind it, other swans, geese, and green ducks began honking, quacking, spreading their wings. Zellie screamed, jumped up, forgot the sandwiches, juice, and blanket, and even Danny who followed quickly behind, both of them startled and frightened, chased by the swan and its minions all the way into the parking lot and across the street.

They ran home, slowing eventually into a tearful stumble. "What's wrong, Zellie?" Danny asked, but she shook her head and couldn't answer. His forehead was creased and he bit his thumbnail, trying to look into her face. But what was wrong, she herself didn't know. His face was a little boy's face, no bones, round and fat, and she could say nothing to it.

At home, Margie was leaning over the railing. "Where's the dog?" Danny asked, and Margie pointed around the back. There, Pearl was standing in overalls by a washtub caldron, stirring its boiling liquid with a plank. "Don't look!" she called to them, smiling as they ran up. "It's for the biology club!" Usually she was proud of her experiments and collected her sister and cousins to watch. "It's important," she would say, handing them each a string, a magnifying glass, or an egg. This time Zellie was already too close and saw, for an instant, a furry paw rise above the surface.

She gasped and ran into the empty house for her mother, or at least a pillow to hide her face. "Wait!" Pearl shouted, dropping her plank and running after her. "Wait, Zellie! It's nothing!" she called, alarmed but also laughing. "They're just cats! And they're dead!"

Pearl could never understand her sister's violent tears, which continued even when the dog came scratching that night at the screen door. Later, when Danny was already an accountant and Zellie herself the wife of a lawyer, she remembered little of Pearl's experiment, only her own search, as if not merely the dog but everything she had ever loved, her grandmother too, had been lost that day—to that boiling caldron, to those great arching wings, to the long thrust of that white neck.

"Now let me get this straight," says Sol. "You and Zelda grew up together, right?"

"Yes," Danny says. "We lived next door."

"Oh, you're the one!" says Sol, and nods significantly before noticing Danny's nervous expression. Nodding again, searching for another fact, he says, "You two—played the piano, am I right?"

"Yes," Danny says, looking down, looking away down the table. They both survey all the platters of fruit, and shrimp on ice, and a huge round challah Pearl has baked herself. Reaching for a wide slice of bread, Sol nods again and says, "Ha! I thought so!"

Danny waves boldly across the patio. "David!" he calls loudly. "David, old man, how've you been?"

"Good!" David calls, waving slightly, standing next to his mother and turning to her. Zellie smiles helplessly, almost shrugs, but she can say nothing, and David must go sit down with them, shaking Danny's hand.

"So there you are, Master Rosen!" says Sol. "You haven't seen the kids, have you? They were looking for you."

"I saw them inside," David says, mumbling.

"Oh, so they're inside? Let me go get them. Excuse me, ladies, won't you?" Laughing, he lifts himself up.

David is glad not to let Danny sit alone; his mother's cousin has traveled alone several hours, though no one seems to have greeted him. They have nothing to say, it seems, but David feels responsible while Zellie is occupied with other guests. Danny has asked about David, David knows; has taken a special interest in him since his father left home, and David feels obligated, even charmed, if not quite grateful. There is a story about Cousin Danny, his romance with a waitress, and how though his mother would never admit it, she had felt abandoned all the same. Again and again she has told the story: how Danny, who played the piano with her, who marched with her in marching band and walked through the woods, became in high school the wild one—escaping onto his horse from the Hebrew school window, bending pennies on the railroad tracks behind their house, fighting with the Irish boys, finally marrying Nell from the restaurant, a shiksa waitress still in high school, as quickly as possible because they had to—Danny who was going to be President, Danny who was going to be rich and famous. "So Aunt Nell isn't Jewish?" David asked; and then, angrily, as if the story should have made it clear, Zellie answered, "Of course she is—*now*."

Now Danny is pale and soft—a balding, round-faced man with smiling eyes; the same man, David tries to imagine, who jumped out the window onto his horse. "So," Danny says, gripping David behind the neck, "how have you been there, my man?" Already David can hear advice, sound, manly advice, stirring up like a storm.

"Okay," David says, as manly as he can, deep-voiced and clipped. "I've been good!"

"Getting ready for college, I guess."

"Well, sort of. I'll be taking the SATs pretty soon. I'm just a junior, you know."

"Just a junior!" Danny says, his voice very low, and laughs hitting him, openhanded, on the shoulder. "Listen," he says, too suddenly. "How about some advice from an old man?"

"Sure," David said.

"I can tell you're not too young. I wish I'd had someone to give me some advice, somewhere along the line." Between each sentence he pauses significantly. "I had to find out a lot of things for myself. You know I was in the navy, don't you?"

"Yeah!" David says, inflecting one increment to many—over-adjusting for a love of battles and ships. Next time, he was sure to get it right.

"Well, there's a lot of things you got to learn out there. You know what I mean?"

"Yeah," David says, almost correctly.

"Like, when guys came up to you and sort of acted funny? You know what I mean?"

"Yeah."

"Fairies."

David can see his mother nearby, listening. She is smiling, but he turns away. "Yeah," he says, nodding, even smiling tightly, as if, like Danny, at a memory.

"Well, I'll tell you, David, if you're in a men's room some-time, or taking a shower or something at the gym, and they come up to you, all you have to do is what I did. Just kick 'em in the balls and run away—simple as that! You can remember that, man, can't you?"

"Yeah," David says without quite enough emphasis, still nod-ding.

"Okay then!" Danny says, holding out his hand for David to shake, and as he grasps that hand, shaking as firmly as he can, David can see his mother across the patio, pretending not to see.

Toward evening, in the near dark of the dining room, the family sits around the table, as if even now they were waiting for something to begin, another meal, another ceremony. Sol, at the head of the table he has avoided until now, is looking at his daughter's pictures of California. "That's just beauti-ful!" he says to her in his full, loud voice, as if to say that by him there are no secrets, or else to enforce, by the rich tone of his voice, a serenity and confidence and fullness through the room. He taps his cigar and pulls at his loosening tie. "Just beautiful." Rose and Pearl sit beside Zellie at the distant other end, watching the last glint of light on the pool; it skims the waveless, almost clear water and is gone. For a moment the water is dark, an open pit in the ground, a deep shadow brushed across the cement. Then, from within, from underneath, a beam of electric light makes it glow suddenly, light blue, transparent again, and the backyard seems all at once quite dark. Surrounded by the night, they are enclosed and protected by the house.

"So what happened to your friend Joanne?" Pearl asks, pouring herself a second mug of tea.

"She's not my friend," Zellie says, still watching the water. "They went to Israel's wedding. They invited his woman over months ago. They're not my friends."

"I never did like Joanne," says Pearl. "I never knew what you saw in her."

"But you could have had your cousins," says Rose, sewing the ripped hem of Lonnie's dress. Her old sewing box has stayed here up north, and she has all her favorite thimbles again, her scissors, her different threads.

"I did have my cousins," Zellie says. "I had the cousins I love, who love me."

"Family's family," says Rose. "They're not your enemies. How do you think Minnie felt, not having her daughter here? I'm going to have to answer for that one."

"Margie is not my friend," Zellie says. "Talking behind my back is not my friend. She was so interested in my divorce."

"Who talked behind your back? Why do you talk like that? She's your cousin. How do you know, anyway?"

"I have my ways," Zellie says, pushing her chair out but not standing up. Pearl smiles at her mother and shakes her head. "What?" Zellie says. "What?"

"Why still be angry, Zel? It's over. It's over and done with."

"Not for me," Zellie says, pushing her chair back in, reaching for the tea. "For me it's not over."

"Well," says Rose, tearing off a thread, "it should be. Enough is enough. Family's important. Some people don't have any family. My mother always used to say, 'Friends are for weddings and funerals. But family's family.' Why do you think we had to have Viola? Still, you could have had Lena, maybe."

"Lena!" Zellie says. "Ma, you never said anything about Lena. How was I to know?"

"She's my friend," Rose says, and shrugs. "She's always loved you best."

"She's in Florida, Mom. Anyway, I didn't know you liked her so much."

"It was for us she moved to Florida. To be near us. She likes a free lunch now and then. She's had a hard life, that girl. The daughter dead—ach!" She shakes her head.

"Who's that?" David asks, looking up from his book.

"Lena Carp, honey," says Pearl. "She came from Europe. What are you reading there?"

"A practice test," David says, covering the page with his arm. "For the SATs next month."

"You're studying already!" she says. "Good for you!"

"He's going to be a doctor," says Rose. "He has to."

"Or a pianist, Mother," says Zellie. "He has to choose for himself."

"First a doctor," says Pearl. "Then let him be whatever he wants."

"Pearl, he's sixteen, for God's sake. They're still children."

"He's lucky," says Rose. "Now's the time, when it's not too late."

"I could have gone to medical school," says Pearl, "and I didn't take any test."

"What do you mean, no test? You were the best in the class. Always. Don't tell me about tests."

"So why didn't you go, Aunt Pearl?" David asks.

Pearl smiles without turning to him, without answering.

"It was the times," says Rose. "She wanted to get married."

"I could have done both, Ma. It wasn't the times. It was the money. For a boy you would have had the money."

"Forget all that," says Rose. "What, do you want to eat your heart out, even now? I'll tell you about schools—"

Sol, at the head of the table, has stood up and is waiting with his arms crossed. "Sorry to interrupt," he says, "but the game's going on, I just wanted to let you know. Come on, Dave," he says, stepping around to hold David by the shoulder. "Let's go on in there."

"—the school of hard knocks," says Rose, finishing.

"I was just—talking with them," David says, nodding to the others, and looks to see if his mother will speak for him. But Zellie, though she watches him at her own end, does not know what to say, does not know what he wants her to say. "Okay," he says, finally pushing back his chair as they all watch, and follows Sol politely out of the room. Sol's daughter, after a moment, bolts after them.

"Well!" says Pearl, turning to Zellie. "So how does it feel, Zel?"

"What do you mean?"

"Being married again."

"I always felt married," Zellie says. "Even when I wasn't. I just had to find someone to be married with again." She can think of nothing else to say, but now that the others are gone the three women are comfortably silent. Pearl reads through the test booklet, asking the questions sometimes out loud. " 'If X equals the number of fish . . .' " she reads, and after a moment impatiently flips the page. Rose is finishing up her hem. Zellie, running her hand across the tablecloth, watching her mother, absently grasps the cloth that spills down onto her lap. Everything—the night, the dark rooms, the family—seems not at all strange or transformed, as she thought it would, but powerfully the same, as it should be.

"Well," says Irene, clearing her throat, standing suddenly by the back stairs with her coat on. "That's everything, Ms.—" and she stops.

"So long, Irene," says Zellie. "Thank you."

"See you tomorrow, Irene," says Pearl.

"Okay, then," she says, starting down, and they can hear her slow, tired steps like a message to them all.

"Did she tell you about her dream?" asks Pearl, after a moment.

Zellie nods. The house, even filled with family, is suddenly quiet: the guests have gone home; the children are dispersed in their various rooms; the pool cleaner still hums, vaguely, across the lawn. In the quiet, she remembers grasping her mother's pleated skirts long ago, holding on against terror, eating an apple, in crowds, at home, at the restaurant, still safe among the folds. What has changed, she thinks, reaching for a piece of fruit even now—an apple again—polishing its dark surface against the cloth, biting in at last, is perhaps only this: that whatever happens now in her life, good as well as bad, she will never again have to be alone.

Down from Providence

Barbara Bauer stood by herself on the platform, waiting for the New York train. She had to be someone's mother, judging by the willing, protective nods of the man across the tracks with a briefcase, who glanced at her quickly and then at his watch, or else by the respectful hovering of the boy students behind her, who would have picked up her bag for her, told her the time, done anything at all for such a woman, dignified but vulnerable in her high heels and mink, if only she would turn around. That she was a mother was somehow, mysteriously, certain. That she was leaving Providence was also certain, though not mysteriously—she was looking toward Boston for the train—and it was certainly not forever, not even for a long time—her bag was too slight, and to the dismay of the boys whose own mothers she resembled, she never once looked around, even for a moment's regret.

Still, her long mink in the warm spring sun and the overstuffed pockets of her weekend bag marked her, to the businessman whose nod she returned and to the boys who wanted to nod but hadn't the chance, as undoubtedly a woman in need of their help, unused to leaving the place where she lived, unused to traveling alone, or by train, or even to gathering herself entirely together for such an independent step. When the train arrived, the boys saw her look around, or rather just begin to turn her head before seeming to stop herself, and even that was hesitation enough.

"I'll take that for you," said one of the boys, quietly assertive; and surprised by his attention but grateful, Barbara acquiesced.

She had a weakness, she liked to say, for young men. The day after she turned twenty-one she married a young musician her parents had called "the gypsy," but whom they tried to love because he had escaped the Holocaust. As a girl Barbara too had tried, through novels and paintings and piano sonatas, to find the romance and beauty that seemed naturally owed to the young, and particularly to girls approaching twenty, but that seemed so absent from Pawtucket, Rhode Island, during the war. Only one man was walking the halls of the music conservatory where she studied in Boston—Erich Bauer, who seemed the vision she had always tried to conjure, with his gentle Hungarian accent and perfect English, his tempestuous Old World style of playing, and his sensuous Jewish lips which, if they never smiled, always seemed to be hiding a happier expression. Barbara signed up as his student, applauded first and last at his recitals, and when the war ended they were married in celebration. Never again did she find the time to practice, busying herself instead with the young lives of her two daughters. Only in recent years did she begin to sigh again with that old, nameless longing, to be more than merely herself, Barbara, Mrs. Erich Bauer, confined by the limits of Providence and Pawtucket; to understand, to strive, and perhaps one day to achieve a glimpse of something great; something sublime. This time it was to her paint brushes and watercolors that she reached, leaving Erich to his own, somewhat obsolete ideas of musical grandeur.

Providence, she thought now—hoping by her own distraction to distract attention away from herself and her suitcase—had certainly changed. Looking back from the blue-tinted window of the train as it curved quickly around to the south, she saw for a fleeting last moment that the ugly city where she had always lived might have seemed beautiful once, an enchanted, quiet haven of colonial spires, clapboard houses, and white churches. Roger Williams, thirty feet high, brown from the passage of time but dignified even now on the side of the hill, had been kind to the Jews when no one else would have them. For that, as a girl, she had loved him, and ever since had defended his city from the disparagement of cynics. For less than that, it seemed, she had always stayed where she was: her husband's career, her mother's loneliness. Now, indeed, Erich Bauer being who he was, unbearable finally in his silence, there was very little more than that old, first love for something little more than a symbol, a statue. Erich could be silent now, forever, admitting or denying his infidelities. This time she was leaving.

Every few minutes, looking up from the book with which she had armed herself against the empty seat on the one side and the whole expanding landscape on the other, she smiled up and then down the train, as if to apologize for being alone, or to pretend she didn't mind. A young man across the aisle looked up from his book at the same time and returned the same kind of smile. He was the one who had carried her bag —handsome, Barbara realized, with his mustache and green eyes. He looked like somebody's son, dressed in a tie and sweater vest some mother had to have knitted, clean and manly next to the earrings and dirty jeans of her daughters' friends. And he was Jewish—that she could see in his face, though it was more than the sensuous lines of the nose and lips, mere features of caricature she disdained and always claimed to overlook in her assessments. It was, she thought—though already she was leaning again into her book, following the words with her finger—

something rather in the expression of the eyes, the anxious slant of the eyebrows, the shadows underneath of study and worry, and above all the piercing strength of gaze that she had always loved in Jewish men, because their grandfathers at least were scholars, holy men, *mensches* who were moral, and loved their families, and loved their wives. Erich's own father was a rabbi; but even so, what had Erich made of himself, his marriage . . . she grimaced away the thought. When she looked up again the young man was looking up as well, and they nodded to each other. He was younger than she had thought, still a student, too young even for Elizabeth, her youngest, who would not have listened anyway, even to a modest suggestion.

"Mrs. Bauer?" asked the young man, high-voiced and deferential.

Barbara looked down and then back up with her former smile, protecting him while protecting herself. "Yes!" she said, and she hoped her cheerfulness would make up for not knowing his name.

"I'm Andrew Chase," he said. "I was at your house for Professor Bauer's party last Christmas. Do you remember?"

Barbara nodded, still smiling.

"I made the cake in the shape of a piano?"

"Oh yes," Barbara said, remembering at least that much; there had been a few cakes wrapped in foil, next to her own desserts. He needed her to go on. "It was very good," she said, wondering if "Chase" could be Jewish. "Are you one of Erich's students?"

The young man nodded, pleased with her recognition, and his need made her forget her suitcase packed in haste, and the empty seat next to her—the whole private trauma she was trying to conceal. "What are you studying?" she asked. She could ask a dozen questions like this and never stumble, never seem distracted by her own life.

"Histology, right now," said the young man, looking down.

"No," Barbara said, indulgently. "I mean with Erich."

"Well," he said, "this semester we're doing all the Debussy preludes. Wonderful pieces. Do you know them?"

"Of course," Barbara said, curtly, and quickly opened up her book again. Instead of reading, however, she looked out the window, and then turned back to him. "I know them very well," she said. "I'm a musician myself, you know. Erich's not the only one in the family. I played the Debussy before he did, in fact. I'm sure I did. What does Erich know about Debussy?"

While she spoke the young man's smile struggled, then fell in confusion. "I don't know," he said at last, when Barbara was silent and looking at him as if she expected an answer. Her face was flushed and her eyes, usually slow and kind, were suddenly fast-moving and sharp. "At least," he said, "more than I do. Are you a pianist also?"

"I am," Barbara said, and aware, suddenly, of sounding pompous, she looked away, this time slowly, to seem modest, and only as far as the aisle, not to cut him off, as if she were looking for the conductor. "I mean, rather, I was."

"I thought so," said the young man, and Barbara turned back to him.

"What do you mean?"

"By your hands," he said. "Your fingers are so long—they're really beautiful."

Surprised though she was by this intimacy—from someone so young it was either ridiculous or condescending—Barbara only grinned, and settled down comfortably in her seat. "Be careful, young man," she said, "you're flattering a married woman!" As she spoke she remembered her morning rage at Erich over the phone, her call to Beth in tears, her packing, her resolution. Now she twisted the gold ring she had forgotten about and stared at her hands. She was afraid she was going to cry. Instead she asked him, "Why ever are you studying histology?"

"I like it," he said. "Isn't that the best reason for anything?" As Barbara didn't answer, he continued. "I'm going to medical school, really. I hate to admit it, though."

"Why?"

"Well, because then no one takes my music seriously. And I am serious about it. I'm sure I'll always play. I have to. Erich—Professor Bauer knows that."

"I'm sure he does," Barbara said, and forgot herself enough to study the boy again, really a young man, who was a musician but would be a doctor. And despite the blond hair, Jewish, she decided, although she was sure her daughters would mock her. She could hardly keep from saying it out loud. "How old are you?" she asked, hoping that that sounded disinterested enough.

"Twenty-two."

"Oh," Barbara said, her voice dropping away. Elizabeth, her younger daughter—it seemed it was Beth, these days—was twenty-four and needed someone older, really. And Carol Anne, her firstborn, was for the moment at least beyond a mother's help, running a small press somewhere in the wild and gentile West—Iowa, which somehow was both a state and a city.

"What?" said the young man. "I don't think that's too old. Listen, you shouldn't give up hope on me until you've heard me. I've only really been practicing a few years."

"Oh—what?" said Barbara, confused. "I'm sure."

"What do you mean?"

"Only that I'm sure you're coming along fine, as you say."

"Why do you say that?" said the young man.

"Why," said Barbara, "because of your hands."

"They're too small," he said, cupping them in his lap and staring at them. "Child's hands."

"Oh, no," said Barbara. "Giotto hands. Masaccio hands. Rembrandt." He looked up at her, confused, but she shook her head at his confusion. "Surgeon's hands!" she said, smiling triumphantly.

BETH'S MOTHER WAS taking the train down from Providence again, this time planned in advance. It was a bad sign. Since Beth had moved to New York her mother had come unexpectedly half a dozen times, showing up at ten in the morning or at midnight, or phoning from New Haven at noon that she would still be there in time for lunch. And each time Beth had had to rearrange her secret, adult life: her twin mattresses lying together on the floor, her women's magazines with ironic names and blatant photos, her picture postcards, her favorite letters, her tuxedo with tails, her painting of herself with David, both of them naked, and all her books with incriminating titles jumping out from the bookshelf, as if illuminated in neon. What actually would happen, David often asked her, if just one time she didn't bother with all of the rearrangement and deception? She was afraid of finding out, afraid of trying to defend herself with words she didn't yet trust, a self-respect she hadn't yet discovered. At the same time she was never quite thorough in her preparations, her secreting away of letters and messages and shameless, amusing sketches. A postcard would still be stuck in the mirror, a picture torn from a magazine would still be staring from a half-opened drawer, and even her most girlish clothes, when her mother visited, were never quite the dresses and high heels Barbara would have liked.

"So what?" David asked her, time after time late at night on the phone. "You are what you are, Beth. It's her problem, not yours." But yet again, now, as he spoke, he shuffled papers together from the floor, and turned the guilty books around, and stroked the back of her neck.

"Let's tell her we're getting married," she suggested.

"Okay," he said, suppressing a smile.

"No, you're right," she said. "It would never work. She'd never believe it for a minute. Anyway, who would wear the dress?"

A question worth answering, perhaps; but perhaps for them the answer was evident. They had met, years ago already, when Beth was at art school and David was up the hill at the university. One day, from boredom, from desperation, or merely by mistake, David had wandered into the art school café—Beth never had found out just why. It was a day of burning cold, and all the crowded tables and chairs were piled high with down parkas, long woolen scarves, and extra sweaters.

"Is someone using this chair?" he had asked, stiff with shyness, pointing to the chair at Beth's table that was piled with garments. No one around her crowded table would speak.

"Well," said Beth at last, betraying her seriousness with a smile only he could see, "actually I was resting my eyes on it. But otherwise, no." David was the only one to laugh. The others at the table, blowing out smoke over their shoulders and dressed, like Beth, all in black because life was brief, and treacherous, and deathward, merely turned away as if they had heard nothing, seen nothing. David ate his bagel and coffee quickly, hunching in silence, looking out the steamy window as if at a view, but the next day he found Beth again, still in black at the same table, and the day after that. Finally Beth had nodded and called him over.

"You must be from up the hill," she said.

"Yes, actually," he said. "How did you know?" She had known from his short hair, his blue Oxford shirt, his blue plastic parka, and from the insignia on every one of his notebooks. But she only hunched her shoulders and smiled.

"I'm gay, you know," he said, soon after that, and Beth had nodded at first—seriously—embarrassed for his sincerity, trying to hide her amusement, so much was his secret not a secret. It was a relief anyway from the other young men she knew, who if they were gay were too silly or too blinded by other boys to see her. If they were not gay they either were the dullest men she knew, or else merely tried to dance her into their celebratory dance of themselves. David would hold her hand, listen to her troubles, laugh at her jokes, and wouldn't seem to mind when she had to be left to herself, hiding sometimes in the studio for days on end.

She could see all that at once.

For him, she was the first one ever to pay attention, to want to hold his hand, to laugh when quietly he made a joke, and to make everything in their lives together seem funny, or important if only because at last it was shared. Finally, for them both, someone could see them as they knew they really were, hidden beneath the persistent costumes and malformations childhood had wrought. They could touch each other, in each other's beds, in each other's bath, one up the hill, one down, safe enough at last to feel being touched, instead of just daring to touch, with bated breath.

"Your skin is so soft," she said, plowing with her fingers the soft hair from his chest down to his thighs, as they lay in bed the first time. "Like a woman's."

"Your skin is so soft," he said, passing his hand along her cheek as no man had ever done. "Like a woman's."

David grew his hair longer, learned to buy clothing on the street; Beth cut her hair, dared to wear pants—his pants—and then his shirts. Though she would not admit it, she loved to find him studying when she appeared late at night at his ground-floor window, his head still bent over vectors and carbon models and diagrams of the brain. Though he would not admit it, he loved everything she drew, all the stray lines and doodles and notes she had left, and he saved every scrap. His drawers were full, and then his walls, not with science but rather with the study of her art, her imagination, her moods. She laughed at his junk, which had been hers; but then her junk was his art. "Beth," he would say, "look at this," stopping her as they walked along to notice a nest of ants, a faded sign, or a rotten apple in the shape of a face. He began to save the stones they had found, and pieces of cloth, and billboards taken from the trash. She had transformed him, perhaps; and now, like her friends down the hill, he would transform in turn everything he saw, her own creation taking on a life of his own.

What did it matter if late at night he still cried for a man's touch sometimes, for a kind of passion that as yet existed for him only in the textbooks he checked out from the library, all from the shelf under *H*? Distracted herself, Beth didn't mind, as long as no one turned away as if she really were taken; as long as no one got the wrong idea. . . .

As they walked along the winter streets—Providence a colonial city silenced by the snow—David might take her mittened hand in his own, both so thoroughly wrapped and rigid that communication that way—fingers squeezing and interlocking, palms pressing close—was token at best, muffled and unperceived at most frequent worst. But then she pulled away.

"What?" he finally asked, after she had separated like this, several times, simply, silently, and, she had hoped, without repercussion. Some approaching group down the narrow, lamplit street might recognize them, or a friend might peer down from a Revolutionary windowsill, through some antique distorting pane of glass. But those silences and empty spaces had weighed more heavily each time on them both, until her withdrawal could not be without its tug, and his question must be asked.

"What 'what'?" she asked him back.

"Why did you take your hand away?"

"I just wanted to."

"What's the matter?"

"Nothing. Someone might see us, that's all."

"So?" he asked.

"I don't know," she said, and sometimes she gave in, gave him back her lifeless hand, and sometimes her hunch was violent enough, even beneath scarves and sweaters, that he could see the warning and keep away. So what? She really didn't know. Perhaps a man might see them together and not ask her out. Perhaps other eyes that might have lingered her way would now refrain, casting glances quickly to the ground. In a world where men and women could hold hands joyously and smile at each other while the world smiled back, why did this seem to her so secretly perverse, so doubly illicit? Only years later did she begin to wonder what it meant that in the wedding she herself kept dreaming, the spouse she had to kiss became again and again Katharine Hepburn, Mary Tyler Moore, and other faces more intimately known, all the women she had loved, while no one seemed especially to be wearing the veil. In other dreams, what were they running to, those childhood friends running across the lawn, their long hair and skirts flowing behind them, while the whole marching band looked on in wonder, in horror? At first, a trip to the gay bar with David, or a march in the Gay Pride parade, was a favor, a dare, a titillating excursion into an exotic, even chic new world. He was grateful; she was at least amused. Some of the women were pretty, some of them sprightly college girls fresh out of Girl Scout green. Some were older, alcoholic, ruined, and Beth looked on them all in horror and in wonder.

"It's not a parade," David insisted. "It's a march, Beth, a protest, a gesture of solidarity and defiance." And they ran through the crowd, holding hands.

Whatever it was, it was soon their shared adventure, of the week, of the year. After college, Beth's hair was always short, her skirts abandoned in the back of the closet, and her friends either interested themselves in her new interests or found themselves wondering why she never called. David too, perhaps, had created something new, sparked in her a new life which, though small and tentative at first, had someday to grow strong and irrepressible if it was to live at all.

Even so, she had never abandoned her mother's dream for herself and her daughters: domestic life; a warm kitchen; a loving husband coming home from work; a child in her skirts (they were still there, the skirts, pushed to the back but not forgotten). After all, she still had that dream of domestic bliss, domestic *safety*—and sometimes the groom, when he turned around, persisted in his masculinity.

Sometimes, on those days, David seemed a happy choice. Of course they could live together; they lived together already. Of course they could love each other through life; they loved each other already. Together they shopped for bulgur wheat and carob chips at his insistence, Pop-Tarts and chocolate bars at hers. Together they piled up laundry and paid their bills too late, and somehow dishes in the sink were put away, floors swept, and the filth around the bathroom somehow swabbed and scrubbed back into moderate dirt. David listened to her records, watched as she sketched scenes from the window. Beth quizzed him on the kidney, and electron theory, and taught him how to sculpt figures out of soap. Was this not love? Was this not love enough, at least, for anyone in this hard life of misunderstanding and isolation? The waitress in the restaurant thought so, as she sneered at their economical choice for a meal. Over the candlelight and white tablecloth they thought so too, the idea swollen and awkward in their throats, moist and unhidden in their eyes. "What's wrong?" they might have asked at such a moment, but didn't have to. They knew. They laughed, and continued with their secrets of the day. On a napkin, as she spoke, David wrote down, "Will you marry me?," folded it, and held it pressed in his palm through the meal. "What's that?" she almost asked, but intuition kept her silent. By dessert he was ripping up shreds, a sacrifice to the flames, and finally crumpled the last scrap by his plate. But coming back with the tip she saw it unfolding there like a leaf, like a flower, like the pleated wrapper of a straw, the blossoming paper damp with sweat, the question, though scribbled and tiny, still intact. Should she take it with her, she wondered, confront him, make him ask out loud? Or fold it up again, perhaps, and hide it away, as proof, as collateral, as souvenir? Look, she might say, you have asked and now you must comply; or else, Look, you once asked, almost, and isn't that, like everything else, worth a laugh? Without even touching it she left the paper there, expecting many times afterwards that it would appear again, on some napkin, or shopping list, or steam-clouded mirror, and that she would have another chance.

Sometimes, however, David's desire for someone else, for a man, for men, made him cold and foreign and secretive, and she hated him. "Aren't men the worst?" she would ask, adding, in his silence "Most men?" After all their complaints he would have to agree, but his complaints, she could hear, were halfhearted, unwilling, and crying out to be disproved.

Only sometimes could she bear to hear the word "lesbian"; other times she refused to let others say it of her, and grabbed David's hand, and hid her tears, and made him promise she didn't seem to be like that. Even now the word conjured up for her all the frightening, humiliating pictures it held for her mother: the obese, the thin-haired, the deep-voiced; as for the sprightly, the elegant, the beautiful among women at bars, at marches, at parties, they still made Beth's heart pound, and still she found herself staring in disbelief.

Late at night, already in New York, when "what if" had

become banal and the neighborhood women's bar no longer seemed so far away, they put their clothes back on, stood wondering too long on the sidewalk, and finally climbed the steps.

"David," said Beth, pressed immobile against a wall by the dancers, "look at that."

David turned to look.

"Don't look!" she said, and David turned back to her, confused. "She's looking," Beth said. "She might see you."

"Beth," he said, "you can't see a thing in here anyway. Which one? That one that just walked in?"

"Yes," Beth said. "I think she winked at me. What should I do?"

"Ask me to get you a drink."

"Okay," she said. "Would you?"

When David slipped off, the woman appeared, a black woman, statuesque, unignorable. Other women turned to look. "What are you doing hanging around with *him*?" she asked, peering down at Beth.

"Oh," Beth said. "He's just a friend."

The woman nodded. "Girls are going to think you're straight," she said, and smiled. "You want to dance?"

Beth could not remember answering, only the blare and dazzle of being led onto the dance floor, pushing between women's bodies, squeezing out a tiny space for two. She smiled, moved her body, and all the while there was David waiting for her in the back against the wall.

Safe enough at last, it seemed, she let herself be carried away.

Already now, awaiting her mother, three hot New York summers and three cold New York winters behind her, all her old fears returned. By now it was a ritual: her mother's flight from Rhode Island, her complaints about Beth's father, the threats of divorce, the tears, the camping out on sofas, the arbitrated phone calls and eventual retreats in shame. At college, Beth had been only a town away, her freshman dormitory the hermitage of a mother whose husband, she was each time suddenly sure, had never loved her, and whose elder daughter, Carol Anne, had run from them both to live what she had told her parents was "an alternate life-style"—Beth knew what that meant.

But Beth herself, younger, forever relegated to the innocence of the youngest child, had had to promise, more than once, that unlike the rest of the family, she would never abandon her mother. And indeed she quickly promised, not knowing anyway quite what that meant. Their intimacy, people said, was unusual, even for mother and daughter; and until New York, where Beth was about to become exactly half her mother's age, Barbara exactly twice as old, they had dressed alike, painted together in the backyard or on the Cape, slept sometimes in the same bed, and talked about colors and clothes, if no longer men and sex, much like two equals, two friends.

"Remember this," Barbara had often reminded her daughter. "The only reason I'm not divorcing your father is because I'm scared. Remember that."

Beth remembered, and each time discounted the threats and fleeting rage. This time, however, so close to the Passover holiday and family reunions, it was different. At twenty-four she was an adept reader of her mother's traumas. The week before, a ticket had arrived in the mail, a plane ticket to Rome, signed by her mother. And no letter.

"Well," said her mother when Beth had called her that night. "Can you go?" And Beth, working at nothing in particular that month, had agreed.

On the plane ride over, a woman with cheekbones and a man's shirt stared at Beth from across the aisle, unsmiling except in the subtle upward thrust of her lips.

"I met a nice young man on the train," said her mother. "One of your father's students."

"Mm!" said Beth.

"Well," said her mother, after a moment. "I thought you might be interested." Beth nodded again, absently. She was leafing through the *In Flight* magazine, concentrating on duty-free gifts but seeing only the woman across the aisle, smiling perhaps when Beth looked away.

"You have your father to thank for this trip," Barbara said finally, and Beth turned to her. She knew what was coming, had known already for a week. Her mother had left her father, it seemed—the trip itself implied everything. Still, her mother needed to explain, to herself and to her daughter.

"What do you mean?" Beth asked, looking away across the aisle, now that she was safely engaged in conversation. The woman smiled, at the corners of her mouth, and nodded her dark head. A streak of gray flowed back from the widow's peak.

"I mean," said Barbara, angrily at the back of Beth's head, "that we had planned this trip long ago. You know how long I've wanted to see Italy. The garden of the Finzi-Continis, the Uffizi, the David, the Jewish ghetto."

At this, Beth turned around. She knew that plans had been made all at once, a week before. "How come Daddy didn't want to go?" she asked.

Barbara grimaced, now that she had her daughter's attention. She turned to look out the window, then abruptly opened her book. "How do you know it was *him*!" she said, and then, remembering that she had said that herself, she continued, "I didn't want *him* to come! Now you know. I'd much prefer to be seeing Italy with my daughter, it so happens."

Beth looked across again, and the woman was reading a thick book. "Did Daddy really want to come?"

"Of course he did," Barbara said, sighing with a confidence she didn't yet feel. "But this is the end," she said. "I've had it."

"Really?" Beth said. She touched her mother's hand, freckled already with the brown, benign but spreading spots of a hand becoming old; she could think of nothing else to say. For twenty years or so she had heard her parents fight, threaten divorce and suicide, reaching for knives or pills, waiting in the closed garage for the car to warm up.

"Really!" Barbara said, proudly now that she had admitted the truth and her daughter still loved her. As if the issue were resolved and their new lives already settled, she turned to her bookmark and read.

Beth leaned down to rearrange her bag on the floor, trying to see the title of the woman's book. *The Bodley Head*, she read, Henry James, and was impressed but disappointed, because she knew nothing of that book, and couldn't smile now in recognition and win that woman's heart.

In Rome, Barbara decided to begin her new life. They had three days. Beth, having in recent memory studied Roman history and Renaissance art, expected to wander through the Forum, contemplate on the steps of the Colosseum, and stand in awe under the dome of St. Peter's. The first day, her mother decided, they would shop. Enthusiastically Barbara bought red Italian shoes, a cashmere sweater, and a long silk dress that she decided to wear right away on the street, though it was Easter week and too cold. Beth too was enthusiastic for her mother's optimism, and sat like a designer in store after store, waiting for her mother to change, applauding or dismissing dress after dress. It was only after lunch, lingering over cappuccino in a piazza with a fountain and dappled with light, that Barbara's enthusiasm drooped and her eyes, focusing in with an old, familiar scrutiny, counseled Beth immediately to be alarmed.

"Didn't you bring anything to wear?" she asked, frowning at Beth's old shirt, bending her head away from the table in symbolic observation of Beth's jeans and sneakers.

"Yes," Beth said, pulling her arms together as if she were

cold. But those quick answers, with Beth as well as her mother, had little to do with the truth. Beth had brought next to nothing of which her mother could have approved. She had one blousy shirt, and old shoes her mother had once bought her; but otherwise, having no money in New York, and a mother whose undoubted love had not often distracted her attention from herself, Beth dressed in the self-effacing, ill-fitting clothes she and her friends had traded back and forth for years.

"Elizabeth, why don't you dress like a grown-up woman?" Barbara asked, an old irritation resurfacing in her voice.

"My name is Beth," said Beth. "Please call me Beth."

"First it was Liz, now it's Beth. Who can remember? I've told you a touch of mascara and you'd look entirely different. You're missing an earring, you know. You look just like a man."

Beth was appalled and indignant, but also ashamed. For the first time—too late, she worried, at nearly twenty-five—she was beginning to like the way she looked: resolutely young, perhaps even unsexed, but also sleek and unencumbered, with the ambiguous attractions of Peter Pan, the strength and freedom of a boy but also that woman's wink, and soft touch. "That's very insulting," she said.

"I'm sorry, dear. Let's start you over again, too. Okay? A whole new look. Now it's your turn."

And Beth submitted, for the afternoon at least, to the other, forgotten reason for her bad wardrobe—her hatred of trying on, trying to fit into those skirts, trying to stand proudly with shoulders back and breasts bared to a world of whistling insults. At filling that image, fitting those skirts, and standing, long-legged, pretty but vulnerable, she was a failure and she knew it.

"I can't believe you don't shave your legs," her mother said. "I'm so embarrassed."

The more she tried, the more homely and awkward she looked.

Every good line of her figure was hidden, every exaggeration and insufficiency enlarged. But her mother was more and more pleased, as if she were seeing only the skirts themselves, or creating before her very eyes a better, more acceptable daughter, the younger woman she herself had been. There they were in Rome, whistled at, winked at, propositioned in a foreign language—and she was too old, the mother of two grown women.

"Why don't you wear it home?" she asked, content and in control, nodding at the salesgirl, slipping her charge card back into her wallet, confident as she could be in the elegant shop though they were far from home, and she had left her husband.

"I don't want to, Mom," Beth said, gritting her teeth and then atoning. "Because I'm cold right now. I'll wear it to dinner."

At dinner, miserable in her dress and hunching her shoulders, she drank two glasses of wine too quickly, and soon they were both talking loudly, pretending they were Italian, then French, Barbara demurring as the waiter described the main course and called them both "signorina."

"Well! I'm not so old, am I!" she said, toasting the future; and Beth suggested, as a joke, that in celebration of her new life they go out dancing.

Barbara held her glass up close to her face, looking into the wine. As if the lights had lowered all at once and the people at other tables had all stopped talking and merely scraped their forks and knives against their plates, the restaurant seemed to her suddenly a dismal place. "I don't think so," she said.

"But Mother, why not?" Beth asked. She herself was already horrified at the idea of some Italian man shuffling her into a corner and forcing his tongue down her mouth. But now she had to pull her mother up out of despair.

Suddenly Barbara smiled, realizing the idea was merely mischief, just a dare. She picked up the watch pendant hanging from her neck and lowered her chin. "It's already ten o'clock!" she said. "I may not be old, but twenty-four I'm not, either. You go out, Beth," she said with another smile, as if it were absurd that her daughter would go out alone, and she were just returning the joke.

"Well," said Beth, "maybe I will." The idea had not occurred to her, but she was feeling very much in a skirt again, vulnerable and ridiculous, and needed an antidote. She had with her a little book from home which listed places all around the world—Rome, Florence, and Venice at least, under "Italy"— where women could dance, if they chose, with women. Rome, Florence, Venice, by chance, was their itinerary.

"Beth!" said her mother. "What are you talking about! You're not going out alone at night."

"But why not, Mother? I go out alone all the time in New York."

"Rome," said Barbara, "is not New York."

Tired as Beth was, that sounded like an epigram, and seemed to her at least a good-enough end to their argument. So, having promised with the last sip of their wine to go out together for sure the next night, they went back to their hotel, and to bed.

At breakfast, over steaming bowls of coffee, Barbara again talked enthusiastically of her new life, and for the first time Beth felt truly concerned.

"Mother," she asked, cringing already from the cruel shadow of her mother's naiveté, "what do you want to do?"

"To do," said Barbara. "I'd like to go to the Colosseum and the Forum. And also I'd like to buy a leather belt. In red."

"I mean back at home, Mom. With your life."

Barbara put down her coffee and looked up at her daughter, surprised. "Why do I have to do something?" she asked. "I'll do what I've always done."

"What's that?"

"I happen to do a lot of things. There's a lot you don't know about me, Elizabeth, since you've been away at school."

Beth put her own coffee down and leaned on her elbows. "Sounds awful mysterious to me, Mom. Do you have some secret life you're not telling me about?"

Barbara listed her activities, trying to describe her life. She took care of her mother in the next suburb, taught ethics to the seventh grade at Hebrew school, and was finishing her degree—slowly, to be sure—in painting at the community college. They had plans to make a studio in the summer, out on the porch. Otherwise she ran her house and, in the summer, gardened. And someday, she said, she hoped she would be a grandmother. There were tears in her eyes, and she drew her lips together.

"Is that a hint?" asked Beth.

"A hint?" said Barbara, straightening up and touching her daughter's cheek. "That's not a hint, it's a knock over the head!" She tried to smile. "I just want you to be happy, honey, that's all."

"I'm happy," said Beth. "I'm happy."

Though in her own life she may have been happy enough, with her mother, in Rome, she was plagued with contradictions.

"Tell me about the men in your life," Barbara asked, as they walked among the fallen, fluted columns and archways leading only to further lawns, and pedestals jutting up without statues. The grass was deep green and uncut, the air was crisp, and the April sky was still a rich Roman blue. Beth thought of a few stories about some of her friends; but her real friends, she had realized by now—and David was foremost among them—were not among those of whom her mother would ever approve.

Once they were. She had liked, well enough, the girls and boys in the high-school marching band, who would dress up every Saturday morning in bright soldiers' uniforms, strong and sleek, with feather pompadours in their hats, and crowd into buses to form a giant letter *P* on the football field at half-time, playing the national anthem by heart, squeezing together on the cold bleachers. Afterwards they would crowd into cars, warm bodies sharing laps, all the girls crowded into backseats.

But now, she supposed, her mother would hate them, the way she already hated David—or not hated, perhaps, but dismissed, rejected, vanquished into irrelevance with an impatient shake of the head, a quick glance up to God. Beth had not chosen her friends that way; indeed, as far as she knew, they had been chosen for just those virtues her mother had taught her to respect: intelligence and kindness. Even so Beth saw, as she tried to think up benign stories, that her mother was already frowning and looking away.

"Are *all* your friends gay?" Barbara said, raising her eyes as if her annoyance were a joke.

"No," said Beth, surprised to realize it was mostly true. But her mother was an artist and might have understood.

"Then tell me about the *men*," Barbara said, sitting down on a fallen column, and tapping it for Beth to join her. "The other men. How about that nice young man?"

"David?"

Barbara grimaced, looking sideways without turning her head, as if the joke were not sufficiently funny. "No," she said. "Come on. The one from Brookline."

Beth remained standing. "You never met him, Mother."

"Yes, but I spoke to him. On the phone."

"Once," said Beth. "You spoke to him once. And I haven't seen him in years."

"Why don't you see him again?"

"I don't know. I don't want to."

"And the other men?"

"The other men, Mother, are just not that interesting."

Her mother slapped the cold, fluted stone. "You think that, Elizabeth, because you want to think that! Maybe it's your own problem instead of theirs."

"Maybe it is!" said Beth, archly, impressed with herself but suddenly frightened of the consequence. Perhaps it *was* her problem; she had thought so for years. She was afraid to look at her mother, and they both stared across the field. Two busloads of Americans were climbing toward them over the stones.

"Ugh!" said Barbara, disgusted, shaking her head, and Beth turned to her, ready either to fight or to cry. "Tourists!" said her mother, and walked quickly away.

They met again on the road, outside the Colosseum.

"Mother," said Beth—whether in retribution, conciliation, or concern, she didn't know—"who's going to leave the house, you or Daddy?"

"I don't know," Barbara said, and sat down on a bench.

"Aren't you going in?" Beth asked.

"In a minute. I'm not much interested in seeing where they killed the Jews."

"Oh Mother!" said Beth. "They also killed Christians."

"So, I should be happy? Why do you ask what am I going to do? You think I can't do it? You think I need your father, the rest of my life? That's a joke! He's the one that needs me, I'll tell you that."

"What will you do for money?"

"I have money," said Barbara, raising her chin. "Anyway, I'll teach. I happen to know Hebrew fluently, and I am a painter. Had you thought of that, Elizabeth?"

Beth was still angry at her mother, but also sadder than she expected. "I had, Barbara," she said, and with her hand held to her breast, in pride, in grief, she went off alone into the arena.

• • •

The day was bright, the stones were warm, and all around her Beth heard the stillness settling down again as if she had disturbed some vast, silent pool, plunging down into it and disappearing beneath its surface. Now she was on the bottom, and every move she made disturbed the quiet, every breath, every shuffle of gravel. Occasionally there was a voice, or a pebble dropping against the stones, but they were far away, as distant as echoes. Across the field, sitting on a stone were two ladies, an old and a young, dressed in long skirts and wide hats as if from a different century—English tourists come to see the sights. High up in the stone bleachers, half-hidden in the shade, a man and a woman sat close together, throwing pebbles—shades of other lovers. And there across from them, high up in the sun, sat a woman alone, as if Beth, or some higher, omniscient force, had preordained that such a meeting should occur, that here where lovers had always met, through the centuries, through all the epochs of art and literature, Beth too should come upon her true love, and rise up, like them, into myth. Taking the stone stairs two at a time, she made her way up.

Even from far away, Beth knew who it was. She could tell, if not by her own intuitive sense of destiny and coincidence, then by the prominent streak of gray in the woman's hair, and by the thick blue book which she held in one hand, now turning a page with the other. Beth's heart beat against her chest, and for a moment she was dizzy. It was the woman from the plane; of that she was certain.

Without glancing up again she walked around to that sunny side, and without a glance she wandered up the steps, turning sometimes the other way just to look at the view and be seeming to take her time. Soon she was standing at just the right row of stones, facing the other way, pretending to admire the view. When she turned around, the woman was gone. As if Beth had tripped and were falling down that flight of stone, she cried out, briefly, sharply, and her voice, pursuing where Beth could not, echoed out across the stones.

"Well," said Barbara when Beth returned, "I'm hungry, darling—how about you?"

Beth sighed and shook her head, and they went off to lunch.

The next day Beth said she needed a book and would go off on her own to find the English-language bookstore. At first Barbara objected. "Why do you need a book this week?" she said. "Look around you! There's more here than in any book." But Beth merely shrugged and arranged to meet her later, at the Spanish Steps.

In the shop, a dirty, dusty place without windows, she went right to the literature section, under "Henry James," but she could not find the book she wanted.

"Perhaps I can be of some help," said a woman behind her, a tall, birdlike Englishwoman, pale-eyed and gray, who might have been hiding out there in Rome until London was safe again for spinsters. She smiled, though, boldly, and seemed to wink.

"Yes," said Beth. "I'm looking for a book by Henry James, but I can't seem to find it."

"Well, we've got them all here in paper," said the woman. "Which one is it?"

"*The Bodley Head*," said Beth.

"*The Bodley Head*," repeated the woman, and stared at Beth, first with narrowed eyes, then wide-eyed. "Look in the back," she said, sharply. "In the hardcovers."

Beth ducked into a tiny, dark room, where the used hardbound copies were kept. There, under *J* in "Literature," she found the book she wanted. Henry James, *The Bodley Head*, bound in blue cloth—but there were twenty such books, all of them with the same name. Randomly she took one from the middle, paid for it quickly, and ran out to meet her mother.

"Well?" said Barbara, hardly turning from her close observation of a painting in progress and also, though his back was to her, of its handsome European *compositeur*. In the sun the Spanish Steps had attracted many Easter tourists, warming themselves, faces uplifted, in the crowded hour before lunch. All around them handsome young people had put down their knapsacks, pulled off their sweaters, and opened up their guitar case or painting box. Looking around at those young men, because Beth had not answered, Barbara asked, "Have you found what you wanted?"

"Yes," Beth said, turning away from the painting, a clown-colored "View of the Spanish Steps." She wondered why her mother could be so interested in such a work. "I thought it was a novel," she said, although her mother was distracted again by the painting. "But it seems to be different stories."

"That's nice," said Barbara absently, and then, as the artist turned around, dark-eyed and curious to see who was talking over his shoulder, she nodded enthusiastically. "*Benissimo!*" she said, nudging her daughter. "Don't you think?"

In Florence they stood together in a field, mother and daughter, listening to the faraway toll of a bell in a tower, and then the silence rippling out after it. Birds twittered clearly in the grass across the valley; a car up the mountain shifted gears. Beth was looking up at the sky, or else at lizards scurrying between the rocks. She was holding her mother's hand, but only pretending, her mother knew, to look where her mother pointed, to see when she pretended to look.

You could lead horses to water, Barbara thought, but you cannot make them remember that their mother had held them in her arms before anyone else, had fed them, wiped their behinds, exclaimed over finger-painted flowers and trees and sailboats long before the era of abstract nonsense, of foreign languages, or art history for five hundred dollars a credit.

Florence—Barbara was having to admit—was a bust. Jammed

with busloads, unbreathable with fumes, unbearably loud and defaced with wall after wall of cheap souvenirs—monkey puppets and painted plates and pictures of the David's genitals, circled in red—Florence, her dream, the Oz of her own and her daughter's childhood, was distinctly not worth the trip. For the third day in a row the Uffizi had closed early or had never opened, and even Beth, Barbara had to admit, had not this time been entirely too quick to condemn. She stared at the Tuscan countryside impatiently—the miniature fields and valleys dropping away in vivid green, the winding brown roads through the vineyards, the purple haze of the mountains—and had to admit, at last, that it was not as she had hoped.

Her daughter was more and more quiet, retreating into her book. Their old intimacy, their shared secrets, their delight in painting and good cooking and beautiful countryside, had all but disappeared. Instead, between them was a silence of impatience and distrust, as if they no longer knew each other at all. And Barbara remembered her own mother like that, shaking her head silently at such a choice for a husband, and saying nothing. Yet, she thought, her mother had been right! Erich had turned out as she had guessed. Perhaps Beth, at least, would be wiser. And here, in the Tuscan hills she had dreamed about for thirty years, they would find the other, hidden Florence, quiet, pristine, and echoing with art instead of buses, sunken beneath the loud, ugly, confusing surface, but reachable, reachable.

On Friday they were off to Venice, where there was not a room to be had. Sunday was Easter, and every Italian, every European seemed to be on vacation, all of them come to Venice for Easter mass. "I told you we would need reservations," Beth complained, looking up on the train from her reading, but her mother, shrugging and looking through her *L'Uomo Vogue*, reminded her daughter that it was after all an adventure, that while they didn't know what they would find, they would surely find something. At the train station they called up one hotel after another, Beth speaking each time in her halting but sufficient Italian, her mother standing nervously outside the phone booth with the suitcase, nodding hopefully at each confident-looking passerby who looked her way.

"Well," Beth said, emerging unsuccessful, "we could always stay on the Lido."

"The Lido!" said Barbara. "Why not! . . . What's that?"

"I don't know," Beth said, "but it was in this book I read. It's where some of the characters stay. I don't know if it still exists."

"Of course it still exists," said her mother. "Venice doesn't change. Venice stays the same through the centuries."

"Okay," said Beth, and found a place on the Lido which indeed still had a room.

It was, as they soon realized, the Venice beach, a separate, nearby island, quiet and still almost empty this early in the season. But the grand hotels stretched grandly along the beach; the casinos and beach clubs and elegant avenues stood in silent expectation of warmer, more social weather. Beth loved the romance of it, the poetry of the empty, lonely villas and the vast, beckoning beaches; but her mother was distinctly unhappy. She wanted the city itself, the civilization she had always read about, the narrow medieval streets and winding canals, overhung with laundry and flower boxes, and Piazza San Marco, and the Jewish ghetto, and the Bridge of Sighs.

"But look," said Beth, happier now than she had been in a week. "This way we approach it every day the way Napoleon saw it—from the water. We're really very lucky, Mother."

"I hate that cold, damp island," Barbara said, as they approached San Marco on the vaporetto. The piazza itself was splendid in the sun, thronged with crowds, bells tolling in the tower and pigeons swirling up and then down again, like a falling echo of the sound. Beth, though she had finished her book, still seemed to her mother more and more distant, and continued to carry that blue book around like a reminder of her mother's insufficiency—that a mother's company was not good enough. So Barbara began to worry, for the first time, what she really would do when they returned, shortly, to their real lives.

Beth was suddenly agreeable to her mother's suggestions, for dinner, for clothes to buy or sights to see; and yet, without understanding why, Barbara still felt left out, rejected; even, somehow, unloved. In the evenings, Friday and Saturday, Beth went out before dinner to wander the beach, as if even there, at the end of the land, she could not escape from her mother far enough. Why or where she wandered, Barbara didn't know.

Indeed it was on her evening walk, their first night, that Beth had nearly fallen, unexpectedly, upon exactly what she was looking to fall upon. As she had walked along, reading again her favorite passages from her favorite story in the book, ignoring the sunset, the glint upon waves at low tide, and the muted shriek of the seagull, her foot caught sharply and she fell into the sand. There, a hundred feet beyond her on the esplanade, sitting with her feet up and one arm stretched out across the bench, still reading from her blue book and pushing her streaked hair back sometimes from her eyes, was the very woman Beth had been dreaming about: the woman from the plane, from the Colosseum, and really, it seemed, from her fantasies. For a long time Beth stayed where she was in the sand, hoping the woman had not seen her. Then, standing up slowly and brushing herself off, she watched as the woman stood from her bench and walked back across the street, into the apparently empty Grand Hotel.

It was a miracle to find her again, perhaps; and yet perhaps it was the most common thing in the world. Tourists commonly started in Rome, everyone knew that, and ended up, many of them, in Venice. And this week, for just one week, was vacation all over the Western world. Thousands, then, must have begun in Rome and ended up in Venice. Hundreds must have come without reservations—three, at least, had come to the Lido.

Just as her mother suspected, Beth was hardly aware during that night, or even the next day, of anything her mother said, or any of the sights and museums they visited.

"What's wrong with you?" Barbara asked, concerned as well as annoyed at her daughter's sometimes blank, sometimes troubled expressions. They were crossing the Bridge of Sighs, and Beth looked neither left nor right nor into the canal below, but straight ahead into a lady's hat.

"Nothing," Beth said.

"Obviously, something's the matter."

"No," Beth insisted, turning to look straight into her mother's eyes. Entrapped in her mind, impatient on her tongue, her real thoughts crept again and again to the edge of utterance, falling palpably against her closed lips. But there they were stopped. How easy it would be, Beth thought, merely to say what was true: she was in love. But how hard it would be from there! It was not even that she had kept her secret so well. Once, years before, she had come home from a party flushed and exhilarated, where the women, Beth explained, had all danced with each other.

"I don't know," Barbara had said. "It sounds suspicious to me."

"No, Ma," Beth said. "I had a great time."

"Leave it alone, Barbara," said Erich, and Barbara had quickly changed the subject.

"Beth," said Barbara now, holding her hand, "whatever it is, you can tell me. I'm your mother, remember."

"I'm very tired," Beth said. "Could we go back to rest awhile before dinner?"

"Of course," Barbara said, kissing her forehead and smiling, as if that explanation had been enough.

Again when the sun was setting, Beth wandered from their hotel with her book, and this time she ran down the beach to the esplanade. The woman was not there. The bench was empty.

She sat down on the bench exactly where the woman had sat, put her feet up against the balustrade, opened her book, and stretched out her arm exactly as she remembered, even turning her head slightly to look where she remembered falling in the sand, in case the woman had looked over that way. For a long while she sat, pretending to read, watching the birds and the seaweed sweep across the beach, until when she looked up a moon had risen, casting even at dusk its reflective path across the sea, like a highway starting at the waves.

"Beth," she heard, almost whispered—"Beth," like a trick of the wind—and a gentle hand touched her shoulder. "I didn't want to scare you," said her mother, sitting down with her on the bench. "It's late, you know. I was worried. Don't you want to go have dinner?"

Beth fell upon her mother's shoulder, nodding while she cried. "Shh," Barbara said, rocking her slightly and stroking her hair. "Baby, what is it?" she said.

Beth pulled herself up and wiped her eyes. "Look," she said, pointing to the moon, her back to her mother. "It's so beautiful here, don't you think?"

The next day was Easter Sunday.

"I don't care," Barbara said, putting on her same low walking shoes and brown travel skirt. "It doesn't matter to me. It's not my holiday. They used to throw stones on Easter." In the vaporetto, however, and then in San Marco, all the crowd was dressed in its Easter finery: elaborate white dresses and Easter hats, the men in dark suits, sunglasses, and shiny leather shoes. The bells in the tower chimed again and again, and the pigeons rose up and circled round, as if time itself were flying ceaselessly, or else were stuck at ten o'clock Easter morning, again and again, forever. To escape the crowd, they walked until they found a poor-looking side street, turning there to find the Jewish ghetto.

Just as they turned, Beth saw the woman she had seen so many times, it seemed, before, and thought immediately of the book she had left this one time in her room, useless now as a prop of introduction. She was leaning against a building, one foot up against the wall, smoking a cigarette and reading from her book, always ignoring the crowd around her.

"Mother," said Beth. "Wait. I'll meet you somewhere. I really want to see the Easter mass."

"What!" said her mother.

"Yes," said Beth. "Don't worry, I'm not turning Christian. I just want to see it, in this great cathedral."

"All right," said Barbara. "But don't you want to see the oldest ghetto in Europe? Don't you want to see where the Rothschilds began?"

"Yes!" said Beth, enthusiastically. "Of course!" But she knew she was unconvincing.

"Well," said her mother, "I'll wander around first, and then I'll meet you at the synagogue at noon. All right?"

"Right!" said Beth, nodding and waving at the same time. When her mother was gone, she turned and almost ran back to where the woman had been standing. Now, this time, she had not disappeared. Out of breath, panting and staring blatantly, Beth forgot that she too was visible, and blushed hotly when the woman looked up from her book, staring back at her. She smirked when Beth nodded, hardly a smile, nodding to herself and going back to her reading. Beth was left standing across the street with nothing to do, nothing to respond to, nowhere to hide. Hitching her foot up against the wall behind her, she tried to read her map.

The woman looked up again, smirked, shook her head, pushed back her long hair, and crossed over to Beth, standing in front of her. "You lost?" she said, and Beth nodded, unable to speak. "Haven't I seen you somewhere before?"

"Yes," Beth said.

"Where was it? Some party?"

"On the plane ride over," said Beth. "And also in Rome, in the Colosseum, and then on the Lido, by the esplanade."

"Really!" said the woman. "I didn't see you there—all those places."

"I mean," said Beth, "I've seen you." She looked up for the first time, and the woman's face was close to her own. "I was —sort of looking for you."

"Well!" said the woman. "What's your name, anyway?"

"Beth," said Beth, and for a while they looked at each other, Beth unable to ask her the same question back.

"Wouldn't you like to know my name?" the woman asked, and Beth nodded. "Ha!" she said. "I'll bet you would! So you've been following me?"

"Well, no," Beth said. "Sort of. I mean, I noticed that we were reading the same book. *The Bodley Head?*"

"What?" said the woman.

"Yes—*The Bodley Head*, by Henry James."

"You're kidding, aren't you?" said the woman.

"No," said Beth. "I saw you reading it. I love those stories."

"Stories?" said the woman. "I don't know what you're talking about. Bodley Head is the publisher. They do all of James. God!"

"Oh," said Beth, nodding, wondering if she was going to faint from embarrassment, wishing that she would faint, and never wake up. "I guess I didn't realize."

"Ha!" said the woman. "I guess not! But hell, I'm going to kiss you anyway." And she did, with fine, chiseled lips and the down of blond hairs that Beth had noticed even on the plane, and dreamt about. "Well," said the woman, "that was all right! See you on the Lido," she said, and walked away, waving before she disappeared around the corner.

When Beth turned around, her mother was standing across the street, holding her hands to her face.

"My worst nightmare," said Barbara, when finally she spoke. They were on the boat going back to the Lido.

"Oh, Mother," said Beth. "It was just one kiss. I didn't ask her to. It didn't mean anything."

"I don't want to hear," said Barbara. "I don't want to know." And though Beth tried to explain, tried to lie her way out of their unhappiness, her mother would not listen. "The ghetto was empty," she said, changing the subject. "The synagogue was closed. Can you believe it? Still afraid of violence on Easter," she said. "Still! When I was a girl, they used to throw stones. Did you know that?"

Even on the plane going back, she shook her head when Beth apologized for so sudden a revelation. "It was nothing, Mother," Beth said. "Just a joke."

"Please," said her mother, "I just can't hear it. My choice is—I don't know—to pretend, or else to die."

"Mother!"

"All I wanted were grandchildren," she said. "Is that too much to ask?"

Back home in New York, Beth called her mother in Providence. But Barbara would reminisce, or describe the plans for her studio or for their Passover supper, but would not talk about what she had seen in Venice, or what it meant.

"Your father's invited a young man from his department over

for the seder," she said. "I think you'll like him. Another pianist."

"I may not be coming home," said Beth. "But thanks."

"What do you mean?" asked her mother.

"Well," said Beth, "I've been invited to one here."

"Oh," said her mother. "Anyone I know?"

"Yes," said Beth. "But I didn't think you'd want to hear about it. Anyway, I thought you were leaving home! I thought you were sick of what you had to put up with, with Daddy."

"I really don't want to discuss that, either," said her mother. "Anyway," she said, seeming to imply both herself and her daughter, although Beth could never bring herself to ask, "I suppose there are worse things in this world."

BARBARA WAS COMING to town again. She had to see Beth right away, if just for a few minutes, and would not interfere in any of her daughter's plans. So said the tape machine, beneath the music and laughter and intimate conversation of thirty people, as Beth stared up at her friends from a floor pillow in her apartment; in all the confusion she had not checked her messages until now.

"Beth!" said David, laughing at her expression from across the room. "Come on, what's wrong with you?" It was a party for her birthday, but she was more and more appalled at the scene she envisioned, her eyes as large and unblinking as if her friends had become, to herself now as well as to her mother, each the perfect vision, one after another, of her mother's nightmare: narcissists, Barbara called them, misfits unwilling to grow up and take their place in the world. Which simply meant, to Beth at least, that at twenty-six, at twenty-eight or at thirty, none of them, for a pertinent variety of reasons, and especially not Beth—just turning twenty-five herself—was married. Wiping clean the slate of all their combined virtues, it was this common flaw that made them seem (at least, Beth thought, to her mother) insufficient, all of them in the same way, and cut from the same color of cloth—invisible.

Most, she realized, were in one way or another artists, although when asked, as in New York one always was, "What do you *do*?" they would have to reply "secretary," or "salesclerk," or "waiter," or worse. Some were poets and wrote book reviews after work for small newspapers in New Hampshire or Florida, staying up late, when they could find the strength, in the rooms they shared in Brooklyn, alone with their manuscripts. Or they were singers or played an instrument, performing in small chamber groups for weddings or bar mitzvahs hosted by parents of their friends, out beyond the bridges and tunnels of Manhattan. The musician friends all lived in the same building on upper Broadway, in single rooms leased for the month, kitchens in the closet, half-tubs of cracking plastic, sharing the urine-smelling halls with indigents and adventurous Columbia students. One woman had sold the copyright to a cookie mold she had designed, and lived all year off the royalties, visiting New York only between her months at artist colonies. Others, like Beth, were painters when they could make the time, or light welders, or sculptors in linoleum. To support themselves they worked occasionally for a month or two laying out magazine copy, or buying clothes for mannequins, or painting raw chickens with a veneer of roasted juiciness for photographic studios. It was from these more respectable jobs that Beth herself could afford her half of the large but dirty loft— a former ladies' underwear factory—with its high beaten-copper ceiling and wide, paint-spattered walls, vast enough for Beth's largest canvas, an abstract some said was a group portrait of her friends: one stroke of black in the middle perhaps was Beth herself; another might have been David.

It was through those jobs as well that she had found her other, more responsible-looking friends, the ones Barbara would have approved of, who were not in Beth's painting, who wore makeup and shaved their legs, who could afford new suits, cabs everywhere, weeks in the Caribbean, tickets to things in midtown—women who in general were looking for men but always came alone, sex for them being too fraught and fleeting to bring along. They sat now on other pillows on the dusty, hard wood floor, paying court to the man or two among them, pulling their skirts safely around their legs and laughing, because Beth was staring vacantly into her lap.

David too was laughing, too hard. He had come with someone new, a magazine picture of perfect masculinity—shoulders like a house, muscles popping out of his clothes—who worked in a bank and had spoken his three words in a high, nervous voice. David, unshaven and underdressed, Beth's mother already knew too well—that was bad enough. Titled and rich though he would be—a doctor!—he had his own special disqualification. Homosexuality was not, of course, his choice, but it made him interesting; whereas being a doctor would make him (so he said) respectable, beloved, and it was (so he said) this time his choice. When he first mentioned it, almost as a joke, a dare, an experiment, his whole family had raised their heads and rejoiced, as if that small word had been all along the secret key to a legacy that now would be his, the password he had had to discover by himself. So he would be a doctor, he would be beloved; but every week he would pull at his already thinning hair, and stare in wonder at Beth's artist friends, and cry for that life. "Why do you think it's so great being a doctor?" Beth often used to ask him, when she wanted to go out in the world, but he still had to study. "Why are you doing it? Are you still so insecure about what your family thinks of you? What the world thinks? The world doesn't care, David. Life is short and then you die. Doctors are boring."

"Am I boring?" he asked.

"I don't know," she said, running her hand through his hair as he stared at inorganic chemistry. "No," she said. "You play the piano. You should be a musician," she said. "A pianist, a rock star—Dave the Rose—anything. I'll get you an audition. But you shouldn't be a doctor."

Soon, now, he would be a doctor.

Maureen was with her tonight as well, her oldest friend from college, and one of the few allowed to say that word "lesbian" ("dike" was still one step too far); she had traveled with Beth all the distance of her transformation, and though tonight she was one of those women in skirts, huddling with them close to the floor, she had just broken off with Lynn, Beth's roommate, a lithe, dark woman of forty. Tonight Maureen had blow-dried her long red hair and come with a man from her office; smiling proudly now, he stood introducing himself and Maureen as well to Lynn, who merely leaned back with her drink against the bookcase and laughed.

"It's nice to meet you," said Maureen, standing up from the floor, not too embarrassed to enjoy the joke. She broke an ice cube in her teeth.

"Beth," called Lynn, excusing both her laugh and her exit, "cheer up, it's your birthday." She bent down in her elegant dress and whispered, low-voiced, into Beth's ear, as if she were kissing her cheek. "It's probably nothing—you know your mother, Beth. She misses you, that's all."

Beth's eyes were still wide open, staring out across the room.

"Maybe she finally left your father," David said, coming over to her with a tumbler full of wine. He sat down beside her, leaving his banker by the long window to stare out at the neon lights of Canal Street.

"She found out about me," Beth said. "I know it."

"Found out what?" David said, his head in her lap. "That you went once to a dike bar? That you dream about Katharine Hepburn?"

Beth could only stare at him, her private fears so casually spilled. "I've done more than that, David. I've had a lover."

"Okay, so what? That was in Greece. It was a year ago."

"And I kissed that woman in Venice. She saw that one."

Beth's friends laughed at this and promptly lost interest, kissed their dates and turned up the music. They had too often listened to such anxieties: "Do I look like one?" "Did she think I'm one?" "Did he?" "Will I ever find a lover I love?" "Will I be spurned by men, ruin my chances for marriage, babies, happiness?" And the song, anyway, was a favorite among them, three suburban sisters singing imperfectly, rhyming haphazardly:

> If you go with that fella, forget about us—
> As far as I'm concerned that would be just
> Throwing yourself away.

"Oh, Beth," said David, taking her hand. "So what? You're being ridiculous. If the issue's only what you do, it's hardly an issue. Do you think that woman called your mother? She didn't even know your name."

"She knew I'm from Rhode Island. My scarf said Rhode Island School of Design."

"Come on," he said, shaking his head and pressing his face into her lap. "Can't you forget it? It doesn't mean a thing."

She was bending over, and only David could have seen the tears in her eyes. "Do you promise?" she asked. Without looking up, he nodded.

Quickly she stood up and pulled him into the kitchen, where it was quieter. No one else was there, and he held her in his arms.

"Don't worry," he said. "I'll take care of things here while you talk to her. We'll play games or something. We'll sing. I'll show them my bar mitzvah album. It's still here, isn't it?"

She hid her face in his shoulder, then quickly pulled away. "I don't want her to come here," she said.

"But why?" David asked. "Are you ashamed?"

"No," she said, resentfully, revealing even to herself how much she was.

"Then what is it?"

"Can you imagine my mother here? She'd die. Or she'd have to kill herself. I just don't want her to get the chance to criticize. You know she doesn't like you, or any of my real friends. I'm sorry to say that, but it's true."

"And you know she's very polite, at least in company. I don't care what she thinks in private."

"Oh? It's not what you tell all our friends."

"Come on."

"How do you like your date?" Beth suddenly asked, pursing her lips.

"Is he the most beautiful man you've ever seen?"

"No," she said. "Do you love him?"

"No."

"That's good," she said, "because there's someone coming I want you to meet."

"Who?"

"Never mind."

"Come on—tell me who."

"I told you about him," Beth said. "My father's student. My mother invited him home for Passover—a nice Jewish doctor, she told me, a perfect catch. 'Boy or girl?' I almost asked her. Well, he's not Jewish either. I don't know where she got that one from—he's blond as can be."

"What do you mean, 'either'?" David asked, absently opening the refrigerator, closing it again.

"You'll see," said Beth. "It was, though, sort of a perfect match. I have to give her credit for that. She said he was like you—she was right." The music spread suddenly down the hall into the kitchen, and Lynn came in to make Beth dance. She wore dresses, she was a lawyer, she had been married (briefly), and all in all Beth's mother approved: "Why don't you get your friend Lynn to take you shopping?" Barbara had suggested. "Why don't you try that kind of blush?" "What a lawyer you would make!"

"I'm a painter, Mother."

"I mean a real job. It's a shame, someone so clever with a pen. Comic books, then—fashion design—animation! You're not always going to have someone like Lynn around, ready to take care of you." Over the phone, her mother and Lynn spent too much of Beth's money talking about fashions, flea markets, remodeling the loft. And Lynn, dancing up now with a gobletful of wine, was really the most dangerous of them all!

When the doorbell buzzed, Beth jumped from Lynn's arms. "That's her!" she said, biting a well-bitten nail, looking around the room. "Turn the music down!" she called down the hall. "Everybody hide!"

Instead her friends laughed. "Beth," they said, "but why?"

"It's my mother," she said. "I don't want her to know."

"Know what?" said David. "That it's your birthday?"

"I don't know!" Beth said, holding both hands to her head. She felt tears in her eyes, and her heart was racing.

"That you have friends?" someone asked.

"That you exist?" said Lynn.

The buzzer rang again. "Never mind," said Beth. "I'll go down. I'll be back in a little while."

"But how do you know it's her?" David called, when she had grabbed David's coat and was already on the stairs. "Call down to her. Ask if it's her."

"It's her ring," Beth said. "Insistent—short but insistent. I'd know it anywhere." A moment later she was coming up the stairs again; David could hear her laughing three double flights away. At the fifth floor she ran up the final flight and pushed open the door. "It's all right!" she called in, to no one in particular. "It's not her! You can come out now!" From the cushions on the floor, from the sofa, from around the table full of wine bottles, candles stuck on plates or dripping down empty bottles, apple cider cartons, Brie wedges, a small birthday cake, and many soft, expensive cookies, her friends looked over at her, unmoving.

"So can you," David said.

"David Rosen," said Beth, introducing him formally, ignoring his remark, "this is Andrew Chase. Andrew, David. What do you know, you're both in medical school. I'm sure you'll have lots to talk about."

Behind her, still in the doorway, a young man perhaps their own age bent his head and smiled. "Hi," he said, offering David his hand, and David, forgetting to smile back, reached out quickly to accept it, holding it there.

"Why?" Andrew asks, as much for a moment's indulgence as for unsatisfied curiosity—all much later, when he knows the answers very well himself.

"Because I knew you loved me already."

"How? How did you know?"

"Because you came down from Providence just for a party. It was obvious. I knew Beth had told you to."

"What else?"

"You were smiling."

"A lot of people smile."

"No they don't. Anyway, not like you. I wanted you."

"You mean, you desired me?"

"Yes."

"How about the banker?"

"You can't love an object, Andrew. I loved you. I loved you because you came all the way from Providence. Because you wore a bow tie to one of Beth's parties. Because you play the piano." Just as much, he wants to add, because you are blond, because your chest is perfect and your deep voice strikes overtones I can feel—any of all the visceral, sexual aspects of his love, the smell and taste of skin, the blush and facets of a cheek. But he will show that in other ways. He has committed himself; one cannot, he has said, love an object. "Because, Doctor," he says instead—they are doctors already—"we both wanted the same thing in life, and we saw it in each other."

"What did we want?" Andrew asks, flattered, curious.

"Ah, that," David says, indicating with a sweep of his arm the two of them in bed, the bedroom itself, their house, and everything beyond. But this is years from now.

Before long the banker said he really had to get back uptown. Most Saturdays he and David ran very early in the park, and he at least had to get to bed. "Okay," David said, walking out with him as far as the stairwell and kissing him good night.

"Was that the rudest thing I've ever done?" David asked, coming back to Beth's corner of the party. A few people were dancing, the music was loud—a woman's voice shouting out the name of her lover, the bass thrumming like a pulse through the floor—and he could speak to Beth as if privately.

"No," she said. "Not by far. There was that time you—"

"No thank you," David said, cutting her off, smiling at Andrew as he sat down with them.

"Who was that?" Andrew asked.

"Oh," said David, "a friend of Beth's."

"Oh?" said Beth. "What was his name, anyway?"

"Very funny," said David, and they went on to those questions of medical-student life: who were the professors David had known? the restaurants? and did he know anything about the psychiatric hospital in town? "Well, yes," David said. "I know Muddler Hospital very well." Though he didn't turn his head, he knew that Beth was smiling.

"Oh, tell that story, David," she said. "The transsexual story."

"No." He shook his head.

"Come on, David, Andrew will appreciate it. He wants to be a psychiatrist himself."

"No, Beth. I don't want to."

"Do you still listen to this music?" Andrew asked her instead.

Beth shrugged. "Why, don't you like her?"

"She used to sleep with girls," David said. "Or so Beth says. Then she got married."

"David!" she said. "Come on, most of our friends went to Muddler Hospital, one time or another. It's a funny story."

"Well," said David, glancing over resentfully. Beth nodded, her eyebrows raised. "They have a five-dollar clinic—it used to be five dollars, anyway—for the unemployed, and for rich kids who don't want their parents to know. The interns get to try out all their theories. One said I'd make a good transsexual. The next one wanted to try aversion therapy."

"To what?" Andrew asked.

"To boys," said Beth.

"Yes," David said. "But I was too scared for that one. So he settled on masturbation therapy. You look at a *Penthouse* centerfold just before orgasm, and then a whole minute before, and then from the time you pull down your pants. And then, according to his graph, I was cured—good student that I was."

"Cured," said Andrew. "Of what?"

David merely smiled, assuming the question must be a joke.

"Of being gay, Andrew," said Beth.

"Oh yes," he said. "Of course. I just thought you meant—there was something really wrong, or something. . . ."

"The next step was to find a woman to have sex with, right there in the office."

"Oh no!" Andrew said.

"Oh yes. He suggested I ask a friend, in fact. He mentioned Beth."

"You never told me that!" Beth said.

"I told him he was crazy—it was insulting, demeaning. He said no, women don't mind at all. Another patient of his had found a woman in a bar, evidently she said she'd be glad to."

"Then what happened?"

David looked over at Beth before he answered. "I did it with Beth, anyway, before long. My shrink slapped me on the back, said I was done with therapy."

There was no opportunity to laugh, and no one spoke. David got up to find a candle for their dark corner and came back with two, stuck onto empty bottles. "It's Friday night," he said, "and we haven't said the prayers."

"Oh, come on!" Beth said. She tried to stop him, but he lit a match to one candle and then held it next to the other until that wick as well took the small flame. The music had finished, and there was enough quiet to hear him sing the prayer, slowly, self-consciously to the end, bending his head but not daring to cover his eyes. *"Baruch Ata Adonai, Elohaynu Melech Ha-olam. . . ."* Beth was embarrassed about having objected to the prayer, now that everyone was listening. David was embarrassed, having pretended it was a joke. If it started as a joke, however, Beth objecting and David smirking, it soon became, despite one of them or the other, a real prayer. Around them everyone was quieter, listening.

"That's very nice," Andrew said. "I never heard that before."

"Except at my house," said Beth.

"Isn't this your house?" he said.

And Beth looked around her, surprised. "Yes," she said. "But I meant, at my mother's."

"This is your mother speaking," said Barbara, distorted but loudly.

For the first time there was no music, and Lynn, standing by the intercom, could hear it quite clearly. "Your mother!" she said, calling over to Beth across the room.

"Your mother?" said Andrew.

"My mother!" said Beth, jumping up. "Andrew! Hide!" she told him, running to the door.

"Hide?" he said, looking to David, and David wondered what Andrew meant behind his unblinking green eyes, his uneven but confident smile.

"She's just kidding," David said, shrugging his shoulders.

Beth ran down the five double flights to the street door, where her mother was standing in her long mink, her suitcase between her legs. Her hair was almost disheveled, and she wore no makeup on her pale, shadowed face.

"Hello, darling," she said, hugging Beth and holding on to her.

"Hi, Mom. What's wrong?"

Barbara only shook her head, still on Beth's shoulder. "That's how you greet your mother?" she said, trying to make a joke. "I've had a long trip," she said slowly, but then found her strength and her speed. "I'm tired. I hope I'm not disturbing you. I tried to call several times, but no one was home. Finally I just left a message. I'm not going back to your father," she said. "This whole thing is his fault, if you ask me. Has he called?"

"Is that what's wrong? You had another fight?"

Barbara shook her head no, but didn't speak as they climbed back up the stairs. Beth carried the suitcase. On the third-floor landing Barbara stopped. "It's something else," she said, speaking quickly, and looked long into Beth's eyes, accusing or pleading. "I found something out," she said, her voice as low as it could get. "I'm more upset than I can tell you."

"What?" Beth said, certain at once of what revelation it would be. She imagined a blackmail letter, hidden right now in her mother's purse: someone had taken a snapshot; recorded a conversation; interviewed her friends.

But Barbara shook her head suddenly and they continued up. Beth was too upset to stop her. On the fourth floor Barbara shook her head again and murmured almost as if to herself, ". . . A lesbian. I can't believe it. My daughter a lesbian—"

"Mother!" said Beth, trying to interrupt her. At that word, all she had ever desired—the soft, curvacious push of breasts behind sheer cloth; the smooth insides of thighs; the angular shelf of hip bones; the smooth cheek; the moist lip—all flashed in front of her, appalling, nauseating.

"You may not know what you want," Barbara said, while they walked. "You have your troubles with men—you'll work them out. All you young people, you're confused, you experiment. I hear it's even chic." Suddenly she turned. "But Carol Anne is thirty, Beth! She's living with a woman. Living together! For a year! I don't even know her name." Gravely she shook her head, and they continued up. "My eldest daughter," she said, her voice very low. "My first child. I'm a goner."

"Mother! What do you mean?" They were almost at the door.

"You just can't know what it's like, Elizabeth, being the mother of a lesbian. It's been a nightmare since she called. Every day I wake up and I wish I was dead. It's killing me." They went into the apartment, and seeing the crowd, she held her hand to her chest. "Oh!" she said, opening her eyes, finding her smile. "I didn't know you were having people over! I'm terribly sorry, Beth—I'll go right to a hotel."

"No," Beth said. "It's Lynn's party, really. She's just having some people over."

"For her birthday," Lynn said, coming over and shaking Barbara's hand, pressing Barbara's cheek with her own and cheerfully kissing the air.

"Your birthday!" said Barbara. "But that's not till next week—oh, I should have known!"

"It's nothing, Mom, really," said Beth; and indeed, as they spoke, the guests became more and more mobile, putting on coats, hunting for record jackets and empty casserole pans. Very quickly, most of them had gone. Across the room, Andrew stood up and walked over.

"Andrew!" said Barbara, as he came up to her, kissing her near the mouth. She kissed him back. "What are you doing down here? I'm so glad to see you. I'll bet Elizabeth is, too!"

"Well," he said, "I had to be in New York this weekend, so I thought I'd just drop by."

"How sweet!" Barbara said, looking from his face to Beth and back. "That's wonderful! And where are you staying? I'm sure Beth has a cushion around here somewhere. One of those futons you people love?"

Andrew looked over at Beth, whose face was red but unreadable. She had promised him a bed, but now, with her mother, it was filled.

"I have an extra bed," David said, looking not at Andrew but directly at Beth.

"Oh," Beth said.

"Well," said Andrew. "That would be fine, thanks. Yes, I have to be up at Mount Sinai tomorrow, anyway. For an interview."

"Well!" Barbara said, nodding. "That's very nice. Very nice indeed!"

. . .

David's car was secondhand and well abused, perfect camou-
flage from the lurking vandals of his uptown street; but once it
had been a new sports car, and beneath all the clear, cold spray
of lights along the East Side Drive—the bridges suspended
above the river, the bright towers of the skyline—it was still
romantic enough an envelope of warmth to make him confident,
as they sped along, that his mood, his intentions were well
known, and that his desires were shared. Still he wondered—
just how would their easy moment together in his cold but
roaring car transform into tension, romance, intimacy? Andrew
was exclaiming over the bridges, the reflected dazzle of the
water, the apartment tower in front of them under which the
highway disappeared. And David had always to keep his eyes
on the road, or to check the mirror—for the moment his own
expression, though supercharged, was safe. He knew that once
out of his clothes he was imperfect to look at; that in bed with
a stranger he could only pretend to sleep; and that he had to
use the bathroom too many times during the night. Still, he
could not say good night often enough to his banker, who to
look at was perfect, who wanted nothing more than to find
himself his own Jewish doctor to cuddle with, to run with
around the park, all personality, even physical traits aside. Still,
something now gave him confidence enough to turn and look,
even stare for a smiling, unblinking instant into the green eyes
beside him. And then somehow—though he had never appeared, to himself at least, gay enough, straight enough, or
handsome enough—he had willed Andrew to lean his much-
desired head toward his own, even to let it fall against David's
shoulder.

"I'm so tired," Andrew said, meeting David's eyes in the
mirror and smiling also. David's arm, levitating precipitously
along the edge of the seat, dislodged with a jerk, and gently
fell.

The arm beneath the sweater was muscular enough; the shoulder above the arm was just as hard; and the chest beyond the arm was sculpted as well—hairless, smooth, and warm, coming right down to it—and easily accessible beneath mere cotton, at least to a hand newly confident, bravely intimate, and full of desire.

"I thought you said you had an extra bed," Andrew said when he was standing in the kitchen, looking into the small bedroom just large enough for David's double mattress. With its heap of blankets and pillows, it fully covered the floor. On the walls and ceiling, on every shelf and windowsill was crowded what seemed to be a collection of junk: rocks in odd shapes and miniature people, paintings found in trash cans, antique hats and canes from attics, flea markets, and expensive boutiques.

"Did I?" David answered, pulling off as if by mistake his shirt along with his sweater. "I guess I meant to say I had plenty of room."

"In the bed," Andrew said.

"In the bed," David answered, falling onto the mattress and sitting back against the wall, his hands up behind his head. All around him were his objects, saved, he liked to say, from oblivion—transformations, buried treasure. "Anyway," he said, "which side do you want?"

"Either," said Andrew, but when he took off his shirt and jeans and lay down in just his Jockey shorts it was on the far side against the wall.

"You know," said David, switching off the light, pulling off his shorts and stretching down next to him, "this way you can't escape." Andrew didn't answer. They lay without speaking, watching the orange flicker of the electric fireplace, a miniature version within a plastic clock. It reflected darkly on their faces and on the mobile high above their heads. The hairs along their legs intermingled, but neither moved. Their arms were parallel, even pressing together, but neither moved. Facing each other then, as if asking a question, as if guessing an answer, they stared unmoving, breathing each other's breath, and finally kissed.

In a moment the phone was ringing. David had to reach for it across to the corner, under the pile of his clothes. The clock, above its flame, showed just after two.

"I just can't keep this up with you," said Beth.

"Hello?" David said. "Who is this?"

"Very funny, David. I can't talk louder because of my mother. Is he there?"

"Yes. Where else?"

"Am I interrupting anything?"

"Well, yes."

"Well, I'm sorry. I'm very sorry. I don't think I can be friends with you anymore. Not like this."

"Please, this isn't really the time."

"Yes it is the time!" From a whisper, she was nearly shouting. "Isn't the time! I can't just keep saying goodbye to you, giving you up like this whenever a handsome man comes along."

"How are you giving me up? This is absurd—why did you introduce us? Anyway, you do the same thing. Men and women both."

"I do not! And walking down the street, who can keep your attention!"

"Who can keep yours! Listen, I'm so tired. I don't know what we're talking about. I'm in bed. I'm naked. Can't we talk in the morning?"

"David, please! You can't just leave me here crying." Indeed she was crying.

"You're home, aren't you? Your mother's there—"

"So what!"

"It's the middle of the night."

"My mother thinks he came here for me. What am I supposed to tell her?"

"Tell her you're not interested. Tell her you're a lesbian."

"Don't say that!"

"Tell her he came for me."

"Very funny."

"What's so funny!" Then he whispered. "Oh, come on. What did she tell you?"

"Nothing very interesting. That my sister's gay."

Andrew had crawled over and put his arm around David's shoulder. "Who is it?" he asked.

"You're kidding!" David said.

"Are you on call or something?" Andrew asked.

"You knew that," said Beth.

"I know," said David. "But it's funny, her telling you now. Considering all your worrying."

"It's not so funny," Beth said. "I wish you would understand that. For her it's a terrible thing. She says she wishes she were dead. How do you think that makes me feel?"

"Is that Beth?" said Andrew.

"Yes," said Beth, sniffling. "Tell him it's me."

David nodded, and Andrew took the phone from him. "Beth," he said, "hi!" But at the other end there was silence. "She must have hung up," he said, and shrugged his shoulders, kissing David again, on the lips, the ear, the shoulder. "What's the matter?" he asked. "Is something wrong?"

"No," David said. "Nothing's wrong."

But turning back again, to Andrew's caresses, to his own explorations and celebrations of a new lover's body, he kept glancing around, even in the dark, absently, nervously, as if the bed itself had become smaller, more crowded, and they were not so alone and private as they had been.

. . .

בָּרוּךְ אַתָּה יְיָ, אֱלֹהֵינוּ מֶלֶךְ
הָעוֹלָם, אֲשֶׁר קִדְּשָׁנוּ בְּמִצְוֹתָיו, וְצִוָּנוּ עַל הָעֲרָיוֹת, וְאָסַר לָנוּ אֶת
הָאֲרוּסוֹת, וְהִתִּיר לָנוּ אֶת הַנְּשׂוּאוֹת לָנוּ עַל יְדֵי חֻפָּה וְקִדּוּשִׁין.
בָּרוּךְ אַתָּה יְיָ, מְקַדֵּשׁ עַמּוֹ יִשְׂרָאֵל עַל יְדֵי חֻפָּה וְקִדּוּשִׁין.

Blessed art Thou, O Lord our God, Who has made us holy through Thy commandments, and has commanded us concerning marriages that are forbidden, and those that are permitted when carried out under the canopy and with the sacred wedding ceremonies. Blessed art Thou, O Lord our God, Who makes Thy people Israel holy through this rite of the canopy and the sacred bond of marriage. . . .

שׂוֹשׂ תָּשִׂישׂ וְתָגֵל הָעֲקָרָה, בְּקִבּוּץ בָּנֶיהָ לְתוֹכָהּ בְּשִׂמְחָה.
בָּרוּךְ אַתָּה יְיָ, מְשַׂמֵּחַ צִיּוֹן בְּבָנֶיהָ.

May Zion and the land of Israel, so long without children or joy, now become glad and joyful with children living happily in the Land. Blessed art Thou, Who makes Zion joyful through her children. . . .

Jill's family, Lutherans from Iowa, couldn't understand the Hebrew. They turned in their seats, stared at the high ceilings of the rich living room, and watched in embarrassed amazement as their blond daughter of the Midwest, Jill Turner, who had waved to them from a float as homecoming queen, now recited unknowable marriage vows in a foreign language, standing under a mysterious canopy among the little group of parents, siblings, and rabbi.

"I do," said Jill, loudly so her grandparents behind her would be able to hear.

"I do," said Warren, quietly, moved suddenly to tears but still impressive in his rented blue tuxedo. After a brief prayer sung by the rabbi, accompanying himself on his guitar, it was time to call them man and wife, the next generation of the covenant, the children of Abraham, diverse and innumerable as the sands on the shore, as the stars in the sky; and to smash with their heels the empty wine glass in memory of the temple's destruction, all of their tragedies through history, all the sadness and fragility of life amidst all its sweetness.

Warren stamped with his foot and then stamped again, but the glass would not break.

"Shit!" he said, good-naturedly but then embarrassed because it was at his own wedding. Still everyone laughed. He tried again, and Jill tried, but they had to unwrap the glass from its linen napkin. It was not a delicate crystal but a small, thick, shotglass, cheap to replace but impossible to crush.

"Zellie!" said Sol, without turning to her, and, facing the crowd, he laughed his deep, public laugh. "For chrissake!" he said. "What did you use that for!"

"It's small," Zellie called out, embarrassed, already running back to the kitchen for another glass. "I thought it would break easier."

The guests murmured, amused, confused, and impatient. Israel Rosen as well, essential at the ceremony as father of the groom, stood under the *huppah* in his dark lawyer's suit, also smiling and shaking his head. He was a small, dapper man who at fifty still looked exercised, groomed, and proud enough of his body beneath his lawyer's gray that he might never have been married. His hair was long and still thick, carefully combed down to his earlobes without a stray tuft. All around him were people he had known for twenty-five years, friends from law school, from Lewiston, Zellie's parents, cousins, nieces, and nephews, his own children, all among the furniture and chandeliers and wallpaper for which he had nodded and written out the checks. Beyond the French doors was a yard he had paid to have landscaped—trees uprooted, other trees planted, a swimming pool dug and filled with the clear water from his own well. Too many times they had dug down fruitlessly, expensively, hundreds of feet into dry earth, until eventually near the surface they struck a pocket, water like cool blood flooding the yard. Anywhere he turned now it was according to his own designs, but he stood without looking around, uncomfortable in the outmoded intimacy.

After a moment Zellie returned with one of her delicate crystals, wrapping it regretfully in the linen cloth.

"No, Zel," called Pearl from the second row. "You should use a light bulb." But it was too late.

"And now," repeated the rabbi, replacing the package on the floor, "once again we break the glass—at least we give it a try!"

This time Warren's foot came down effectively, and everyone heard the shattering crystal.

"Mazel tov!" shouted Sol and the rabbi, and all down one side of the room came echoes and repetitions of their wish for good luck. Jill lifted her veil and the bride and groom embraced. Sol kissed Zellie, taking her in his arms, Zellie kissed Warren and his bride, and all around people were kissing, embracing and wishing good luck. Only Israel, standing out in his dark suit, remained awkwardly alone, crossing his arms and then uncrossing them. He had declined the tuxedo himself, as by now all of Zellie's family knew. Except for his strong resemblance to his sons—the dark hair, the narrow face—he might have been in the wrong house, at the wrong party.

"Mazel tov!" said Beth, coming up to the *huppah* and kissing David, who was standing stiff but handsome in his own rented outfit. "*Kaynahora!*"

David turned to see if she was joking; indeed, she was distinctly half-smiling, crossing her arms as if to hide herself and the long linen dress Zellie had bought her in Jerusalem. "You're next!" she said to him, unquietly in all the confusion. "You're going to make some lucky man very happy!"

"Thank you," he said. "So are you, I'm sure." A roomful of relatives were watching them, nodding to David as they crowded up toward the wedding party. They looked at Beth, they looked back at him, cocking their heads, raising their eyebrows.

"Two years in bed with him," said a voice close by. David turned around, always prepared to hear himself the subject of any whisper; but Gloria, waiting nearby in line with Pearl, had her back to him. "And still she's wearing white!" she said. "It's a travesty."

"Ha, ha!" said Beth. "Just you wait. I might get married after all, you know."

"Shh," David said, whispering in her ear. "Everybody's listening."

"So?"

"Dad," David said, taking Beth's hand, "you know Beth."

"Of course I do," said Israel. "How have you been, Beth?"

"Fine!" she said. "And you?"

"Oh, fine, fine. How is your art going? David tells me you're beginning to get somewhere. It must be tough."

"Well," she said, and looked to the floor as if she were too shy to say. But really she could think of nothing.

He smiled and turned slightly, as if someone else were approaching.

"At least he didn't bring his woman," said a voice, very quietly and far away. David stood stiffly, listening. "I'm surprised he came at all."

"I never said I didn't want to get married," said Beth, whispering again.

"No, you just want to have a girl or two on the side."

"Yes. What's so bad about that? You'll have your lovers and I'll have mine."

David shrugged, and went to kiss some of his aunts, Gloria, Pearl, Minnie, Ruthie, and Ida, who had come up from Florida. They were moving out slowly onto the porch, where long tables had been set up with a buffet at one end. It was the middle of May, and already, by noon, it was hot in the sun, the orange trumpet flowers already wilted and fallen in great heaps from their vines. When David came back, Beth was no longer smiling. She was sitting alone in the front row of folding chairs, her face long, her eyes reflective as if with tears; beautiful to him, and even knowing what would come, irresistible.

"What's wrong?" he asked, looking around to see if anyone was watching. He was frowning impatiently but finally sat down with her.

"Oh, nothing," said Beth. "Only my mother would die if she saw all this. It's all she ever wanted. She's taken to reading bridal magazines in the supermarket. I saw her pick one up and she was embarrassed. She won't ask me anything about my own life, but I have to hear about every wedding in Rhode Island. My cousin Cynthia got married last month in Cranston. Oh, David! Would you like to know what her dress was made out of? Crêpe de chine, with little flowers all along the collar in pale blue and gold—"

"Then why do you keep telling her about men, if you don't want her to plague you so much? It seems like you bring it on yourself."

"We named the dog Sammy, like theirs," they both heard, but they didn't turn around. ". . . get us used to Jewish names." David smiled, glad for the distraction; but Beth was undistractable.

"But David," she said, and reached down to pull at her stockings, "I don't talk about men anymore! Besides, I can't tell her anything about my real life. It's not like with your mother— she leaves you alone. The minute I mention a man's name my mother asks me all about him. A month later she's still asking. Any acquaintance, even my landlord. And now, with my sister—I'm all she has left, she says. Her last hope. She asked about my friend Jo for a year, until I said she was a girl. She should have seen her face fall."

David was distracted; he was hardly listening. In the city she would have known why—a handsome man walking down the street, turning the corner, bending over to tie his shoe. Invariably his eyes would stray to the tight pants or the cut of a jaw, his smile fading like the afterglow of a flash. She hated it, felt belittled, demeaned, canceled out, and always determined that she would not, in fact that she did not, respond that way herself to a beautiful woman—at least if anyone was with her, at least if she could help it. But David seemed to have no compunction, even here; here, though, in the bosom of his family, where no man in his powder-blue suit could have been interesting or handsome or unrelated enough, it was a mystery. "Does your mother do that to you?" she asked, trying to draw him back. "I mean, plague you about women?"

"No," David said, still shifting his eyes, looking for a place to anchor them.

"I know," said Beth, "You really have it much easier than I. Your parents aren't sophisticated, but at least they leave you alone."

"My mother doesn't ask me about men either, Beth, or anything social. Except maybe you sometimes, shyly. She can't bear to really know about my life. Who I really am. I certainly couldn't have brought Andrew here."

"But you just met him!"

"I know. But I couldn't have."

Beth tried to look at him without sneering, or crying. He had gotten her into this, she considered, taken her along this far in aberrance if not perversity, even to wearing a long dress while secretly, simultaneously, longing for women. Once she had loved all the Beatles, had smiled at the nods of handsome men, had taken her choice between a dozen eager college boys. But now when it was convenient for him, when she had merely kissed women in secret but had no love, she was being left by her only guide, stranded, dumped; and having come even this far, she was sure there was no way back—each kiss was stamped like a scar across her past, and anyone, looking closely, would finally see it.

"Would you have wanted him to come today," she asked, "instead of me?"

"Beth," he said, "of course not. Anyway, it's not just me. My mother wanted you to come also."

"I know!" she said, sighing and turning away. David stood up, about to leave. "So how *is* your life?" she said, reaching up to him. "I mean your love life. My gift from Providence. Have you spoken to him?"

"Andrew?" He sat down again. "Yes, I have, actually."

"You have? Are you two in love or something?"

"I don't know, Beth. What does that mean? Yes. It was a nice weekend. I'm sure I'll see him again. But he lives in Providence."

"So what? So he'll transfer."

"And meanwhile, what? Life is short, Beth. I'm lonely."

"David!" she said, too quickly, betraying her impatience. "So what am I? Chopped liver?"

"You know what I mean, Beth."

"No, I don't know what you mean. I'm lonely too." Already it was an old conversation, and they followed along its familiar ruts as usual without being able to turn, or stop, or remember the pained look in each other's eyes; in their almost memorized exchange, the real feelings were easily forgotten. But Beth had not forgotten how far she had come, and how far they had come together. Only a few months before, in the fall, she had cried about her fate, and he had held her hand, and on his afternoon off had taken her out in a rowboat in Central Park. For two nights he had not slept, and sometimes seemed to be half-asleep; but still he had sounded sure of himself.

"If you do what makes you happy, Beth," he had said, "you won't be unhappy. You won't regret your life."

Already he sounded like a doctor; but how could he know! She had sat in the stern facing him, watching the yellow and brown leaves shake down in great gusts from the stunted trees. "I want children," she said. "I know that. Whatever else I want, I won't be happy unless I have that, David. A normal life, without people staring all the time, and hating the lesbians, or always wondering 'Is she or isn't she?' I'm tired of it. I want a husband and children. What if we had children?"

"I don't know, Beth."

"Just *if* it happened? What would it be like?"

"Oh, well, *that!*" he said, smiling; and throwing back his head, accepting for a moment the conceit, he described their imagined life together: the two of them making dinner in some safe, quiet kitchen, or walking along the beach, a small child between them.

"And after dinner," Beth continued, leaning forward eagerly, "we'll tell her stories in bed, and we'll take picnics, and draw together."

"Wait," David said. "After dinner, who's going to clean up?"

"Both of us."

"And the diapers?"

"Oh, *that*. I can do that, David. You just don't know that part of me. I just haven't been inspired yet." She had gone even farther than that. "I'll be a good mother," she had said—she cringed now at the memory. "You'll see, David, I would."

Then she gasped, staring at the trees. There, on a peninsula just beyond the bridge, two men were facing each other in the shrubs, only yards away. One of them knelt down and disappeared behind the leaves. David stopped rowing, transfixed, and until she doused him, not so playfully, with water from the lake, they had drifted toward the shore.

"Beth," he said, fully awake, taking up the oars again at last, "you don't want me."

He was saying the same thing now. His anger was identical, as was his belief that he could know what she thought and what she wanted. She looked around, forgetting where she was.

"You want someone straight to play at being straight," he said.

They were in his family's house, now she knew; in his living room, where he had played the piano, waiting to grow up, wondering, as she herself had wondered, What will I become?—while all along it was obvious.

"I don't want to pretend anymore," he said. "I did it too many years. Anyway, according to you I couldn't pull it off."

"That's not true," Beth said angrily, but then became quieter. "Anyway, I'm sorry if it is. I mean, I'm sorry if I said it."

"Let's go outside," David said, nodding toward the door. "We should mingle."

"Wait," she said, holding his arm again. "At least you have to find someone for me." With her nails she pressed into the blue cloth of his sleeve.

"How about her?" David said, pointing to one of the brides-maids, a friend of Jill's from high school, with blond hair in two flip curls at either side of her face like the three other bridesmaids, the strong shoulders of a farm matron, and the wide, rosy cheeks of corn-fed good health. Ignoring him, Beth wondered if indeed she knew what he meant, what she meant herself. Her chin was pressing into her chest.

"Oh, Beth," David said, looking finally into her eyes. "I do love you. I know we love each other best."

"Then what are we going to do? How can you leave me?"

"Leave you?" he said, and seemed truly surprised. "Beth, I wouldn't ever leave you."

She could only look at him, squinting a tear away.

"David!" called Zellie, coming in from the porch. When she saw them she grinned. "Beth!" she said. "Where were you two? We just cut the challah and said the Kiddush."

"I'm sorry, Mom," said David. "I didn't notice. We were just sitting here."

"Well, they want to take some pictures in here." She stood a moment watching them frankly, open-eyed, as if sitting there with their knees together and holding hands they were already posed for a photograph, frozen, absent, a moment from the past already captured and transformed. "I'm so glad you came, Beth," Zellie said. "You look so beautiful in that dress."

The bridesmaids were filing in around her, followed by Warren and Jill, sweaty but happy, who stood again under the *huppah* with rigid smiles, waiting for the portrait to be snapped. The room was crowded again as the different scenes were re-enacted—the blessing of the couple, the giving of the ring, the breaking of the glass (successful and unsuccessful, with the accompanying smiles and frustrations)—and different combinations of portraits composed: the couple, the wedding party, the bride's family, the groom's family. Meanwhile, just outside, the band was tuning up, and hors d'oeuvres on huge round trays were making their first rounds. Rose, in a flowing spring dress, stood for a moment with Minnie, Ruthie, and Ida, the three of her sisters who were well enough to come, each of them proudly arching her back and smiling for the instant of the flash, their faces lifted bravely as if into wind. Minnie was a blonde this year—her name, too, suddenly transformed into Minnah, more fashionable, rejuvenating and unique in her Miami building—but Ruthie was a darker brunette than ever. "Ruthala," said Rose, while they were frozen with their smiles, "why aren't you blond like us? Look how young Minnie looks!"

"It's Minnah, darling," said Minnie, nodding perpetually, only somewhat smiling.

Rose turned from her with a quick grimace, returning to her smile. "Next year you should be blond like us." Then Pearl, Zellie, and Margie stood with the aunts, and then it was all the family, clustered around the bride and groom.

"Wait!" Zellie said, when they had all become rigid and ready. She stepped out of the lineup and took Beth's hand. "Beth," she said, "come on," grinning and winking. "Hurry up now—you too!" And Beth had to press into the portrait from the side, squeezing David's hand violently behind their backs as they smiled into the future.

She hadn't wanted to come. She was made nervous, she said, being treated, by David's mother at least, like the next in line to the Rosen genes and the Rosen fortune—ambiguous prizes Beth had mostly imagined for the amusement of their friends. But already she had a dress from Jerusalem and a string of pearls gotten cheaply in Hong Kong. For David their friendship had the tonic effect of placating his family, calming them, convincing them, at least for the moment she was among them, that their boy might wind up uncomplicated after all. But for Beth it had no such charm. She had told her parents early on exactly what David had told her, and though her mother had been friendly, cheerful, even motherly toward him, alone with Beth her lip would raise with hidden fear and outward contempt. "What do you see in him?" she had asked. "Why do you need him so much? Why are you so obsessed? Why don't you find a man who can love you? I mean *really* love you." She was afraid, she said, of where his private parts had been, what diseases they had been exposed to—she herself would never risk it. David seemed, in fact, to cast Beth not in the comforting, conventional shadow of a man's girlfriend but rather in the radical, suspicious light of a freak show. His own mother called them "humanists"—at that they laughed.

Now they danced together, fast and slow, they kicked their feet and clapped their hands with Zellie's aunts, part of the big circle of dancers, and then, suddenly, accidentally, they were part of the inner circle, all the groom's family dancing around them, faster and faster in the opposite direction. In the swirl of faces, David was sure he saw Minnie wink at him. Ruthie nodded. Rose, clapping her hands from a chair nearby, looked directly at them as they passed. Even Zellie, kicking with one arm around her sister and one around her husband, seemed to be smiling a message directly at them.

Afterwards Margie stood next to them, holding a hand to her Mexican necklace, catching her breath. "So, David!" she said, pausing and smiling as hard as she could. The lines parenthesizing her mouth became deeper, as if she were used to trying so hard. Sometimes, she seemed to say, things were taken wrong in the family, despite good intentions; and by her smile she tried to assure him she had only good intentions. "It looks like you're going to have good news too, one of these days," she said, nodding toward Beth.

"Yes!" David said, matching her smile, nodding also, but feeling ashamed. Beth too smiled broadly, falsely, and walked away. A thousand times already life had asked him to lie—as a child, as a young man, now as an adult—and he could lie immediately, thoughtlessly, nervous inside but outwardly smooth, knowing it was for everyone's sake, for the general peace. It was easier that way, Zellie had said, reminding him to take out his earring. "But Mother," he had said, "Beth's wearing the other one. We're a set." Why cause problems? she had said. Why announce to the world you're one thing or another? You're not a thing, David, she told him, a member of a club. You're a person.

Now any shame, any shock would be his alone, and he would

bear it, and bury it slowly. No, no! he wanted to shout, flailing his arms, calling attention, refuting himself—his false self— but also his family, forcing the truth on his aunt and on all of them, as if there in the middle of his family he were confronting the whole world. Indeed, coming back, he saw them again as the whole world, with all the old power and omniscience and importance he had grown up among and almost forgotten. Even his sister was a part of it, that privilege, that power; even, strangely, Matthew—anyone still close enough to Lewiston, still inside Lewiston, the old streets and old houses. But David seemed tacitly to be left out. I am this, Aunt Margie, he wanted to say, disenfranchised anyway from their invisible kingdom, already with nothing more in that world to lose. I am this and not that! Look, I have a hole in my ear, as if that mattered. No, Beth is not my good news. I mean—he hesitated, he halted, grew confused, and in the universal confrontation he had silently imagined, he lost their attention, they turned, they wandered away—I mean she *is*, but not the way you think. It has nothing to do with marrying her, and dressing everyone in suits and pretending to be what everyone expects and hopes! The hole, after all, is in the left ear, which is all right these days, everyone has it, it doesn't mean what you think—although it's true, what you think happens, by chance, to be right. But—he resumed, then paused, catching his composure and silent breath—what you want, my aunt, cannot, no, must not be!

"She's a lovely girl," Margie said, sitting down on the old swinging sofa and patting the flowered plastic next to her.

"Thank you," David said, sitting down.

"Have you known each other a long time?"

"Well, Aunt Marge, we met in college. It's a long time for me."

"You seem to get along very well."

"We do."

"My Robert's doing very well," Margie said, still looking in David's face for some clue—of interest, of boredom, of his own secrets. "He's a lawyer now. Did you know that?"

"No," David said.

"Yes, it's a good business," she said. She pushed a few times with her feet, rocking them both, but unevenly. When her side went forward, his side went back. "He has a lot of clients. Still not married, though. But we're hoping. Did you ever meet Gail?"

David shook his head.

"She's a lovely girl—I don't know what's stopping them. It's so far away, San Francisco. But it's what he wants. Have you ever been there?"

Suddenly she was staring at him, still grinning, and David was sure this was the trick question, the San Francisco test, the real reason for her story about her son, the hidden trap at the end of the maze.

"No," he said, his heart thumping as if this too were a lie. "But I hear it's beautiful. I'd like to go sometime."

She nodded. Now perhaps she knew, perhaps she had her information. He had heard of San Francisco; he would like to go; it was almost an admission of his aberration. Why else would a young man (except her Robert who had his Gail) want to leave his family three thousand miles behind for a strange city where the men dress in leather and open flower shops? Why not New York, so much closer?

But that same instant he saw himself condemned, he saw too, as if a veil had slipped from a statue, that it was only David condemning himself, taking the imaginary accusing finger always poised in the air nearby and pointing it around to his hiding place; that sitting there with him was only his Aunt Margie, his mother's cousin, whom he had known forever and forever had heard criticized, just a middle-aged lady with her hands in her lap, uncomplicated, unsuspicious, unfrightening, almost too short to rock the sofa with her feet—only her toes could reach to the floor. His grandmother had rocked on this sofa, his mother had grown up on it, and here he himself had taken many unsuspicious childhood naps, waking up on the sweat-slippery plastic. For years his mother had complained, had railed against her cousin and run around corners, held up newspapers, and hidden behind potted trees, but here on the sofa with him was Aunt Margie now, just another aunt, another cousin, as innocent as could be, looking on him fondly and nodding because he reminded her of someone.

"You look just like your father, you know."

David nodded.

"If you go," she said, "be sure and look up Robert. He has lots of room, he'll be glad to see you. You're cousins, you know."

"I will!" David said, jumping up in a sudden rush of goodwill to find his mother, and the others in the family he hadn't seen in a long time, wondering now if he would see them as they were, and be free.

Lonnie found Teddy in her room, holding on his lap the large mirror from her wall, etched with all the faces of the Beatles. "Oh, hi," he said, high-voiced despite his football player's chest. Sitting down, he was just her height.

She didn't say a word.

"You want a line?" he asked, deep-voiced again, trying not to be embarrassed and continuing to chop with a razor blade. Lonnie merely had to shrug, accepting the straw and the line of white powder without admitting anything. Afterwards he left, and as she looked around her room it seemed already much friendlier. The pink carpet stretched away to pink walls; the pink walls reached up to contain the pink ceiling. And stretching across, like a circus net after a fall, the pink rope hammock still rocked with its catch of stuffed animals from when Teddy had brushed against it, going out.

She opened her thick notebook on her desk and in tiny, secretive lettering began to write—the date, the event, and under it this most recent crime. Already, at sixteen, she had been recording evidence for years, and the notebook was more than half full. She would have written good things as well, she supposed, if everything good in the family had not been used up long ago, when Stevey, the firstborn boy, the best-loved grandchild, was young. Now he was already grown up, that time was gone, and no one cared so much anymore. Even Stevey's afghan was better, was real wool and all of a piece; Lonnie's was artificial, shiny wool and leftover colors, and smaller than the rest—her grandmother's hands were already arthritic then.

After a few minutes, though she would have taken any excuse to stay where she was, far away from the party and safe behind her own door, Lonnie had nothing more to write. The notebook was up to date. She sucked on her pen, looked again around the room, flipped with her thumb the wide margin of unused pages; but finally she shook her head and walked out, carrying the notebook with her. In the foyer she found a guest list on the desk, and was copying out the names of the bridesmaids when Zellie hurried past her into the empty living room. A moment later Margie appeared down the hall, looking from left to right and bending down to peer through doorways as if she were lost.

"Hello, Lonnela!" she said. "And how are you!"

"Pretty busy," Lonnie said, bending over her work.

"Oh," Margie said, and shook her head slightly at the unexpected rudeness. "Well, then, where's your mom?" she asked, smiling again, and Lonnie, ashamed that her rudeness had been caught, smiled back at her and pointed, cheerfully, into the next room.

"Zel!" Margie said, and even from where Lonnie was sitting she could hear her mother's gasp. Before they could come out again, Lonnie opened the heavy front door and sat down on the front-porch swing, alone and safe again, waiting for things to write.

In the living room Margie said, "You look beautiful, Zel! Who would guess we're as old as we are?" There was no answer. "Well, it's a lucky day, isn't it?"

"Yes," Zellie said, as sullenly as her daughter.

"She's a lovely girl, that Jill. I was talking to her just now. And she seems truly interested in Judaism."

"Yes, she is."

"That's something. And David's friend, too—what's her name?"

"Beth," Zellie said. "Beth Bauer."

"Yes, they seem very happy together. She reminds me a lot of Robby's girlfriend. You've met her, haven't you? Robby's Gail? She'll be a lawyer."

Zellie nodded and quickly turned away, as if they had already said goodbye.

"Anyway," Margie said, "I'm glad for you. Believe me, from Robert I know, I bet you were nervous."

Zellie was almost through the door, but she was still too close to miss Margie's ending:

"With these sensitive boys you never do know, do you!"

Outside on the front lawn, all was quiet. The light was strong, and underneath the big tree a web of pale shadows spread across from leafless branches. Lonnie pushed back and forth on the swing, wondering how she might escape, where she might go, and if anyone, after all, would even notice. She could not hitch-hike to New York, to Europe, to California. It was all too far away, too dangerous. She knew no one; she had no money, only her mother's Bloomingdale's card. There was no place to go. She did not know the world. She was trapped.

Suddenly, from around the rhododendron hedge came the sound of human suffering, a heaving, grunting complaint, and the slow skid of a heavy load along the gravel. Irene appeared, still in her fancy dress, dragging over her shoulder a canvas sheet that was loaded, as far as Lonnie could see, with dirt.

"Hello, Irene," she said.

"Hello," said Irene, and glared for a moment at Lonnie, who was sure she had said something disrespectful again. Was she not allowed to swing, perhaps, on the day of a wedding? "I was just taking these extra pachysandra," said Irene. "Far too many's there already. All choking each other out. It's a damn shame, I tell you that much."

Lonnie, not knowing what the name described, could tell anyway from the tone of her voice that Irene was angry at being caught. She had never not been called "honey" before. Standing up to look at the loot, Lonnie could see that indeed the sheet was filled with plants. "I'm just going to take them to my car," Irene said. "Just a couple extra plants."

"Does my mother know?" Lonnie asked.

"She will," Irene said. "I guess." She hesitated, watching in case there was more to say, then turned and continued slowly down the driveway. Lonnie ran inside, leaving her notebook open on the swing. It was not to tell her mother or anyone else that she turned and ran but because, staring wide-eyed and confused down the steps so long into Irene's abashed and resentful eyes, she already knew it was the last time they would ever, either of them, really look.

On the porch there was a commotion of pastel dresses, and all of Jill's friends were crowding around the steps. Rice was thrown, cheers were called out from all sides, hands were raised and waved like heavy shafts of wheat.

"Go on, Beth," said Pearl, gently pushing her toward the stairs.

"Go on, dolly," said Rose.

Beth turned to David, her eyes wild.

"What," Lonnie said to her brother, "they're leaving already?" But David was listening only to Beth.

"David," Beth said, "come on, you want it more than I do!"

"Want what?" Lonnie asked, turning to see where they looked, and as she turned a pile of flowers smacked her on the face.

From all the women on the steps there came a groan, unanimous and indiscreet, but then the older voices laughed again and shouted their goodbyes.

"Oh no!" someone said. "How old are you? Thirteen?" It was a girl Lonnie had never seen before and never wanted to see again. She kissed Lonnie on the cheek. "Well, congratulations," she said, and turned away, shaking her head.

"For what?" Lonnie asked, dropping the bouquet down onto a chair. "For what?"

All around there was laughter and confusion, and no one answered.

ON THE OLD street behind the town hall, Irene lives now with a Haitian man and five of her children. The others are still in Granada with their grandmother and aunts, who deposit her checks from America and tend to her various investments. She will not say just what investments these are, nor how many children she has, preferring to keep her mysteries to herself.

Dropping her off one November day, Zellie got out of the car to walk down the buckling sidewalk, some of its fractured slabs pushed vertical by weeds and frost. The traffic at the corner was the same as she remembered, constant but far away, beyond the squeal of children swinging up and back in the dark playground. The swings were old, like the ones she knew, and no tree or grass could grow even now in the shade of that huge municipal fortress, still barred and wired from when it was a jail. A dark little girl in braids ran around the corner, abruptly stopped and stared at her, then ran inside to Irene's side of the house—one of Irene's children Zellie had never seen. Across the street her own childhood house still had the same black shutters, the same bay windows in front, the two narrow doors in between, though the backyard was now a parking lot, and the front porch had been replaced with cement steps. Once it had seemed expansive, the yard, the street, the huddling-together of buildings, elaborate and significant and stretching out in every direction. Now the quiet seemed to imply a for-gotten, abandoned place, someplace hidden and original, almost miniature, a frontier become a center like the wood in the middle of a tree, alive and vulnerable once, now encircled and encrusted by years and years of outward growth. Here we were born, someone might say, pointing to the narrow ring near the middle. Here was that hard winter; here the fire; here the drought. Once she had imagined she would go far away, to New York, to Europe, but after all here she still was: here I grew up; here I had children; here I stayed. A girl in braids could open the front door right now and it could be Zellie herself forty years before, years flowing so smoothly away they might never have gone, except that too much evidence clinging to her proved it: the station wagon; the stockings and wool skirt; the fur coat; even though she couldn't see it, her own older body, too heavy now and full of aches; and her face, which other people must see, and judge, and presume about. "Still so pretty," they said even now, meaning it, "such a pretty woman"—but implying as well the surprise, because time had after all flown. She might have walked inside right now, waiting for the screen door to slam behind her in the same old way, heard the radio in the corner, run her finger along the pink table in the kitchen, across the dark seams at either end. "Hello?" she used to shout into her tin can, the string stretching out the window and across the porch, disappearing again at the window next door. "Is anybody there? Can you hear me?" And very clearly she could hear Danny shouting back, "Roger! I can hear you! I can hear you! Over and out!" Too conscious, suddenly, of what that little girl must see, coming out of the house again—a big car and a curious, overdressed woman in the middle of the street —Zellie turned away.

"Aunt Zel!" she heard, and the name seemed odd, remembered, calling her back. A door did slam, and on the ugly cement steps someone was waving to her, running over without a coat. It was Matthew there, Pearl's Matthew, wiping his hands on his overalls. He wore no shirt.

"Hi, Aunt Zellie," Matthew said, stopping short, shy as soon as he approached. Across the yard he had been a man; now he was her nephew again.

"Hi there!" Zellie said, wondering if she should kiss him. He was unshaven; she bent to him but hesitated, and they did not touch. "Matthew," she said. "What are you doing here?"

"I thought for a minute you were my mother!" he said, holding himself and jumping up and down in the cold. "Then I saw your car."

"How come you don't have a coat on?"

"It's inside."

"Inside—inside there?"

"Yes," he said, looking past her as if he were ashamed, as if he had admitted something. "Didn't my mother tell you? I have a room here for a while. It's okay."

"Here? In our old house? This one here? Number twelve?"

"Yeah," Matthew said. "Didn't my mother tell you?"

"I thought you were home again. I mean at your parents' house."

"I was," he said. "I just moved in here. I like it."

"Matthew, did you know we used to live here? Our family?"

"Yes. My mother told me. Do you want to see inside? See my room?"

"Sure!" Zellie said, embarrassed at her own enthusiasm, stepping quickly onto the sidewalk and then running back to lock the car. She was still too surprised to be shy or suspicious. Indeed, just a night or two before she had been to Pearl's and saw no sign, heard no clue of Matthew in the house, and assumed that as usual he had fled somewhere, gone out on the road, even shown up again at her own parents' door in Miami, two cents to his name, unshowered, unshaven, afraid or unable to go home to Pearl and Mel. Sometimes he had stolen from them. Sometimes he had stolen a car from town, or a wallet, or disappeared from a drug deal along with the pile of cash. Strangers still called Pearl after midnight, threatening, cursing. "We know he's there," they said, and Pearl snapped back, "No, he is *not*!" Zellie, sitting there, had heard the whole thing. "Well," said the voice, "then we're coming over, gonna get *you*."

By the time Matthew had made his way south, Zellie knew, he had each time no trace of hidden wealth, no smirk of success nor even a guilty distraction; dirty and ragged, the only possible proof of his crime was having come at all—"for a visit," Rose called it. Rose and Max let him shower, fed him supper, opened their sofa sometimes, or sometimes gave him money for a hotel room and a plane ticket north. If he was a dreamer, as Pearl said, a schemer, smart whenever he wanted to be, it was only for the moment: all the money must have gone into movies, steak dinners, desserts, drugs, and bus tickets south.

But now he had his own room, and he was proud of it. "In here," he said, holding the storm door for her.

"Are you sure we're allowed?" Zellie asked.

"Oh yeah. No problem." They both shrugged and walked inside. Instead of a wide living room there was now a dark, narrow hallway leading, she saw, through a door into what had been the kitchen. There were four doors now, and one of them was the door to her own room. She put her hand on the old glass knob but withdrew it quickly, remembering it was no longer her own. Once she had fled there, from the empty house, from small injustices, from family fights, or she had run out, waking up from Nazi dreams—Jews pushed into ovens and burned up, babies murdered, old people stripped naked and shot into open pits, Nazis breaking through the bedroom window, right there in New Jersey.

"What's in here?" she asked, pointing to the door.

"I don't know," Matthew said. "Someone else. Mine's downstairs, at the end."

"In the basement?" Zellie asked, and regretted it. But Matthew only shrugged.

There were footsteps on the stairs, the same heavy footsteps she remembered from her father coming down in the morning. At the end of the hall a door opened and a small, heavy, balding man stood facing them, only an undershirt covering his belly beneath his suit jacket. Behind him, Zellie could see the room that had once been her mother's kitchen. Inside there was a sofa, and beyond that a television, flashing blue and white onto the walls.

"Mrs. Green!" he said, wiping his hand on his pants and coming forward. "How are you, Mrs. Green! I just heard your son's voice out there and I thought I'd come take a look how he's doing. How's it going there, Matthew?"

"This is my aunt," Matthew said.

"Pearl is my sister," Zellie said, coming forward and holding out her hand.

"Okay!" said the man. "Your boy here's doing just fine too, I'd say. How's the work, old man?"

"Fine," Matthew said.

"What work is he doing?" Zellie asked, sorry too late to have asked over Matthew's head.

"Doing dishes," Matthew said. "At the Chinese restaurant."

"Not too bad," said the man. "I've done worse myself." They all stared for a moment back and forth, no one remembering to smile. "Well, goodbye there, nice seeing you, Mrs.—" he said, nodding.

"Friedman," Zellie said.

"Yeah," said the man, and stepped back into his room, continuing to watch them.

"You know, Matthew," Zellie said, anxious suddenly in the cramped and dirty hall, "I think I'll come back another time to see the room. I only had a second, really—I have to pick Lonnie up at school."

"That's okay," Matthew said, nodding, but squinting also.

"Next time I'll come see your room," Zellie said, already back at the door, turning the handle. "Okay?"

"That's fine," Matthew said, following her. "Only, do you know where my mother is? I was trying to reach her."

"No," Zellie said, "I don't," still smiling and shaking her head as she turned from the glass door, where her reflection merged with the empty branches outside and the dark hall within. She was glad to breathe the cold air again. "Next time I'll come see!"

"Okay," Matthew said, waving after her. "Thanks for coming by, Aunt Zellie. I'll see you! If you see my mother, tell her to call me."

Zellie waved, then hurried to unlock the car. Inside, she gunned the engine into gear and shot forward too fast, the wheels throwing out gravel. When she turned the corner, Matthew was still standing outside on the porch, and she honked to him twice quickly: for not having said more, and for not having gone downstairs to his room. Quickly she was under the railroad bridge, past the old hotel, and on the highway, still wondering if he could have heard or understood her—that she had not meant to run from him, her sister's child; that it was her own life and not his she could not bear to see there; and that, despite her honking now and her promise, she could never again visit that old house.

JUST WHEN THE past might really be dead, when the silence in the morning safely dampens the traffic outside and whatever dreams linger, David's phone rings too early for anything good. For two days he has been at the hospital, sleeping a few hours when he could. Now it is Thanksgiving Sunday, and he is alone; his hands still smell of chlorine soap and rubber gloves. Timidly, on the fourth ring, he picks up, an instant before the machine that imitates his voice. Timidly, to whatever trouble or possibility it will be, he says hello.

"David?" asks a male voice, familiar, intimate, half embarrassed, the voice of any number of men he has known. "It's Matthew."

"Matthew!" David says, sounding right away glad and accepting, as he has been trained—no trace of sleep, of fatigue, of indecision.

"It's been too long," Matthew says, loudly but hesitantly. "I've been thinking about it. I think we should get together for once. You know, and have a good time. Go to a movie, or something."

"Matthew?" David asks slowly into the phone, as if he were asking himself across ten years. "Where are you?"

"Home," Matthew says.

And David repeats, "Home. At your parents'?"

"Yeah, I just got in. I thought I'd come into the city, go to a movie or something."

"Oh. Well, let me call you back, Matt—okay?"

"Well, I'll be in the city, so I'll just meet you somewhere. How about Port Authority? Pick me up at one?"

"Well, I'll have to see," David says, sitting up, scratching his head, looking around for an excuse. "I'm sort of busy. Can I call you?"

"Sure. Okay, I'll see you then, David. I think it's good we're going to get together. One o'clock at the Information, okay? I'll see you."

"Matthew?" David says again. "Matt?" But the question is met by a new silence, stretching out beyond the city.

At first, getting up, making coffee, craning to see up the air shaft whether the sky is blue or gray, David is resigned to do a good deed, since a good deed has fallen so heavily across his path. To step around such an incident would be unkind, he thinks, even cruel. And—he has to admit it—there is nothing he must do, no one he must see. The narrow rectangle above the window is dark but seems to be the unclouded color of sky, a sky for running around the reservoir under, or wandering around downtown, looking for romance to wink from a restaurant window or from an unexpected crossing of the street. It is a treasured day off, when he doesn't have to run to the hospital by eight-thirty in his tie and jacket and doctor's robe, but instead can sit until ten or eleven o'clock completely naked if he wants at the kitchen table, reading, drinking coffee.

Back on his bed again, he picks up the phone, stares into it, and dials a number he has forgotten for years. Three days before, at Thanksgiving, he was again with all the family—everyone but Matthew—too ashamed for once of his own chronic absences. Happily, persistently, they asked about life at medical school—"Are you a doctor yet?" Mel asked him; "So why do I cough so much?" asked Max—knowing those answers would be safe, the attention not prying or critical. Once Rose would have asked, had asked many times: "So when are you going to find a girl?"

But no more. The years have made her shy. David the doctor is also a nephew, a cousin, a grandchild among many nephews, cousins, grandchildren, and his moment of attention was quickly, safely dispatched. Max leaned back in his chair, looked up at the ceiling for something to say, started to hum. With other cousins they talked of marriage, of money, of football, but with David, too often alone as far as they can see, they clung to his career. Now he imagines them whispering: Why not send him Matthew? Give them both something to do. Davey wouldn't say no, alone so much—as the phone rings back in Lewiston, thirty miles away.

"Who is this?" demands Pearl, drawing in a breath.

"Hello, Aunt Pearl," David says. "This is David."

"Davey!" she says, her voice suddenly warm, indulgent, relieved. "I thought it was someone else. We've been getting a lot of calls. Matthew's friends, I guess. How are you?"

"I'm fine," he says, already holding a hand guiltily over his eyes. "Listen, Aunt Pearl, I wonder if you know anything about Matthew's plans today?"

"Matthew?" she asks. "No—but he's right here, you know. He came home after all. Would you like to speak to him?"

"Yes. I guess. Thanks." His voice rises with just a hint of suspicion. "He called me, you know."

"He did? Matthew did? Just a minute, dear." Her voice is surprised but quickly grateful. "Matthew!" she shouts. "Guess who's calling! It's David."

"Hi," Matthew says, quickly, guiltily into the phone.

"Hi, Matt. Listen, I've been thinking about—what we're supposed to do today. You know, meet in the city?"

"Yeah, one o'clock."

"I've been thinking. Let's make it for another time, okay?"

"Like when?" Matthew asks. His voice is slow, all suspicion, disappointment.

"Oh," David says, pulling his hair while he hesitates, and clamping his jaw. Too many seconds go by. With anyone else he would already have excused himself, made up words to fill the gap. But for Matthew he can think of no story, no words to cover the truth. Once, they both know, they were exactly the same, and built a tree house in the woods where they would live when they grew up. "Well," David says, "How about two-thirty, Matthew, or three o'clock? That'll give me more time."

"Sure!" Matthew says. "Sure, Dave, that's fine. I'll see you then, okay? Two-thirty."

"Okay, Matthew. Bye."

"Okay."

Matthew hangs up the phone; David hangs up the phone, and then falls down onto the pillows, trying to smother himself back to sleep.

Later, on Forty-second Street, he parks in the lot for ten minutes, because there is no place to stop. A giant of a woman calls out to him, hooks her finger wildly for him to follow. She wears a short skirt, fish-net stockings, and high heels, and her white, pointed breasts are bare. "Honey," she says in a deep, man's voice, "you want a date?" And David looks away but still shakes his head no.

Inside by the information booth is a man smoking a cigarette, jeans black with grease, curly hair unbrushed, face swollen.

David walks up and touches his arm. "Hi!" he says, and Matthew bends down right away for his knapsack, not looking David in the eye.

"How are you?" Matthew asks, when they are safely in the car, waiting in traffic.

"Oh," David says, "fine. How are you?"

"Great," he says, nodding. "This your car?"

"Yes."

"It's nice."

They drive across town, back down Forty-second Street. "What do you want to do today?" David asks, and Matthew falls heavily against the seat with his head thrown back, blowing out smoke.

"How about *Galaxy of Terror*?"

David looks over, confused by this large man, bloated, overweight, muscular, who is his cousin. The down on his cheeks is now rough, dark whiskers, badly shaven and sparse. When last he looked at him they were sixteen, and Matthew was strong and slim, clever when he wanted to be, a man while David was still a boy. "Touch this," Matthew had said, grinning in a boathouse and holding his erection. His blue eyes were reckless then, but seductive. Now, to David's silence, those same eyes become alert, distrustful. They are blue but also red, and look out through slits.

"*Galaxy of Terror*?" David asks. "What's that?" And Matthew explains it's a movie.

"Sort of a cartoon," he says. "I saw the ad."

"Okay!" David says cheerfully, but he is more and more resentful; not only his time but his mind must be wasted for the day. He is sure Matthew's family has planned this excursion, hanging their albatross on the weakest member. Call up your cousin David, he can hear them say. Go to a movie. Have a nice day.

"There's one at six," Matthew says. "Eighty-sixth and Third."

Looking over from his driving, David is impressed that suddenly his cousin can be so sharp. But soon he is leaning back again with his eyes closed, and David can think of nothing to say. In the hospital he tells jokes, looks into people's eyes, holds their hands. Now he is afraid to take Matthew back to his apartment: afraid for his stereo, his piano, his color TV. Instead he parks on Fifth Avenue, blocks away.

"This where you live?" Matthew asks, looking back at a door-man.

"Nearby," David says, and they cross the street into the park.

They walk through piles of leaves in the sharp afternoon air. With anyone else, David thinks, even alone, he might have been happy. The day is cold but bright, and runners are running, squirrels are scurrying and dogs race by, freed from their leashes. But Matthew sees none of it; he walks next to David with his head down, smoking and watching the leaves. "Hold on," he says, and they sit down at the nearest bench. With his legs stretched out into the path, his head thrown back, he seems to be asleep. His cheeks, once cherubic, are pockmarked and pale. His lips, once full and seductive, are colorless. David looks at his watch, crumples a leaf, tries to be patient.

"Are you okay?" he asks, impatiently.

Matthew nods but doesn't answer. Then suddenly he stands up, waiting with his jaw dropped open, his lips parted, as if he were trying to remember an older, simpler smile.

"Now what?" he asks.

The men who run past in their nylon briefs are lovers, handsome, lean runners whom David has followed, at least with his eyes, many times in his own revolutions around the park. One of them touches the other, lightly on the back, just a gesture, a quick, private reminder for both of them which David, too, has noticed, and feels excluded from. Quickly he leads Matthew the other way. Once, watching two men kiss on a street corner, he had stood too close, too long. "What, does he want me to kiss him too?" said one to the other—and David had fled, the answer being so urgently yes.

"So do you party?" Matthew asks, looking up at the trees.

"Yeah," David says, lying. This third year of medical school has kept him studious, but even now he is ashamed to say no to Matthew about anything. Exaggerating his nod like the cool boys from their high school, he waits as Matthew lights a joint, loudly sucks in the smoke, and holds it out to David with his fingers stretching delicately, as if for a teacup. The cool boys were Matthew's friends; they laughed about him, David knows, but paid for the joints he procured and the pills he stole. They were tough-talking, strong-shouldered, and rubbed at their crotches without shame.

David sucks in the smoke impatiently, and soon the world is heavier, funnier, and smaller. Distrustful but interested, he feels himself sliding down.

Just as the clock strikes three they wander into the zoo, and stare up as the iron animals emerge from their clock chamber. The bear holds the cymbals, the lion a trumpet. Out one door and back in through the other, they turn stiffly on their track without playing, and disappear. After they are gone, David and Matthew continue to stare up at the motionless doors above the archway, listening to the chime.

"Wow," Matthew says, and David nods in agreement.

"Yeah," he says, and cannot stop himself: "Wow," he adds.

Farther on, they stare at birds and goats and monkeys without talking, Matthew waiting patiently each time until David is ready. But at the great apes Matthew peers in, fascinated. An old gorilla stares over his shoulder from the corner, humiliated, enraged, and David has to look away.

"Matthew," he says, "so where have you been?"

"Didn't my mother tell you?"

"No," David says. "I've been really busy. You've been away?" He has not asked a question about Matthew for years. The stories have always come to him anyway, but now, he realizes, they were only fragments. Matthew was in jail, out of jail, home again, stealing a toaster, a fishing rod, a ring, until finally he was locked out of the house, threatened through tears, forced to leave; this could not have been all.

"I was in Florida," Matthew says.

"Florida! How was it?"

Matthew shrugs, looks away. "It was all right." When they are out of the park, back on the street again, Matthew looks up at the luxurious buildings as if he were looking for one window in particular, David's window. "How about you?" he asks, blinking, his words slurring together. "So what are you doing?"

"Well," David says, "you know I'm in medical school."

"Oh yeah." Matthew nods, and for only the second time they look in each other's eyes. "So how is it?" Matthew asks, and this time it is David who shrugs, looks away as if he were watching the traffic.

"It's all right," he says, but then turns back, touching Matthew's army jacket for emphasis, and feeling, for his own secret pleasure, the coarse, male fabric of it. "Remember that time we got lost in the park, and built a dam?"

"Oh, yeah," Matthew says nervously.

David starts to laugh, but stops. "That was funny, wasn't it?"

"Yeah. Where's this place we're going, anyway? Eighty-sixth and Third. You know, the movie."

"This way," David says, vaguely directing them across the street. "And remember all those bricks we found? We were digging for something—worms, I think—and we found all those bricks in your backyard, in the woods. We didn't know what they were for."

Matthew leans for a moment against David's arm, and then pinches him, hard, grinning as if it were a joke, until David pulls away. "How far is this place?" Matthew asks.

"Not too far," David says, rubbing his arm. "Don't you remember, Matt? We thought we'd discovered a secret civilization or something. We were going to dig up the whole place and get famous, remember? And we drew pictures of what it looked like before the earthquake? Matthew, come on—you have to remember!" He takes Matthew's arm, hooks his hand intimately around the elbow, even begins to lean his head on Matthew's shoulder. Then quickly he pulls back, straightens up. "This way," he says, turning away.

Outside the theatre there is a poster for *Galaxy of Terror*, a benign cartoon painting of astronauts exploring a new planet. "Great," Matthew says, looking around as he pays for his ticket. "There's no line." David stares at the poster a long time but finally pays for a ticket as well. Inside, the lobby is huge; an escalator takes them up to the farthest of four theatres. Remembering their childhood of movies together, *Treasure Island* and *Swiss Family Robinson*, David offers to pay for popcorn, soda, or anything else Matthew might want. But Matthew refuses, shaking his head. "I have to sit down," he says.

The movie, when it begins, seems to have started in the middle. There is no introduction, no narrative, no music, and the film is not a cartoon. Nine astronauts, all of them women, zip up their space suits and load their space guns. Carefully they leave their space ship to study the new planet, and each, one after another, is slowly raped and mutilated by strange, inhuman, snakelike creatures creeping up to them in the dark, piercing their space suits at the crotch. "Now what could be in *here?*" says one of the women, opening a mysterious door.

David covers his eyes, drops his head, holds a finger in each ear, and hopes that during the intervals between attacks the dialogue will pick up and the plot finally begin. But each time the scene is the same, and he can hear the new woman screaming. Matthew is leaning back in his seat, his eyes almost closed. In the audience girls scream, their boyfriends laugh, and both shout across from one to the other.

"I'll be back," David says, touching Matthew and running down the aisle into the lobby. He wants to cry—his eyes are full and his breath is choked—but he is too embarrassed; the ushers, sullen and silent, are staring at him. One of them, an old woman in tight black pants, hurries over as if to stop him.

"Stop!" she says. "You can't get back in without a stub." David nods, tapping his pocket, trying to be friendly and not to cry. "Good," she says. "Otherwise, you know—" and points with her thumb.

In the men's room he pretends to urinate, but after a while there are others pretending to urinate as well. "Oh, man," says a large, unshaven man, staring down into the urinal and shaking his head, then looking over at David before staring down again. "Oh, man," he says, jiggling. All the urinals flush at the same time, and David hurries out. For an instant in the mirror he sees himself—hair mussed, eyes red and swollen, as if he were in costume behind that grotesque face. He cannot wait in the lobby, where the ushers raise their heads and watch him; even there the screams come through, loud and articulate.

Back at his seat, he nudges Matthew, who seems to be asleep, although one of the women is screaming and spouting blood. "Let's go," David says, without whispering. "I have to go." And Matthew nods, opening his eyes.

In the car neither of them speaks. Matthew leans against the door while David squints through tears to drive. It is dark, and the city is alive with moving lights, but the air is cold and quiet, as if there were no such movie. "You can just drop me at the Port Authority," Matthew says.

"Matthew," David asks, remembering other suffering faces looking up unexpectedly and calling him "Doctor." "Are you all right?"

"Yeah," he says, "I'm all right. You can just drop me at the bus."

It has been several years since they have spoken, and David cannot imagine when the next time will be. He is afraid to end in silence. "I'm sorry I had to leave the movie," he says. "I'm just really tired."

"That's okay," Matthew says. "I thought it was a cartoon."

"Oh well," David says, and Matthew echoes him:

"Oh well."

The traffic at the Port Authority is loud and aggressive, and a cab leans on the horn as David pulls up to the curb.

"Okay," David says, hesitating to come to a stop. "Goodbye, Matt," he says, and can think of nothing else. "See you!"

"Yeah," Matthew says, smiling with closed eyes. "See you."

And David pulls away into the confusion of cars, looking back in the mirror to see him one more time. But already Matthew is gone.

A year later, when Matthew was dead and the family stood in its fur coats and cashmere scarves for a Christmas funeral, David sobbed at the graveside even after the others had finished. Embarrassed, he tried to stop, imagining that the silent grief of parents and brothers could only resent his louder, lesser grief, because after all he had everything, while Matthew had come to this. Two perfect children, the rabbi said, cousins born at the same time, one with problems, one without, and in front of everyone he had stretched out his palm to David, the one who was left.

Even the day before, when Warren had called, low-voiced but stoic, with the news, David had not come near to crying. "What was that all about?" asked Andrew, coming out naked from the bathroom, drying himself from the shower.

"Matthew," he had answered absently, wondering if Andrew would remember this name from David's past—a game they played, trying to stump each other with references to their lives before each other, hoping all along that nothing would be forgotten, that everything in one's life would be known and preserved in the heart of the other.

"Matthew . . ." Andrew had said, distorting the name with a yawn, still heavy-lidded and unshaven, leaning over with his arms around David. "Oh—Matthew the thief?"

Aunt Margie came up to him. As a child he had kissed her, and she him, but now they merely smiled. "You know you're missing a button," she said, pointing to his coat, and he thanked her. As it was lowered down, the coffin slipped from its ropes and the lid bounced almost off. "Leave it," said the rabbi quickly, waiting, when the others had gone, for the men to chop further at the frozen ground, here where all the graves had familiar names, all the people from Rose's stories chiseled into stone: Esther and Theodore Levin, Flora and Sasha Berensky, Leonard Minkoff and both his wives—like a quieter, reconciled community of everyone who had been alive here once, and carried on now silently, patiently, along the paths and neatly ordered rows. Then only David and Margie were left, facing each other across the grave, throwing in another handful of dirt, listening to the traffic. Margie squeezed her eyes closed, wiped away a tear, and seemed unaware the others had gone. A pebble bouncing resonated loudly; shoes ground into the gravel of the path; already in the parking lot an engine roared into gear, and even Rose, struggling with her walker, had passed by her own plot without a glance. Still they waited, and David remembered what he and Matthew had dug up long ago, those bricks of a lost, ancient city, imperfect and crumbling, indecipherable, while his aunt stared across at him, at his chest, at his imperfect row of buttons, also shaking her head at so great a loss.

The Four Questions

TRAVELING UNDER THE river, David explains about the ten plagues suffered by the Egyptians—blood, frogs, locusts, and so on, up to the worst one of all, the slaying of the firstborn. Andrew, who was born a gentile himself but didn't know until college that it was even a category, listens intently. He is going home to David's family for Passover and doesn't want to be thought a snob—or worse, an anti-Semite—for not knowing. By the time the train sighs into Hoboken and opens its doors, he is already chanting the four questions in Hebrew, in his sweet Broadway baritone that makes David's quieter, broken voice sound embarrassed and uncertain.

A smiling woman, stepping out of the train with them, shakes her head at blond, gentile Andrew and nods briefly at David, as if to say what a lucky young man David is, with such a friend. "Ach," she says, "a regular *hazzan*!"

"And you don't even know what the words mean," David says, shaking his darker, bespectacled head and hurrying away toward the stairs.

"That's not true," Andrew calls after him. " 'Why is this night different from all other nights.' Isn't that right?"

"I guess so," David says. "Then what?"

Halfway through the turnstile, Andrew kisses him before he can turn away, an aggressive but also an expressive kiss meant to be indulgent. "That's what I'm waiting to hear," he says, smiling in a way that years of being charming have made subtle and potent. But then he is serious: "You're not nervous, are you?"

David pushes through the turnstile, not answering until they have bought their tickets and are on the train, an old commuter line with wicker seats and dark-metal chandeliers. Outside the windows, black with grime, the train yard and then the poorest, burned-out slums pass slowly in and out of view. Here it was that the family, as he knows it, began: Hillside Terrace, Rose Street, Charleton Street—streets that no one he knew would walk again; no one dared.

"I'm not nervous," he says. "They know you're coming."

Andrew takes his hand and says, "Don't worry." But when the conductor comes by they separate, as if naturally.

Away from the city they ride, and soon there are trees and backyards, suburbs even Andrew has heard of, radiating farther and farther into the woods, into the country. At the station the commuters disappear into waiting cars and are gone. Only David and Andrew remain.

"Andrew," David says, "please don't force the issue."

Indulgently Andrew nods, looking out for the car that will pick them up. "Who's it going to be, honey?" he asks.

"Please don't call me that now, okay?"

"Lonnie? Flying in on the traveling bed?"

"I don't think she's home yet. She would die if she ever heard that, Andrew." Lonnie, throughout her childhood and now throughout vacations from college, has been prone as much as possible, and it is her brother's joke that her bed has wings and wheels—watching TV or whispering on her private telephone, she waited away her childhood with "General Hospital" and

Pop-Tarts. David waited away his own adolescence as well, hiding in a marijuana fog, plucking at a guitar, nodding gratefully when a chord came out right. Sometimes, in passing, he would notice his younger sister. Sometimes, from the TV room or over a bowl of cereal, she would notice him.

"Warren?" Andrew asks.

"No."

"Muggsy?" he says, trying to coerce David's smile with his own.

"I hope not," David says. "And please don't call him that." (Sol is called Muggsy by his wife's children to their friends because of his likeness, in face and dress and size, to a hit man of the thirties.)

"Baby, of course not. I'll be very good, you'll see. I call him Sol, right? Or Dad?"

It is Sol's Fiat that soon turns into the parking lot and speeds around to a sudden stop.

"Oh no," David says.

"Well, hello, boys! This is a surprise!" Standing up from his driving crouch, Sol likes to see people's faces when he rises to full height from the tiny car. He is wearing the white tie David once bought him for Father's Day as a joke. "I didn't know you'd have your friend along with you, Davey. Mom didn't say a word. She said your friend Beth might come."

"Beth couldn't come," he said. "You remember Andrew, Sol. I've told you about him."

"Sure I do! How have you been, young man!" He reaches an oversized hand across the car and firmly shakes Andrew's hand, his head cocked, his eyebrows furrowed in concentration. "Sorry about the squeeze, boys. It's only a short drive, though. Can you take it?"

Andrew sits doubled over on David's lap, talking to Sol on the way home about foreign transmissions, diesel fuel, and the rigors of medical school. They are in their last year together at the same hospital—which Zellie explains proudly to her friends, and bravely to Rose. Sol too is proud of David the doctor, and seems willing to be proud of Andrew as well, asking about diseases and late-night emergencies with equal interest. "So how's tricks?" he asks, after a pause.

David is silent, trapped or hiding under Andrew's weight, but Andrew twists himself around. "Tricks!" he says, squinting to understand. "They're okay!" David rolls down the window a final half-inch, leaning out.

"Primrose Lane!" Andrew says, as they turn onto that street. In shame David closes his eyes, but Sol says, "That's the one!" The street is a narrow country lane, covered by branches from either side, reaching across and mingling. Halfway down is an enormous, solitary oak, darkly symmetrical in the middle of a field.

"That must be the tree where David used to play!" says Andrew. David used to hide there when his parents were fighting, and once, as Andrew knows, he spent the night there, freezing on a branch.

As they slow down to look at the tree, David squeezes Andrew's arm. "Well," says Sol, "I guess that was before my time," and finally they stop altogether, Sol's large features relaxing into daydream. "What do you know, Davey? It's been almost ten years, your mother and I are married."

"Really!" Andrew says.

"Yes, sir!" says Sol, surprised at a response. "And I don't regret a minute of it." As they climb out of the car, Sol holds on to the roof again, extending his hand across. "Andrew," he says, "I'm very glad to meet you. Let me shake your hand, sir. I'm glad you're here."

Standing in the driveway, David bites his nails, tearing off each narrow end and spitting it out. He has heard about this moment in other people's lives, when the child comes home

with the unacceptable lover. Once—at least in this suburb—
the egregious mate was merely gentile, a ringlet-laden cheer-
leader like Jill, blond as a movie star, quiet, pretty, converted
even, but still, to all eyes, a shiksa. Now, around kitchen tables
and through narrow bedroom walls, the horror stories have
changed. The nightmare possibility these days is not blond but
black or brown. A shiksa might convert—but a *schvartze*! It's
okay, says the mother in the joke, sleep in the master
bedroom—I'll just have my head in the oven. There are still
no jokes about the *faygeleh* son, coming home with his "friend."

Zellie waves from the kitchen window, pushing it up to greet
them. "Hello, boys!" she calls down. "Come on up!"

She meets them at the door, looking behind them down the
steps. "I thought Beth was coming," she says.

"She was invited to one in New York—that guy she's seeing."

"I see," Zellie says, frowns, but quickly kisses Andrew as
well as David. From the first Andrew has attracted her as a
son-in-law. "Why not give him Lonnie's number," she had said.
"It couldn't hurt." A month later she asked again. "Sorry, Mom,"
David said, "but you know he's not Jewish." "So?" she said,
"I'm a liberal. So he'll convert."

Now she says, "I'm so glad you came, Andrew. Have you
ever been to a seder?"

"Not many!" he says, shaking his head, following her into
the kitchen.

"It's one of the only holidays celebrating freedom," she says.
"That's why the holidays mean so much—to me. The Jewish
holidays, I mean. Do you know the others? Rosh Hashanah?
Simchath Torah? Purim? Hanukkah you must know."

Andrew smiles, and David tries to copy that smile, sharing
in the holiday spirit, and changing moods, he hopes, by changing expressions. It is exactly what he told Andrew to expect,
but he did not expect to be implicated himself in the simple,

private rituals of his family. He had wanted to rise above all the embarrassments of coming home, to see each difficult moment instantly in perspective, a small, meaningless wince already forgotten in a month, or a year. Once, he thought distance and time would be enough. At the hospital they call him doctor now, and in stores the clerks treat him with deference at last, if he remembers to deepen his voice: he thought that would be enough. But stepping through the door he is once again the child he used to be, transformed in a second back to his smaller self. Even hearing the words as a TV script far away, he cannot help speaking when his turn comes.

"David," says Zellie, "is something wrong? You look sick."

"Mother!" he says, like a child despite his man's voice and his man's coat. "Andrew knows about Hanukkah." He considers running out into the woods, or up the stairs, but already Andrew is standing next to his mother in the kitchen. Quietly he closes the door, taking his place between them.

"In my own family," Zellie says, "we had three seders—first night, second night, and one on the last night. Tomorrow it's in Newark, but I don't think David's coming. At home we just do this one."

"Wow!" says Andrew. "Three seders! That sounds like a lot of work." Simply, his arm is around David's waist, and for an instant Zellie's face is stuck between expressions.

"Work?" she says, shrugging her shoulders, and turns back to the Cuisinart, guiding pared apples through the plastic tube. "It was for the family," she says, "it was part of life. My grandmother used to say—David knows this—'Work is sweet.' "

Her hands, David notices, are pale and freckled, wrinkled already like the kid gloves she has worn every Friday night for years—fine, shallow wrinkles everywhere, as if the skin has been softly shattered. Her knuckles are more prominent, even swollen, and the veins stand out.

"Mother," David says, "Andrew and I are looking for a place together."

"Hm!" she says, and turns on the slicer for a few, very loud seconds.

Zellie has changed since her son appeared unexpectedly one weekend from college, sat her down in the kitchen, and slowly steered them into a conversation about sex. She is pleased with herself these days, even impressed, shaking her head at the cruelty and intolerance of other parents. David too is impressed with her, and grateful, remembering as well the first year of their new lives—he as the gay son, doctor or no, she as the mother of such a paradox.

"High school was hard," he said.

"I know."

"I never fit in."

"I know, I know. I hoped it wasn't too hard. But what could I do? I worried for you, practicing so much, alone. I didn't want to pry."

"I know."

"I was alone myself, growing up."

"I know."

So much they both admitted to knowing, while still each admission was surrounded by silence, padding them as much as possible and fighting that fall toward revelation. Near midnight David ended, staring into the dregs of his tea. "I loved her," he said. "Actually, we slept together."

"I know. I knew that," Zellie said, flushed and embarrassed despite herself. "Mothers aren't so naive, David!"

"I know, but I wanted to tell you. And I also wanted to tell you that . . . I'm attracted to men . . . as well."

At that timid truth, or else just at the relief of finally getting there, Zellie sighed in her chair as if she had been punched.

"I could kill your father!" she said, suddenly vehement, standing up and slamming the window shut. "I told him he should have played catch with you all those times! He laughed at me." Tearful a moment later, she asked, "Isn't it just loving yourself too much, maybe?" She wept—the first time ever in front of a child—left the room, walked back in and then away again. Finally she stood at the doorway, her back straight, a hand clenched in front of her as David sat motionless at the table. "Can't you wait, at least, before you decide?"

"Oh, Mom," David said. "Wait for what?"

"Until your grandparents die," she said, crying again, blowing her nose. "It would kill them to know."

Before the Cuisinart is fully silent the doorbell rings, the dog barks, and the front door opens.

"Well, hello, Solly!" calls a voice very much like Zellie's, cheerful and unhesitant.

"Oh dear," Zellie says, wiping her hands. As she runs to the front hall, David regrets having embarrassed her. She runs with some effort now, but still enthusiastically. He wants to run after her, but her own parents have come in, and Andrew is holding his arm. It is Andrew he hugs.

"Which one is that?" Andrew asks, moving toward the hall.

"Wait," David says, alarmed, but stopping him gently. "Ma Rose and Poppy Max, I guess." The dog, a disheveled soft-coated terrier, runs into the kitchen on clacketing nails, announcing the new arrivals. These days he too runs with some effort. David squats down, but the dog, seeing Andrew, runs to him.

"Hi, Sammy!" Andrew says, and Sammy humps his leg.

"Hey!" David says. "Hey!" And Sammy retreats back to the boy who left him years ago for college. Patiently and chastely he waits for a caress. "Do you love me?" David asks, holding Sammy and staring into his dark, discreet eyes.

Reaching down, Andrew strokes David's head. "Of course," he says.

In the hall Zellie greets her parents, who retired to Florida but returned after ten years when the last of their new friends all died, three in a week. They had gone south already old but still strong, and were at first the youngest couple at the bridge and canasta evenings. Now they are feeble and afraid—of the cold, of slipping on the snow or a loose rug, of driving in the dark, of every subtle ache that might spread into pain for the last time. Surprised to be alive this long, they consider themselves incredibly old, although Rose will still not admit that she was born before the new century, at least two years before Max. Everyone in the family knows but pretends she is the younger one, even celebrating her birthday on the fourteenth of May instead of the real date, the thirteenth, a date she never liked. It is undeniably spring now, and there will be another birthday after all. They had guessed the winter would kill them.

Zellie has never seen her mother's new wheelchair, her latest humiliation, and with Sol she exclaims over it, praising its evident comfort, its amazing features—three speeds and reverse, manual ease, foldability for the car and stairs. She helps her mother off with her fur coat, hangs it up in the closet next to her own. Both are sable, with deep black stripes and high collars—almost identical, it seems, although one is new and the other thirty years old. The shoulders are padded and always full, as if the two women were still standing in them, huddling close together. For a moment, Zellie presses her face into the fur.

Sol is slowly wheeling the chair, and Rose sits back with a sudden, determined grin. "You're something, Solly," she says, and as they pass the closet she calls out to her daughter, "This is quite a guy you've got here, *mamela*, you know that?"

When David comes in with Andrew, he sees his mother still

standing in the closet, her back to the room. "Hi, Poppy! Ma Rose!" he says, kissing the cheek Rose patiently offers, and her skin, even wrinkled and powdered with blush, is as soft as he remembers. "When did you get this?"

"It's new!" Sol says, standing behind the chair with Max, who continues to grip the handle. "This baby'll leave my Fiat in the dust. Look at it, Davey, three speeds. We'll have to race her after dinner—what do you say, Ma Rose?"

Max smiles for the first time, revealing beautiful but new teeth. David looks down until Sol has finished. "Ma Rose?" he says. "Poppy? This is my friend Andrew."

"How do you do!" says Rose, extending her hand formally. "How do you like my racer?"

"I like it!" Andrew says, shaking her hand a shake too many. Max says, "Young man," and nods his head, looking away.

Zellie calls out from the closet, "Andrew is in medical school as well, Mother. Remember?" and Rose nods respectfully, eyebrows up, while Max hums quietly to himself. "Another doctor!" Rose says, and David himself nods, too emphatically.

Months before, Zellie had told him, "She's very modern, David. You'll see. It's Poppy who doesn't understand, maybe, but my mother knows how things are. She likes to live and let live, I'm telling you." A day before the seder, Zellie called to remind him about his earring. "For me," she said. "Please. It just calls attention."

"But everyone knows, Mother. What does it matter?"

"It matters to me."

"But Mom," David said. "It's in my left ear. It's okay."

She didn't answer. Until this minute David has forgotten, and now it is too late; Rose has seen the one speck on his body he would like to have kept hidden. Quickly her eyebrows raise again, her head turns away. Zellie points to her own ear in pantomime.

"Your earring," she whispers a minute later in the dining

room, and they stare at each other, David's face a blank, as if he doesn't understand. The earring, a birthday gift from his sister, has absorbed in its tiny proportions all the anxieties of myth and taboo. "She should have minded her own business," Zellie had said, but now, quietly, she says, "Please," and after a pause David pushes the diamond stud from his ear.

"What's that in your ear?" says Rose, wheeling over a moment too late.

"What, Ma Rose? This? It's just the tip of my glasses."

"Oh," she says, "I thought maybe it was an earring." And Sol pushes her chair across the hall, changing the subject abruptly in his deep, theatrical voice.

Andrew has found the "Stairalator"—a chair on a track—and after strapping himself in, he gently rises up. David races to stop him.

"They can hear," he says, and Andrew smiles for further explanation. In the kitchen a woman is laughing—Zellie, or her mother, or both. When she was sick, David explains, his grandmother lived upstairs, and hates to remember. Never again, she says, shaking her head not just at the Stairalator but at cancer, helplessness, and old age. It's no good, she says, it's a lie. "Later," David whispers, and for the first time he is kissing a man in his mother's house.

Upstairs they tour the rooms, saving the guest bedroom till last, with its king-size bed from Zellie's first marriage, and all the fancy but retired sheets and pillows and lamps. Even the pictures there are from before: her family, her children, even, in group portraits, Israel, their father. It is there, David has promised, they will spend the night. From the shelf in the hall he pulls down several books, opens a cover, and hands it to Andrew. On the title page is Zellie's name—"Zelda"—written alone at the top, bereft of a last name, waiting perhaps for a new one. Andrew merely nods and hands it back.

In the bedroom Lonnie is spread-eagled across the huge bed, her eyes closed and her mouth open, nodding to the beat from her Walkman. At eighteen she is as small as a girl, and except for the many gold rings through her ear, her spiked hair and torn sweatshirt, she might pass for a much younger sister. They lie down on either side of her before she opens her eyes.

"You hiding too?" she says.

"No," David says, "I just wanted to show Andrew where we're going to sleep."

"No you're not!" she says, still nodding to the music no one else can hear. "Mom sent me up to take my stuff out of the closet—for Warren and Jill, she said."

"No!" David says, pounding the pillow. "That's not fair, Lon, we're here first."

"Don't tell *me* about it. I'm just up here hiding. Please don't say anything to Mom, David. It would just upset her." Since David became the problem son, it is Lonnie who counsels and moderates, worrying for their mother when they are not fighting. First it was David, but he has fallen from that grace. From her college dorm, she calls her brothers with secondhand advice, concern, and complaints, while on all sides they whisper to her, David, Zellie, and Israel too, sometimes. For David the reversal is still new, and in gratitude he touches her small hand, finally holding it.

"I guess we should go downstairs," he says.

Lonnie gets up as well, grinning grotesquely. She asks, "Does my smile look real?"

In the master bathroom, Zellie is now dressed in her white skirt and blouse. She is leaning across the sink to the mirror, brushing blue powder on her eyelids.

"Mother," David says, "can we talk for a second? About who gets the big bed?"

"Please," Zellie says, not turning around. "Do we have to have this one now?"

"It's just that we're here first and all."

"David," she says, and his name, well articulated and low on her voice, is an unexpected sound. "They're married." In silence he watches her leaning toward the glass. He has no answer, and wonders what he could say, what he used to do, so she would turn and hug him. When she does turn, the brush is still poised in her hand, and in her pearls and mascara she is just as David remembers her, leaving for parties late and frantic, the perfume lingering.

"Do we have to deal with it now, David? It's Passover."

"Come on, Mom," he says. "We're married too."

"Come on," she says, smiling, but squinting also. From the living room they hear the piano, and then Andrew's unhesitant voice, singing in Hebrew.

"Okay," David says, and in his man's shoes and his man's suit, he feels too big to be standing there with her. "Next time. Okay?"

Before he goes out Zellie stops him for a moment, kissing him quickly. "I'm doing all right," she says. "Aren't I?"

Andrew is playing Passover songs from an old book, singing instead of Hebrew the English that passes for translation. To a dark old melody he sings:

> Pesach time is here my friends,
> Pesach time is here.

Entering the formal room, David is afraid to look up, afraid to see his grandparents shaking their heads, their lips raised, their eyes held up to God as witness. They will interrupt, shout their disdain across the room, and then Andrew will know.

But Rose is sitting by the grand piano, singing along intermittently in Hebrew while Andrew sings the English. At the end she laughs. "And now," she says, " 'Had Gad Yah.' Do you know it? About the lamb at market." As he starts she claps her hands, singing fast to make all the English words fit the verse:

> He slew the ox
> That drank the water
> That quenched the fire,
> That burned the stick
> That beat the dog
> That ate the cat,
> That ate the kid, the only kid.
> Had Gad Yah, Had Gad Yah!

And David is filled with pride, for this old song, and for his lover, brilliant, he remembers, and handsome, he sees, and gentle beyond question, beyond complaint, it seems, who can sing, smiling and unselfconscious, with an old woman, while the others sit watching, eating peanuts from a dish. Andrew winks when David sits down, and David's relief is entire. He has not pretended, he has not hidden himself or compromised. Andrew's wink is like a big, wet kiss in front of everyone. Could they get up now and dance? Could they stand in the middle of the room and embrace, slowly spinning? Even the earring in his pocket is not entirely a defeat. Pressing against his thigh, it is his gift to them all.

"That's wonderful," Rose says, cutting off before the last verse. "You'll have to help with the four questions, young man."

"The four questions!" Andrew says. "I know that one!"

Zellie has appeared at the door, holding her blond grandchild up against her cheek. "Look who's here, Esther sweetie! There's Ma Rose, and Poppy, and Grandpa Sol, and look—there's David's friend Andrew playing the piano!"

Esther looks around, clutching her farm lunch box, then turns to hide her face in Zellie's neck. Everyone is charmed by her shyness, and for a moment each face reflects the same surprised affection, unhidden and quick, until Esther looks up again and they all stiffen, smiling or looking away. What will she remember of this night? they wonder. The bright chandelier? The elegant piano? The wheelchair? A few blurry faces nuzzling up with a kiss? Or only Zellie's perfume, a soft neck that hides her from all the excitement?

"Zelda, please, it's too much for her all at once." Jill comes up from behind and takes her daughter from Zellie's arms. Esther is carried across the room, lowered in one arm to kiss Ma Rose, then Poppy Max, Uncle David, and finally Grandpa Sol, who swings her way up in the air and says "Whee!" At each face Esther squeezes her eyes closed. But with her mother she doesn't complain; they sit next to David on the couch, and Jill sighs deeply, a message he ignores. She has joined the temple Sisterhood, Zellie said; though according to Warren she finds the meetings more tolerable stoned and giggling. At first, even to David, they seemed ideal parents for the first, revered grandchild, perfect guardians of the blood, keepers of the family flame—all the old sacrifices. Zellie stands at the door with her hands clasped at her waist, and David sees in her gaze both the wish and the fulfillment. He imagines her whispering, though her husband is not their father: We have given them everything, themselves in our own image, and they will remember us.

Then, as if he has guessed right all along, Zellie grins, throws out her arms, and Warren, her firstborn, walks reluctantly into them, into everyone's view. At twenty-nine he has a child, two cars, and a ranch house and goes to work every day at five for Sol's contracting company, building shopping centers. He looks middle-aged already, balding, soft where he used to be hard from lifting weights. He is surprised to be so completely grown up, at least in all the accoutrements he always imagined—the car, the house, the baby—and makes jokes about it to David sometimes, holding his daughter on his knee.

"Hello, everybody," he says, grimacing while Zellie holds him in her arms, kissing his cheek.

Uncle Mel and Aunt Pearl arrive, with Stevey between them. Still lively and cheerful—through breast cancer, Matthew's death—Pearl is frailer than David remembers, and smiles through a face newly old. Mel, taking her coat, has seemed old for years, as if only now, in his sixties, he has grown into his true, elderly self. His tie and jacket, pulled from his closet again after thirty years, are back in fashion—narrow and severe. His eyes never seem quite focused, and he mutters jokes from years of being ignored. Since his heart operation he is often amused or confused, though exactly which is a mystery. Either the Levin matriarchy has beaten him down—that and his son's death—or else he found in Pearl, long ago, the vital complement to his hidden weaknesses. No one remembers him as a young man, although there are stories of their courtship, and they still often kiss each other's hand. Still, he has gone on too many fishing trips, perhaps, sitting all day in small boats, and put his feet up too many nights in the den, silently watching football.

David shakes his uncle's hand and kisses his aunt. "This is Andrew," he says.

"Well, isn't that nice!" says Mel.

"How you doing there, Big Dave?" says Stevey, boldly holding out his hand just like his father. At thirty-two he still looks like a boy, a charming, accomplished boy, a first and favorite grandchild, who still can throw a ball or shoot a basket like the best of them. And now, besides, he can drive a sports car, and sign checks from his father's firm. To Andrew he nods as he shakes his hand, frowning in a businesslike way.

"Hello, Andrew," says Pearl, politely. "We've heard all about you." Her smile is indulgent, her gaze gentle; for the first time David the doctor is not a reflection of her sister, nor a mirror held up to her own children. Steven is still a boy; Matthew is dead; Teddy a clerk somewhere in town. But David—David, the perfect son, has come home with a man. Still holding his hand, Pearl says to Andrew, "I knew him *when*!" smiling with affection.

The table extends almost all the way across the dining room, from the marble hearth almost into the kitchen. On every other china plate is a blue prayer book, and in the center is a huge tray of fruits and flowers, crowned with a pineapple. Andrew stands behind a chair, hesitating.

"Anywhere, anywhere," Zellie calls over her shoulder as she runs past. Jill sits with Warren at the far end near Sol, but Esther's highchair is near the kitchen. Zellie comes in with a bowl of apples chopped with wine and nuts, and Rose leans across to Andrew.

"*Haroseth*!" she says, vehemently.

Mel leans forward as well. "That's the mortar that built the pyramids," he says. "You know what we mean by that, Andrew—a symbol."

"Cut it out, Dad," says Stevey. "He's not an idiot! You know, Andrew," he says, leaning over confidentially like his father. "The ancient Hebrews were slaves."

"Sure," Andrew says. "I know!"

As she passes, Zellie touches him lightly on the shoulder, shaking her head. Behind her follows Irene, dressed up in black and carrying an enormous tray of little plates.

"Irene," says Rose, "so what do you think of my daughter's table? Have you ever seen such a feast?"

"At your house, Ms. Levin."

"Irene," says Pearl, "will I see you tomorrow?"

"Of course," Irene says. "Eleven, you said."

"Okay then, eleven. You promise?"

Jill, who has had Irene only since the fall, still looks away unless Irene speaks first. "She so pretty tonight!" Irene says, looking across at the baby as she puts down a plate. "Thank you, Irene," Jill says, meeting her eye for just an instant.

Everyone is seated except for Lonnie, who still has not appeared. Zellie calls her name from the bottom of the stairs and quickly takes her seat before there can be a scene. Soon Lonnie trudges down the stairs, shuffles to her place between Andrew and the baby, and at last pulls her headphones down to her neck.

"I thought you were going to get dressed," Zellie whispers.

Low but unquietly Lonnie says, "I am dressed."

Sol stands up at the head of the table, white yarmulke on his head, white prayer shawl on his shoulders. His face is deep red. "I just wanted to say—" he begins, but starts to cry, and chokes over the words. "My family," he says, gesturing down the table on both sides. He hesitates, sobs, and covers his face, while down the table others are quickly moved to tears as well: Zellie, Pearl, and Rose, Max, his eyes closed, Irene in the kitchen, David, even Mel and Steven.

Jill and Warren look away, into their laps.

"I'm very happy," Sol says, sitting down again on the extra pillow.

" 'On Passover,' " he reads, " 'we celebrate the exodus of the Jews out of slavery in Egypt, explaining to our children, so that their children will understand, and explain.' "

David holds Andrew's hand under the table. They are leaning close together, their shoulders and knees touching. Zellie stands by her place and lights the candles with a prayer, her hands held close to the flame as if for warmth. Then, covering her face with her hands, even rubbing her eyes, she prays, silently, for secret, private things. Everyone tries to guess: for the starving Africans, Lonnie thinks, or Russian Jewry; closer prayers,

Sol thinks, for her parents, for him; for Sol, her parents think; for Esther, David thinks, or else, though he dreads the thought, for him. All of them are covered, surely—husband, parents, each of her children—with a whispered word. Even Esther next to her leans forward, staring wide-eyed into the small, perfect flames.

"Amen!" Zellie says at last, clapping her hands, suddenly grinning, and makes her way around the table, loudly kissing each cheek.

"Zellie, will you please?" says Sol, as she lingers, kissing him. "I'd like to get started with this." Slowly, proudly, he reads through the prayers, stopping once at the mention of children, wiping his glasses. His own children have fled, to California, to Wyoming—cowboys and Indians, he calls them. Now, at the head of the table, in the big chair he avoided until after the wedding, he reads from the Hebrew with tears in his eyes. The others turn pages, touch their forks, take a glass of water.

"Let's go on to the English," Zellie suggests, but Sol keeps reading, holding up the bitter herb, the shank bone, the matzoh, each of the symbolic foods on the silver plate they bought in Jerusalem. With each explanation he looks directly at Andrew.

"This horseradish root, Andrew, the bitter herb, represents the bitter times of our slavery, when every meal was degraded, and every day was sadness. For we too were slaves. Today, wherever slavery remains, we Jews taste its bitterness."

Before the bitter herb can be passed around, Esther spills her grape juice and starts to cry, thrilled but then appalled at the mess.

"Esther!" Warren calls from down the table. "Be quiet!"

"Ah, honey," Zellie says. "Sweetie, don't cry, we'll clean this up right away and get you another." She picks Esther up into her lap. "Your father spilled things, too," she says.

Jill drops her book onto the table. "Zelda, it's all right. Just leave her alone, please," she says. "She has to learn to sit through dinner."

Zellie looks up as if she is going to speak, but then bends down and only murmurs to her granddaughter, while Sol continues with the Hebrew. "Honey," she says, and points quickly to the spill. "Lon, will you get paper towels for that, while I hold her? We'll just blot it up real fast and then leave it till after."

Lonnie hesitates, then pushes back her chair and goes off into the kitchen, slamming cabinets. Jill stands up and hurries to Esther.

"Sorry about this," she says. "I'll take her."

"No, no, it's okay," Zellie says, still holding Esther's legs as she is pulled from her grandmother's arms, surprised into tears again. "Wait!" Zellie says, but a shoe comes off, and half a sock. Finally she has to let go, and presses her lips with the back of her hand. Soon Jill is at her seat again, Esther squirming on her lap while the sock and shoe are restored. Warren bangs the table, and Esther is still. Meanwhile, across from them, Max has lifted his cup, chanting in Hebrew.

"Hm!" Andrew says at the end, but Max looks away, at his plate, at his wife, at the picture window, blackly reflecting the room. Finally he turns to his first grandson, child of his retirement. "Okay, Stevey," he says, almost with his back to Andrew, "you're next!"

"My, my," says Mel, as Lonnie returns heavily to her seat, tossing a wad of towels onto the stain.

"Not like that, honey," Zellie whispers.

"Then you do it. She's your granddaughter."

Zellie looks up across the table, but Sol is turning pages, continuing with another prayer. She crumples the paper, sponges up the juice from the cloth, and leaves the darkened ball on her plate. "Irene," she whispers into the kitchen, "can you help me?"

"For chrissake!" Sol says, suddenly interrupting his chant, and his prayer shawl falls onto the floor. "How do you expect us to get through this with all the goddamn interruptions? Goddamn it, Zelda!"

In the silence everyone stares down into the pages, as if great terror were waiting just behind the window, close beyond the quiet of the night—all the history remembered at Passover, inquisition and holocaust, slavery, families blotted out—all that might be ushered in with a sound. "My father's prayer gown was like that," says Rose, pointing to the shawl. "We buried him in it. My mother said, 'Go get Papa's *kittel*,' and we said, 'But why, Mama? His *kittel*?' 'Yes,' she said. 'That's his shroud.' "

Loudly Warren clears his throat. "So," he says, "when do we get to eat?"

And the family laughs. "That's my Warry!" Zellie says, and they move in their chairs again, going on with the story.

" 'We were slaves in the land of Egypt—' "

"And now," Zellie says, interrupting Sol by mistake, "the four questions!"

Warren looks up from his book. "Will you cool it, Mom?"

"Now," says Sol, "we come to the four questions, which, according to tradition, should be posed by the youngest member of the family. Lonnela, you're on."

Lonnie is leaning on her elbows by the candles, moving a finger slowly back and forth into the flame while everyone watches.

"Lonnie," says her mother.

"What," she says.

"Come on, honey."

"Well!" says Sol. "We should really ask Esther, but I think she's still a little shy. What do you say, Lon, should we ask your competition?" He holds Esther's chin with two fingers, leaning over with a loud kiss.

Lonnie's finger stops too long in the flame, and she jerks it away. Then, stretching out her fingers, she catches dripping wax on her palm.

"We'll all say it," says Pearl. "Okay?"

"Lon, don't do that," Zellie says, touching her daughter's hand. "What's wrong?"

Lonnie is frowning so hard her cheeks resemble her mother's, older, even jowling. "Nothing," she says.

"Well then, come on."

"Come on, already," Warren says. "I want to eat."

Max leans his body toward Rose, without turning. "Maybe she forgot," he says.

"Oh well," says Mel. "Little Lonnie forgot her lines."

"She's just embarrassed, Mel, can't you see that?" Pearl winks at her niece, whispering to her husband. "Too many people. Leave her alone."

"Of course," says Mel. "She's embarrassed."

"She's not embarrassed, already!" Zellie says. "It's just family." To Lonnie she whispers, "What's wrong, honey?"

"You want to know?" Lonnie says.

"Yes," Zellie says. "What?"

"You really want to know?"

"Yes."

Looking up at her mother, then down the length of the table, she says, "It's such a fake here. This whole thing. You just show off all this religious stuff for strangers, and they don't even give a shit."

"That's nice language, missy," Sol says.

"Who's a stranger?" Zellie asks. "Who?"

"No one cares about this! Why are you pretending! I'm not going to be fake, just to make you all feel better! I'm not!"

"Who's a stranger?" Zellie says, hitting her plate by mistake. "Just tell me who!"

With a loud scrape Lonnie pushes back her chair and runs

into the kitchen. "You don't care!" she calls back. "No one cares!"

"Well, well," says Stevey, but then he is silent.

Zellie studies the flowers. Whenever she is not smiling, her lips are drawn together, and she looks, unexpectedly, her age. Esther is the only one to move, wriggling off her mother's lap and running into the kitchen as well.

"What's wrong with her?" Rose asks, and Zellie quickly glances the question away. But Rose continues. "Hungry," she says. "My mother always said, 'Eat first, then ask questions.' Eleven daughters, you think she didn't know?"

"Let's eat," Warren says. "We'll finish this stuff later."

"Well?" says Sol, looking at Zellie. "Should we eat?"

"You want to eat?" she says, holding up her palms. "Eat!" She points to the line of plates on both sides, each with its waiting, smaller plate of gefilte fish in jelled broth, crimson with horseradish. Lonnie, reappearing, walks calmly back to the table. In her hand she carries a can of Tab, which she pulls open and empties slowly into her wine glass, up to the extreme edge.

"Well," says Sol, "but if you think we should wait, we'll wait—"

Behind Zellie there is a soft crash, and then the wail of Esther's tears. She has tripped on the rug, and her plastic farm animals have spilled from their barn.

"Baby!" Zellie cries, rushing to her, lifting her up.

"Zelda!" says Jill sharply, rising from her chair. "I can take care of my own daughter." But Zellie has already turned away, with Esther in her arms. "Zelda, I can take care of my own daughter! Zelda!" Slowly Zellie turns back to the table, giving Esther up. "Thank you," Jill says.

"Mom, will you stop it already?" says Warren, while his mother stands with her arms at her sides. "She's got to learn how to behave," he says, and snaps his fingers. "Esther, get back here, and sit down!"

Esther goes back to her father, who sweeps her onto her mother's lap. He holds out his finger until she stops crying.

Zellie sits down as well, holding her chin in her hand, staring straight ahead.

Sol laughs and says, "That's your mother!" But when he meets Zellie's gaze across the table he stops smiling. She stands up again, walks to the door, and loudly turns the bolt.

"Hey," says Sol, rising from his seat, "Zellie, where are you going?" But before he can stop her she is out the door. "Christ!" he says, "that's your mother!" and follows her out.

At the table Max is humming, tapping his fingers on the cloth.

"Stop it, Max," Rose says.

Jill is holding her forehead. "Should I go out there?" she asks, and Warren shakes his head no.

"You know about Elijah?" says Rose, leaning toward Andrew across the table. "Ask the boy about Elijah," she says, pointing to David.

"I know," Andrew says, "you set an extra place, in case he comes."

"Or any stranger," says Rose. "You understand? That's why you open the door. Tell him, dolly," she says, pointing to David, then to Andrew, then to the door. "That's why you open the door. Now where'd she go, your mother?"

"Actually," says Stevey, "it was to show the goyim we weren't eating Christian babies!"

"Goddamn," Warren says, as the door opens again. Zellie walks into the kitchen, and Sol returns to the table, grinning. "Okay!" he says, clapping his hands. "Where were we?"

"The four questions," Andrew says.

"Ah, yes, the four questions. *'Mah nishtana'* is right!" And he winks at Rose.

"Andrew!" says Mel, looking down the table, his eyebrows raised. In his face is the benevolence of a man who has hiked and fished and camped out for thirty years with whatever children happened to come along. His smile hides his eyes. "You're so smart, you know what that means?"

Andrew clears his throat, winks at David, and begins to translate.

Sometime during the meal, the father is supposed to hide a piece of matzoh—under the pillow, behind the flowers, in somebody's purse. At the end the children search for it, inspired by the promise of remuneration—Passover *gelt*. Once it was a quarter, later on a dollar, then five dollars, until this year college tuition was mentioned, humorously but with another wink down the table, implying the lawsuit pending between Zellie's two husbands. By prior arrangement Lonnie found the *afikomen*, but she threw it down at the mention of her father. This year for the first time Esther was old enough to play, and after Lonnie won it was Esther's turn as well, Sol holding her on his lap until she patted the flat protrusion in his pocket. Abruptly, Lonnie disappeared upstairs.

Andrew had been holding up a large, unbroken wafer of matzoh, running a finger along its serrated brown rows of bubbles. He turned to Pearl but addressed everyone. "You know," he said, "this matzoh is just like the wafer." Pearl's smile continued, but her eyes became glassy, and no one else responded. "You know," he said, turning at last to David, "the sacrament."

Now, in the moonless mid-evening, the men watch baseball in the den, while just beyond the window David and Andrew swing back and forth on the porch swing. Through the glass can be heard the squeak of the chains on one side, and on the other side the occasional cheering of the men. Each time the swing falls back the chain squeaks, and David and Andrew become visible through the window. Andrew's arm is around David's shoulders, but otherwise they hesitate; the romantic image wavers on irony already, and they want to feel the simple, sweet part as long as they can.

"Are you upset about all the fighting?" David asks, knowing just how low to speak for privacy. Andrew is surprised by the question, and David has to explain.

"Really!" Andrew says each time, shaking his head. "I didn't realize." After a while he asks, "Did they like me, do you think?"

"God damn it!" Warren shouts from the other room. Far away Esther cries, and then is silent.

"Yes," David says. "I'm sure they did."

It is an April night, still too cold to be outside without coats. But to touch inside would still be a spectacle, and to hide upstairs would be rude. Here they sit undisturbed, undisturbing, though each arc of the swing reveals them to the room of men. David touches the window once, twice as they swing, remembering the hard, thin separation, through which the yellow light spreads onto the porch and beyond them into the yard. Andrew's hand in David's is also hard, gripping and confident, a doctor's hand, a surgeon's. They lean together, and then, as the swing falls back, remain embraced.

"What do you think?" Andrew says too loudly, pointing to the window. "Can they take it?"

David whispers in his ear, kissing him. "I forgot about them," he says.

Then a door slams, a car starts up hard, and two headlights quickly sweep the yard: Warren's car.

"I can't believe it," David says. "They're leaving." Together they watch Warren's car turn onto the street and out of sight. "I guess that means we get the big bed."

"I guess they forgot about us," Andrew says. "I wanted to say goodbye to Esther." Again the yard is dark, the one huge oak visible only by its wide trunk. Above them, bare branches stretch out black and hidden.

"My mother's afraid of her," David says.

"Who?" Andrew asks. "Esther?"

And David takes his hand again, closing it around his own. "Jill," he says, as Zellie opens the heavy front door, standing in the new wedge of light. She is holding an afghan, woolen squares she knitted with her mother long ago, waiting for Warren to be born. For a minute she waits, politely, then steps out smiling to face them.

"I brought you this," she says, coming forward, unfolding the blanket to cover them. "I thought you might be cold."

FROM HER OWN seder Beth had to run away: from the rich Scarsdale neighborhood in which it took place, from the family that welcomed her, and above all from the first son of that family, who had asked her out there, hoping to impress at once both his family, with his artistic Jewish choice, and Beth herself, with the economic and ethnic charm of his background. Right away, as soon as the invitation from his mother came, she had known that her own mother would love him. With his mustache and his size-eleven shoes he was just the portrait she had painted on her walls every adolescent night in the shoebox-sized room of her childhood, alone and sleepless in her narrow bed, before sleep could change the scene—the walls like overblown petals fell away, and there, across green fields, running to her, were her friends, her girlfriends, whom already she loved and had always loved. In the flesh, this male vision, Glen Katz, knew how to kiss on the cheek, take her arm in his, and hold open the door. His voice was low and resonant. He was wealthy himself, a corporate lawyer, and already had asked her to live with him in Brooklyn Heights, in the vast former church converted—its stained-glass saints preserved above his bed, a mezuzah nailed to his door—into a bachelor's home. All it lacked, he said, proudly tapping one of the remaining pews, was a bride to feather his nest. What he could not learn was that sometimes Beth could not bear to be touched but had to sleep, when she chose, far away on the other side of the bed, or else escape late at night in a cab he would pay for, back to her own room and her own bed across the river. He would try to acquiesce, rub her shoulders affectionately, but soon asked her anyway—was she protected?—nuzzling up provocatively until she had to squeeze her legs together. So rather than spend that Passover night in the unused children's wing in Scarsdale, she put on her coat while the elders were still drinking coffee and smoking cigars around the long table, and pleading illness of a general and inconsistent nature, begged to be driven back.

The next night she was at David's, who at least had never wanted to possess, who had never in their lives together staked a claim or asserted a prerogative. Even his worthless but treasured artifacts, from thrift shops, from stacks of trash on street corners, from flea markets and street fairs, would be carefully wrapped as a gift if someone had praised a clock, or lovingly held up a water pistol or a piece of clay. That he would be a doctor was absurd; even he knew that. In his doctor's robe at the hospital he looked embarrassed, childish, caught in the act. Often when she came to his apartment he would be lying asleep with his clothes still on, or bending over in a chair, exhausted, even crying. "No sleep," he would say, smiling, and then go on crying.

Opening the door now, he was glad but unsurprised to see her, and pointedly avoided asking about the night before. They held each other under his down quilt, but even then she didn't feel safe. "Please," she said to him, knowing he would understand, "unplug the phone."

But he was on call, he said, and besides—he didn't finish his sentence. "You won't have to speak to him, Beth," he said, "if you don't want to," and he jumped up himself when they were in the bath together about eleven o'clock, in case it was Glen, her lawyer. But it was a man from the hospital who loved him, one of the orderlies, and he brought the phone into the tub rather than offend the voice at the other end. He kept holding up a finger to say he'd be off in a minute, but after a while the water was too cold to bear, and still he held the phone in the vicinity of his ear, head back against the tub, eyes closed.

"Why didn't you just say you were taking a bath?" she asked him later, when they were both naked in the kitchen, cooking oatmeal.

"I don't know," he said. "It didn't seem right."

"You can never tell these people no." He looked at her too long, accusingly. "It's not kosher, you know," she told him, pointing to the oatmeal. "*Pesachdik*, I mean." Rather than answer he stared into the bubbling pot. She herself, it was true, could not quite say no to her lawyer—or any man, really, who vaguely fit her mother's dream.

"Beth," he said, still looking down into the bubbling, primeval mess, "what would it be like if the world were like this?"

They huddled in bed, but Beth couldn't sleep. There were muted, untiring traffic noises from Second Avenue, and sometimes a beam of light swept through the room from the kitchen. Beth knew all the irregular whorls of the ceiling; but illuminated suddenly and briefly they were again mysterious to her, like an ocean or an uncharted map. A silver mobile lit up sometimes; she had made it herself: human body shapes suspended by themselves, an arm, a breast, a foot. The clock, luminescing, said after midnight. Within it the miniature fireplace was still glowing with an unmoving, electrified flame. No matter how she closed her eyes in his apartment it was always too light to sleep. Finally she crept up to turn off the flame, and when the switch clicked David said, "No, Beth, leave it on." She jumped, and gasped. Lying perfectly still through all her turning and restlessness, he was fully awake.

"It'll burn out," she said, and hurried back under the covers. "You can't sleep either? I'm so glad!"

"Why?" he said, not nearly so glad.

"We can keep each other company."

"Beth, what's going on?" he said. "What's up with you and—"

"Nothing," she said, quickly turning over as if to sleep.

"Do you like having sex with him?"

From deep in the pillow she answered. "Yes, I do. Well—"

"Well what?"

"Well enough." She turned back to him. "But he wants me to be his girl, or something like that. He wants me to hold his arm when we go places, and to like him all the time. And I just can't. I always think it's just what I want until I have to do it—until I'm introduced as his girlfriend, or I'm there pretending sex is the most incredible thing in life. In his life, maybe."

David merely scratched her arm, held straight up like a sleepwalker's. "Who have you loved?" he asked.

She thought of her usual list, but then had to cross the whole thing out. "You," she said.

"Who else?"

"Oh, I don't know. I thought I loved some of the others. Gwyn—no. Nyla—no. Jessica."

"Jessica you loved."

"Oh, but they weren't good enough!"

"Good enough for what, Beth?"

"Oh, you know what I mean, David. You've dropped a few yourself, through the years."

"So what are you getting at?"

"Oh, David," she said. "Face it, there's no one we like as much as each other. And I want to have a child before I die. I know you do too—it's what we always talked about. So what do we do about it?"

Now David turned over heavily, away from her, and she tried to count the freckles across his back. "Beth," he said, far away, "you're only twenty-six."

"Almost twenty-seven, David."

"So what's the big deal? You have a long time to work it out."

"You don't understand, David." She poked his shoulder. "It's not true. Women have to start thinking about children. How long is it going to take to find someone to love, decide to have a family, and then try to do it? After thirty-five it gets dangerous, you know."

"You're twenty-six, Beth."

"Anyway, suppose I die young?"

For a while he didn't answer, and she thought he might have fallen asleep. Or else he was pretending to sleep. How else, she wondered, could he so easily ignore their shared past, when he too was scared, and grateful for a friend? They had lived together, grown up together, planned all kinds of futures and laughed at the possibilities. She would indeed like to have a child before she died. Women with children, she knew, were holy, protected from malice, degradation, the first ones saved on sinking ships. The world accepted them and loved them, and Beth wanted to be among them.

"Beth," David said at last, "what are you talking about?"

"Just suppose I was sick with something, David, and only had a year. Would you have my child then?"

"Yes," he said, and with that she was going to let him sleep. But in the hallway there was a jangling of keys, and they could hear the first old lock turning in the door . . . then the dead bolt . . . then the police bar.

"Who's that?" she said, pulling the blanket up to her neck. David didn't answer, until the light went on in the kitchen and Andrew's voice called out to him. "David? You there? Anyone home?"

"It must be Andrew," David said.

"He has a key?"

"Hi," Andrew said, standing with the light behind him in the kitchen. "I couldn't sleep without you." He raised his arms, leaned against the doorway, and smiled. Then he saw Beth.

"Beth!" he said, and stood up straight, the keys dangling from his hand. "Hello there."

"Hello," she said. She was embarrassed for him, but also angry, and said nothing more.

"I'm sorry I barged in," he said. "I tried calling earlier, but the line was busy. I thought I'd just come on over. I guess I'll just go on out." He turned around and was almost out the door before David reached him, naked and vulnerable.

"Andrew," he said, "wait a minute. Why are you leaving?"

"What are you talking about?" Andrew said. "I'll see you later. Good night."

Beth could only hear them whispering. "Put something on, at least," she heard Andrew say.

"Well, come away from the door," David said.

A moment later Andrew had gone. David got back into bed, pulled the quilt up around his head, and said nothing.

"What was that all about?" Beth asked.

"Nothing," David said.

"Oh."

"He's jealous, I guess. He doesn't like me sleeping with you."

"Oh?" Beth said nothing else, but snorted once, thinking

how sexual claims were the most presumptuous of all. She had slept here more times than she could count. "I didn't know he has keys," she said, but David didn't answer. He seemed already to be safely asleep.

"DAVID," SAID ZELLIE, and he could hear, even over the phone, the relief and pleading in her voice: that it wasn't Andrew answering, that now she didn't have to pretend anymore.

"What, Mom? What is it?"

"Aunt Minnie died."

"Oh," David said. "I'm sorry." There was snow falling outside, lighted by street lamps, and the city was silent.

"I loved her very much."

"I know, Mom. I'm sure you did."

Zellie was crying. "I was very close to her, growing up." A moment later she had recovered. "I have the most beautiful granddaughter in the world," she said.

"I know," said David. "She is."

"I have her for the weekend," Zellie said. "Could you come tomorrow for a while, while I go to the funeral?"

"Yes," David said.

"Could you come alone?"

"No," he said.

In the car she was cheerful and attentive, asking Andrew about psychiatry, and the mental health of two-year-olds raised by grandparents, if necessary.

"Well!" Andrew said. "I don't know! It can be fine, I guess. I mean, as long as there's love, of course, and intimacy. I mean, I *guess*—what do you think, David?"

"Of course," Zellie said, already thinking of something else.

"You know," she said, "I can't help thinking about you two as well. I just can't help not giving up hope, at least for David. It's just the way I am, I can't do anything about it. The way I was brought up."

In the backseat, Andrew unrolled the window and rolled it back up.

"I mean," she said, "it's such a shame about you boys, wasting such wonderful genes. And you'd be such good parents, that I can tell. I'd be happy if you two brought up Esther, I'll tell you that much."

"No," David said.

"Yes I would."

"What did she mean by that?" Andrew asked when they were in the car again, alone this time with Esther. They were going to the Christmas wonderland on the Lewiston green. David turned to Esther in the backseat.

"This is the "whee" hill, Esther. We used to go 'whee!' over the top. Ready?" The car lifted over the crest of the hill, and together David and Esther said "Whee!"

"Does she still want you to marry Beth?"

"I don't know, Andrew. It doesn't matter. She loves you too."

"Not like her," Andrew said. "That other woman."

"Look, Esther," David said. "This is where Grandma used to live. And Ma Rose and Poppy Max." He turned down the dark street, driving slowly by the old house. "Look!" he said. "Right there." Esther looked out from the furry hood of her parka, saying nothing.

At the green they parked in a snow bank and had to crawl out. The ground and the trees were covered with new snow. All around were huge cut-out objects: a two-dimensional jack-in-the-box ten feet tall, a winter sleigh, a giant toy soldier. In the center a cottage had been set up, glowing, beneath its snowy roof, into the dull winter light. At the door children were in line with their parents, waiting to talk to Santa.

"This is wonderful!" Andrew said, jumping up on a rocking reindeer. "Come on, Esther sweetie, let's take a ride."

David handed her up, but she began to cry. Andrew descended, and they took their place in line.

"I love this place!" he said, and several children turned around.

"I always hated it," David said. "We always felt left out. Like we had to enjoy it, even though it wasn't for us."

"Why not? It's for everyone. What are you going to ask for for Christmas, Esther?"

She shrugged.

"A dolly?"

"Yeah," she said, shyly.

"A big dolly?"

"Yeah."

"Do you say yes to everything?"

"Yeah."

Andrew hugged her, and lifted her up until she screamed. He put her down.

"I would like us to have a kid, though," David said. A parent turned around, and David stared back.

"Though?"

"Though obviously, it's not so easy," he said, more quietly. It was Esther's turn, and she walked up confidently to the pillow-stuffed man in red, turning around to be hoisted up by him. All around were heaps of toys and dolls, trumpets, tricycles, drums, water pistols, and darker, more threatening artillery. The stockings on the mantel were stuffed, and little automated elves too slowly raised and lowered their plastic arms, up and down, as if in their hammering and sewing they were thinking of something else. David and Andrew listened, but there was music playing, and Esther was whispering into the vast white beard.

"Why do you want to be a father so much?" Andrew asked.

"What do you mean?"

For a moment Andrew turned away. Then, turning back, his face tense, he said, "You still have to prove you're a man so much? You're still so insecure?"

"No," David said, and turned away himself. Then, as if to himself, he said, "I could always have one with Beth."

"No you couldn't," said Andrew. He stood up and turned to him. "I'd leave you."

"But why?"

Esther was still on Santa's lap, but Andrew, in his summer shoes, stepped off the path into the snow, leaving deep prints behind him.

They caught up with him near the manger, in the middle of the snow, Esther on David's shoulders, David galloping like a horse. "Whoa!" David said, slowing down. "What's this?"

"The manger," said Esther. "The Christ Child in the crèche, Mother Mary and the kings."

"Where'd you learn that?" David asked, but up on his shoulders she didn't answer. "And who's that in the back?" he asked, pointing to Andrew, near a sheep.

"That's Joseph," said Esther. "And the animals."

"Cut it out," Andrew said.

David put Esther down. "You know," he said, "you're even more adorable when you sulk."

"Leave me alone," Andrew said, and turned his back on them.

"Come on, Andrew, what's wrong?"

"I can just see Beth pregnant. Anyway, how can you even consider that! At this point?"

"Andrew, why not? It's the only way I can think of, at the moment. I mean, we could splice our genes, I guess, and try one of those peritoneal pregnancies. I'd have your baby, if you want. But that's still risky."

"David, for chrissake! She doesn't want me in your life. She'd have all the power. You'd be miserable. I'd be miserable! I'm not going to put up with that for the rest of our lives. I hate it here," he said, a moment later. "My feet are cold. Can we go?"

"You think I like it so much?" David said. "I'd like to steal this baby—it'd save a lot of trouble." He tried to pick up the baby Jesus, but it was concrete and too heavy. He laid it back down.

"For who? For us? There's other ways to have a kid than stealing it."

"For the Jews, Andrew," David said. "For the Jews."

WHEN BETH WALKED into the gallery there she was—the woman from her dreams, she thought, remembering, after a moment, that that dream, like all dreams, must have begun somewhere more substantial. The gray streak she remembered, also the unsmiling, acquisitive regard, seeming to approve without any admission of desire or vulnerability. But the exact moment from the past, as well as the degree of intimacy of their intercourse, remained shrouded in uncertainty, confused as it was with her present, renewed excitement. The woman was standing at the desk, talking with the receptionist. Beth wandered past the enormous, pale canvases lining the walls and stood for some minutes before one that seemed to be entirely white. She could not hear, from across the room, what the woman was saying, but neither could she ignore her voice, low and untimid, nor the intimate, lulling response of the other woman. She leaned closer to the canvas. There seemed to be no paint, no brush strokes visible, nothing but the monotonous, artless bumps of the canvas itself. The women laughed, one high, one low, and

Beth bent closer to the painting, to see if some subtle pattern or symbol might emerge. When she looked up, the woman was already out the door.

"Excuse me," Beth said, hurrying to the young woman at the desk, "I think I know that woman who just walked out. Do you happen to know her name?"

"Yes, actually," said the woman. "She's a friend of mine."

"Oh," said Beth, and was silent, hoping the woman would continue. But she turned back to her papers. "Where would I know her from?" Beth asked, wondering almost to herself.

"That depends," said the woman, looking up again and smiling. "She's been around." Her blond hair was cut short and thick, like a Dutch boy's, and when she smiled Beth could see she was not so severe as she pretended, nor so grown-up. "Where have you been?"

"Well . . ." said Beth, beginning to answer, and then realized she was safe. "You mean, all your life?" she said, covering her smile with her hand, and though she blushed at her own daring, she was also proud.

"Yes," said the woman, looking down and back up again. "Maybe that's what I meant."

"That's what I thought," Beth said, and turned away to the paintings once more, suddenly taking her time.

Her name was Cory Reed, and just before six o'clock Beth was back again. This time she was expected. Cory saw her come in, but betrayed her distraction only through the slightest smirk while talking with a last, lingering visitor. As soon as the visitor left, however, and the door had been locked for the night, Cory turned around suddenly so that her face and Beth's were only inches apart.

"Now what?" she said, and before Beth could answer, Cory had slipped away and was motioning Beth into the back room. "Here's where we leave our coats," she said. "And store the etchings." She put on her jacket and stood in front of Beth. "You want to see?"

"Well?" said Beth.

"Well," Cory said, and kissed her lightly on the lips, so lightly it might have been only her breath. "I'm glad you came back," she said.

Beth had no words. She could only nod, and kiss her as well.

In bed, in Beth's bed, Cory was passionate and untentative, and only late at night did Beth look up to notice the lights of Canal Street flashing in the dark. It was a relief to feel at once strong and attractive, to forget manners and poses and still be loved. For three nights they hardly slept, breathless, exhausted, intensely content, stumbling out of bed only to use the toilet or pour each other glasses of juice. On the fourth night Beth jumped awake, trembling.

"What is it?" Cory asked, stroking Beth's hair while still almost asleep.

"I can't do this," Beth whispered. "I can't do this anymore."

"Do what?" Cory asked, yawning. "Stay up so late? I can't either. Tomorrow I'm going to have to go home."

"No," Beth said. "I mean something else. I mean—" But Cory was already comforted, already asleep. Beth crept out of bed and into the living room. In the dark, counting the holes on the telephone, she dialed David's number.

"Hello," she said, "David, am I bothering you?"

"No," he said. "No. It's okay. What's wrong?"

"Are you asleep?"

"No," he said. "I don't think so, anymore. What time is it?"

"Three o'clock," she said.

"Oh God, why did you wake me up?"

"David," Beth said, "I can't do this anymore."

"Do what?"

"Be a lesbian."

"Okay, so don't. Good night."

"It's not that simple. She's still here. In my bed."

"Who?"

"Cory."

"Does she know you're changing?"

"No," Beth said. "Not yet."

"Well, what are you going to do?"

"I don't know. I don't know."

"Well," David said, "call me back when you decide."

"Okay," Beth said. "I will." And she hung up, still sitting there in the dark.

The next day Cory went home, and David invited Beth out to Lewiston. To his surprise she accepted.

"Why so surprised?" she asked.

"I don't know," he said. "It's not the sort of thing you like to do."

"Well," she said, "I'm changing. Anyway, I wanted to be with you alone for once. I never get to anymore, now that Andrew's around all the time."

"Beth, you've been pretty busy yourself."

"Only for the past week. I'm talking about a year, David. Two years. Last year you were up in Providence every free second. Anyway, for me, it's over."

"What do you mean? I thought you had a great time."

"I did. I mean, at first. Then the whole thing horrified me. The life I'm leading."

"Does she know it?"

Beth shook her head. They were driving through the Holland Tunnel, and she was watching the ceiling and the walls for cracks. "I'm getting too old for this," she said, and wiped a tear from her eye. "All the running around, and staying up late, and being so lonely."

"You weren't lonely this week."

"I know, but it's not the sort of thing that could last."

"You just met her! How could anyone know?"

"I'm tired of being so strange! I'm growing my hair long again."

"You think that'll do it?"

"And I'd like to get married, and have a child."

"No you wouldn't."

"This is something you don't understand about me, David."

"Well, good luck," he said.

"You used to want to also, David. Or so you said."

He didn't answer, squinting as he studied the sign, then cursing as they turned off at the wrong exit, descending into Newark. Now they were lost. The ramp expired in weeds and potholes. A school playground, fenced in barbed wire, was lit up as if it were night. A man stood in the middle of the street, watching as they approached. No window was unbarred, no advertisement unfaded. People turned to stare at their white faces, at their dirty but fancy car, low to the ground, accelerating loudly.

"Beth," David said. "Look for a sign in English, will you please? That was a long time ago. Anyway, I told you it wouldn't work out. I guess I've changed."

"I guess you have."

"Listen," he said, "how would you feel if I marched in the Gay Pride march with Gay Fathers?"

"I'd divorce you in a second."

"Well," he said, changing gears, "there you have it." And they pulled into a gas station for directions.

Out on the highway again, Beth continued. "Well, how would you feel," she asked, "if I married Glen Katz?"

"I'd hope you'd be happy. I doubt it. Look," he said, pointing to the park, "that's where my grandfather proposed. They went rowing on the pond, and neither one could swim." The pond, across the park, beyond the highway, was still covered with a last, thin layer of ice. The trees were black and frozen, the earth gray. Neither Beth nor David could much imagine that scene, a summer's day, lovers just after a war, bow ties and straw hats, long skirts and parasols.

"So you wouldn't care, David?"

"Beth, we've had all this before."

"Oh," she said. "I guess that means you wouldn't." She waited for an answer, but David was tapping the steering wheel and nodding his head, keeping time to some silent distraction.

In Lewiston he rummaged in the attic for books, while Beth called her answering machine and returned her calls. Cory had left two messages, and though it was Beth's intention to ignore those calls, at least for the weekend, she was moved, after the second innocent, amorous monologue, to respond this one more time. . . .

"Beth!" Cory said, answering the phone at the gallery. "I'm so glad you called—can you hold?" Before Beth could agree there was music, or not music but a sort of underwater sound, a dripping, a plunking. In a moment Cory came on again. "Sorry about that," she said. "I miss you terribly."

"I miss you too," Beth said. "What was that sound on the line?"

"Oh, that's a tape. It's an opera, called *Lots of Good Fish*. It just came out. Beth," Cory said, "let's meet tonight. I need to."

"I want to," Beth said, "but I can't. I'm with David, at his parents'."

"Oh," Cory said. "Well, how about tomorrow?"

"I'll have to see."

"Can you hold?" Again as Beth waited there was the same underwater fantasy. When the back door opened and Zellie appeared, a bag of groceries in each arm, Beth quickly hung up the phone. Too late she regretted it. Picking it up again, she was already cut off.

"Beth!" Zellie said. "What a nice surprise!" Despite her grin she looked sad, as if she had been squinting and preoccupied. Putting the groceries down on the table, she asked, "Where's David?"

"Upstairs," Beth said, standing up quickly. "I'll go get him."

In the attic she said, "David, let's go somewhere."

"What do you mean?" he asked, still bending into a box. "I have to get these old histology books. Thank God we never throw anything out."

"Driving," said Beth. "Or let's go walk in that park you like so much."

"Beth," he said, straightening up, "what's going on? You never like going outside."

"You see," she said, "I told you I'm changing. Let's go to where those soldiers lived."

"Where are you going?" Zellie asked, when they were downstairs again and putting on their jackets.

"We thought we'd go out for a while," David said.

"But I just got home," she said, following them. "I was hoping—where are you going?"

"To the park."

"Not to those horrible ducks?"

"Do you hate birds too?" Beth asked. "So does my mother."

"How is your mother?" Zellie asked, stopping them at the door.

Beth shrugged, and looked outside beyond the house, at the old snow on the lawn, at the dark pit of the pool. "She's okay," she said. "I don't speak to her too much. We're having our troubles."

"That's too bad," Zellie said, and stood aside, letting them pass.

In the park, David was lost. Men in tricorn hats were standing in the damp, thawing field, aiming their empty muskets and firing. Women in long skirts stood by a fire, stirring a caldron.

"It's not the same," he said, "since the bicentennial. All the roads are one way. And paved. When we grew up there were no signs. Here," he said, pointing to a lane of dirt and grass, "this used to be a road, it went right by the Wick house. You know about Tempe Wick, don't you? Now you have to walk to it."

"David," said Beth, not looking where he pointed, as they walked along. "I have something to tell you. I think there's something wrong with me."

"Something I don't know about?"

"David," she said, "I'm serious. I've been dizzy a lot."

"Are you pregnant?"

"Hardly. But that's what I wanted to talk to you about."

"This is where Tempe Wick lived," he said. "She hid her horse in the bedroom. We had a tradition of picking apples here in the orchard, before they put up the fence. Or maybe just once or twice—but it felt like we were starting a tradition. Now you can't go in there."

"Come on, David, why won't you listen to me? What if I'm dying?"

"Come on yourself."

"If something's wrong with me, you said we could have a kid."

"Nothing's wrong with you, Beth."

"Well, I'm going to the doctor about it. Will you come with me?"

"Of course," he said, and really looked at her for the first time. They were doctor's eyes, scrutinizing an object. "Are you serious?"

"Yes," she said, "and if I die, I want a huge memorial. Okay?"

In the house, Zellie put the groceries away and soaked two chickens in a pot, now that David had come home. It was a rare-enough event, with his new schedule—never sleeping, staying up all night, waiting in the emergency room, taking care of people. And psychiatry was no surprise to her, though she was glad of it. Less blood, she thought, fewer terrible things, although the stories David sometimes told her made her shudder. As for Beth coming with him this time, and not Andrew—the upstairs was far away, and whatever her children did, they did. She was glad not to know about it, not to ask questions. It was enough that they were there.

When the phone rang and Barbara spoke her name, Zellie was at first confused. She was looking for her daughter, Barbara said—was she there?

"Oh, *Barbara!*" Zellie said, remembering, and promised to give Beth the message. "I'm glad the children have found each other again," she said, after a moment.

"Yes," Barbara said.

"I mean, they're both so unusual, and—gifted."

"Yes," Barbara said, even lower.

"Do you think they're sleeping together?" There was no answer. "I mean, romantically?"

"Frankly," said Barbara, "I hope not. I think the whole thing is pretty peculiar. It's a shame," she said. "A terrible shame." She was crying.

"Oh, come on there, Barb!" Zellie said, clutching the phone and speaking confidently. She had suffered too much herself once not to help others now. "Really, you have to remember there's a lot that's worse in this world. That's for sure!"

"Oh, really?" Barbara said. "Like what?"

"Well," Zellie said. "You can start with my sister's son. He's dead."

Over the phone there was heavy breathing. "Would you ask Beth to call?" Barbara said. "I really have to go."

"Of course," Zellie said. "Of course. And Barbara, please call again if you want. Okay?"

"Of course," Barbara said, vehemently, as if Zellie had done her some good. "Of course!" And just as vehemently, she hung up the phone.

"Where do we get to sleep?" Beth asked, when they were at the house again. "In the big bed?"

"Actually," David said, "I wasn't planning on spending the night. I just wanted to get those books."

"Oh, but David! We have to! I canceled a date to come out here."

"I thought you canceled it anyway?"

"No," she said. "I expected we'd stay."

"Beth!" Zellie said, calling to them from the library. "Your mother called!" At the staircase she caught up with them.

"My mother!" said Beth. "I wonder why? Well," she said, dropping her head and looking dejected, "I guess I'll just wait and call her tonight, when we go back."

"Go back!" Zellie said. "You can't go back tonight—you just got here! I'm making chicken soup! Sol isn't even back yet from his meeting. I was hoping to get some time with you, David. Did you visit those swans?" She made a face, hissing like a swan.

"No," David said. "We went to the soldiers' huts instead. I don't care, Mom. I'll spend the night."

"Not if you don't want to," she said.

"No," he said. "I do. I do!"

At night, in the big bed, David called Andrew, and Beth called Cory, both of them murmuring and whispering and guessing at the meaning of each other's silence. "Did you tell him we're sleeping in the big bed?" Beth asked.

"Yes," David said.

"I don't know why you need permission. I slept here before he did. What did he say?"

"Not to do anything he wouldn't do."

"Isn't he clever."

David turned off the light, and they lay for a while far apart on either side of the bed.

"What's the matter?" Beth asked.

"Nothing. What's the matter with you?"

"Nothing. How come you're afraid to touch me?"

"Afraid? I'm not afraid, Beth. I'm just tired. How's Cory?"

"Fine," Beth said. "She loves me. She wants to marry me."

"Why don't you?"

"I told you why not. It's not what I want."

"How do you know? You like sex with her—and you don't with men."

"That's not true! Anyway, sex isn't everything, David. Other things are important in life as well. I don't even remember what I like, or what I don't like, for that matter."

"Do you like this?" David asked, rolling onto her and treating her roughly. She laughed and pushed him off.

"Is that what *you* like?" she asked. "With men?"

"Frankly," he said, "yes."

"Well, then," she said, "you can have it." And she rolled on top of him, tweaking and bumping.

"Oh, please!" he said, and not too long after she said the same thing to him, quietly this time in his ear.

IN THE PARK, you take your chances. Everyone does—the joggers, the kids on bikes, dog walkers, boys cruising for sex, drugs, or an easy bicycle, mothers with strollers and straggling firstborns, seniors from the East Side struggling in with walkers and nurses dark-skinned, bored, trusted, and leaned upon. This time David and Andrew come in behind the rat.

"It's real," David says, pointing with his chin, but Andrew is looking around at all the smiling spring, right off West Sev-

enty-second Street—flowers and trees, not to mention the jog-
ging men already stripped down to nothing at the first warm
breath.

"My God!" Andrew says a minute later. "What is that?—is
it real?"

"A rat," David says; its thick white tail hangs straight down
from the puff of white fur, nestled under the man's ear. The
man and a friend converse, ignoring the world, while three girls
clutch at each other and jump away. "A rat!" says one. "Oh,
my God!" And then the next: "That's so gross!"

"Is it real?" Andrew asks as they follow the path, the two
men and the rat still close ahead. But the tail finally curves up
affectionately; emerging from the fur, a rat face turns to nuzzle
up at the ear. "They're dangerous," Andrew says, "aren't they?"—
as a runner stops, pulls down his headphones and turns to them.

"A rat," he says, shaking his head in disgust. "That's just
great. All we need." And he disappears down the arbor. Casually, Andrew and David follow his sweaty back, thick with
muscle.

"Hey, homos!" shout some boys from the woods, but Andrew is looking back at the rat tail, still amazed.

"Hey, fairies!" they still shout, in a muffled way among
trucks accelerating and trees blocking the distance that mingles
with meaningless sounds near and far. They run a few feet,
excited, but then stop before the trees thin out. Too close not
to have been heard, they hang back cautiously, stay in the
woods. The two men arm in arm must not be timid, but either
challenging, or deaf—any closer and they might turn around
with men's faces, seeing only boys in the woods.

"Can you believe that?" Andrew asks, and David only shakes
his head no, meaning yes.

"You come from New Jersey," David says, "you know what
lurks in the woods"—and he gestures behind them to the boys.

You come from California, you have no idea. You think of palm trees, hummingbirds, geraniums blooming in winter. This— he assures Andrew, stroking his neck—is no disparagement. For such visions he was first in love; and still is. Even in a world of many desires, this is not a love to exchange.

Out on the street again, they are safe among the cars and roller skaters.

"Why do you think they do it?" Andrew asks.

"I don't know," says David. "For kicks. For a laugh. To get attention." Andrew smiles, nods, and takes David's hand in his own. "You know, Andrew," David says, "I don't think they think about it, till someone gives them trouble."

"You mean," Andrew says, "you think it's just a pet for them?" He looks straight ahead, his profile etched against the slight green of the trees, even as one of those big radios swings past and they are flushed in the sound. David's trial has been solitary: Andrew has seen only the rat. His innocence, David thinks, has saved them both many times, and so one last time he calls it perseverance, concentration, courage. You follow someone's gaze, but you can only guess.

At the bridge is the rat man again, his pet still on his shoulder, his friend at his side. Andrew turns to follow them into the Rambles, but David pulls him back. The path there is uneven, dark, hidden and roundabout, and suddenly David needs large spaces, the broad, open avenues where other couples wander into evening.

"Jason was mugged here," Andrew says, as if the Rambles did not evoke to them both, always, immediately, men standing in the shadows of the trees, waiting for sex. Every time they walk here Andrew says, as though he has just thought of it or as if either of them could have forgotten, "Jason was mugged here"—kicked many times in the face by boys no longer boys shouting "Faggot, faggot."

"Again?" David says.

"No, just that once. It was after dark, though. Is that why you won't go in?"

"I've been," David says, "—plenty." But Andrew knows this is not the truth; David found him early enough.

Andrew takes his arm, laughing. "David," he says, "you just want the rat man for yourself!"

They have come up to the meadow where only men lie down in the sun. It is April, though, late afternoon, and only a few have spread their blankets and tanning oil. Still, David hides behind a rock until Andrew scouts the field—this because of the banker, who spends his summers there. Because of him, and a year David hates to mention, he always hides at first behind this rock.

"Chicken," Andrew says, pulling him back. None of them, he says, are blond.

Up at the Great Lawn they stroll around five softball games and Brearley girls running races. Soon, passing them, a lady from the East Side grimaces, her still-young face contorting, fluid and frustrated. She would like to call out, to expostulate and share her disgust with someone else, anyone else—the rumpled old man on the bench, even those boys over by the tree, smiling at her for reasons of their own. But too quickly she is upon them, and there is nothing she can do but grunt, huff, and then she is gone behind them. David turns as she turns, returning her grimace. A mutter like hers, a shake of his head—an impotent victory.

"What?" Andrew says, hearing his grunt.

"Nothing," David says. "They're out to get us."

"Who?" he asks, and grandly David waves to the fields of baseball, to the old West Side couples, arm in arm like them, and even, immoderately, to the painters with their easels stuck in the grass by the castle pond.

"All of them?" Andrew asks, and David must concede here

and there a wink, a smile, a nod in passing which must mean thank you, bravo, God bless you.

But behind the museum are the rich kids hanging out, twenty in a row, leaning on the slanting glass around the Temple of Dendur. Arms outstretched behind their heads, or cotton skirts wrapped and held carefully around knees, they are skittish for entertainment, shouting and laughing for attention, even from a distance.

"Hey, now, cut that out!" yells one of them in a fatherly tone, and Andrew looks over that way. "Yes, you there!" calls the boy. "That's reprehensible, you know. You should be ashamed!" It is the big, handsome boy in a sweater vest and tie; David has not looked, only guessed by Andrew's incredulous stare.

"I can't believe it," Andrew says. "I mean, they're all smart, educated."

After an empty laugh, David kisses him on the cheek. "He's just feeling bad," David says. "College acceptance. Pimples."

"Inordinate interest in boys," Andrew says, recovering. "And young men holding hands!"

Near the carousel they find a bench beckoning and make their way there. "Ain't that sweet, now!" calls a voice, and then, still unheeded, the double whistle, ascending and descending, of sexual attention. And because Andrew is still just watching birds and little children, as innocent, as absorbed, David is ready to concede once again that perhaps the derision is a compliment: that any sexuality exposed to the world must incite and accept all other sexual response, all jeers, and release, and attraction.

"Turn around," Andrew says, "you won't believe this."

The rat man has returned, having wandered south through the Ramble while David and Andrew rambled north. He and his friend and his rat sit across from them on another bench now, face to face. The rat, sniffing and domestic on the bench, wanders timidly to the edge and then back. A gentle, innocent rat, David is thinking, when the rat man nods to him also, smiling perhaps because David has smiled at his rat. Nice rat, he is ready to call out, but stops himself. Instead he whispers to Andrew, "It looks like a nice rat."

Up the path come the whistlers, big boys on fast little bikes. "Rats!" they call out. "Rats!" and as they speed by they throw sand at the bench of the offending creature. The rat man jumps up, swearing, and his friend also, chasing them for a few steps before giving up, swearing, brushing off dirt.

On the bench there is still dirt, but the rat is gone. "Stewart!" calls the man, bending over the bench, over the leaves, shuffling through the prickers and the daffodils, calling, "Stewart—here, boy—Stewart!"

In the subway Andrew says little, hardly even reading the posters. David strokes his neck, holds his hand, but Andrew is strangely absent. "Look at that woman," David says. "Look at those two men!" and Andrew looks but says nothing, his expression alarmingly David's own, squinting from the nearness of pain.

"Can you imagine?" David asks. "All those flowers out in April? The dogwoods, the cherries? All those beautiful men, so naked?"

"I wonder about those boys," Andrew says.

"Forget it," David says. "They're harmless. They'll grow up and get married. They'll go to Harvard."

"No, the little ones," Andrew says. "In the woods. Did you notice? They start so young now."

"Andrew, Andrew," David says, rushing them above ground to the rush-hour traffic, afraid now of what he has wrought. "What was your neighborhood like when you grew up? Weren't there always little boys in the woods?"

"Yeah," he says. "It was great. We built forts and stayed there all day. It was a wonderful time."

"I'm sure!" David says, trying to obliterate what he has pointed out, erase it from memory and time. Next time, he swears, he hopes, he will be silent altogether. Coming home now in the sunset and sudden cold, it is only Andrew's hand, he thinks, that saves him. "It must have been a wonderful time!" he says, trying again, and this time Andrew seems to have recovered, and nods, reminiscing. There is still enough light left, after all, for a quick walk around the old neighborhood.

THE LITTLE ONE will never remember, is what Rose thought to herself when Zellie slammed the station-wagon door and walked around to the driver's side. Today her daughter walked, Rose could see, as if she carried a burden, almost stooping; but that was all right. When Rose was fifty, she remembered, she already felt like an old woman—more than thirty years had gone since then. Zellie snapped the seat belt across her own lap, then Rose's, and as they raced away from the apartment house Rose could again see each room, each corner she had filled one more time—the last time, it turned out—with the old chairs, the old tables, the pictures and the books. It was empty now; it had never really been their home. They had moved there knowing it would be the last one, knowing it would be the end. That was now. But at fifty, Rose remembered, she was still working eight, nine hours a day at the restaurant, her feet so swollen by five o'clock that she had to stand behind the counter in her bare feet. At least back then she could stand there; it had not really been what an old woman felt. *This* was what it felt like —helpless. It was not true what they said about old age; it was no good, it was a lie. And how many years had it been, working that hard, feeling trapped? At eighteen Max had gone to work at the hotel; at twenty Rose was pregnant. Before that she had slaved for her sister—"I need her, Mamma," Flora had said, and that was that, at sixteen she had moved away from her parents forever. Even now, with Flora so many years dead, it made her angry. "You put them to bed, Rosie," Flora had said, insinuating, smiling from the beginning. "You're so good at it." Still, you had to do what Flora said; she was like that. Anyway, she had done it, and here she was. At least her daughters were married to wealthy men, men who had gone to college and had half a chance. Already their children had children—Rose carried the pictures with her—though Esther, the little one, had been just a baby last time, and would not remember. But Rose remembered everyone, her parents, all her sisters, as if they were all still around somewhere, nearby and living; remembered old Esther Levin easily, fifty years dead, a strong woman, her mother-in-law, not the kindest, nor the wisest, but she might have lived longer. They had never much gotten along, now the child had her name. No, Rose thought, thinking of her mother-in-law, of her own great-grandchild, and of herself and Max as well, smiling from the beach in Miami—she remembered all of them better than pictures. Pictures never gave you the right feeling; they were always insincere, or tried to make something permanent out of a smile or a scene that had only lasted a second. And Max would never take a picture without someone in it, so Rose was always made to stand there smiling—by the Eiffel Tower, by the Spanish Steps, by the place in London where they cut off the heads. Now, with Max gone, she was left with those pictures of herself alone, all with the same happy face. She could remember how Max himself had looked at each different place, but he had been on the wrong side of the camera, and remembering was like seeing a ghost there, where no one else could see. Even so, she had saved all the pictures, labeled them, loaded up her carousel until flipping back and forth now there was no beginning and no end.

Past the old hotel now, under the bridge, past the old street, the store where the restaurant had been, past the town green, the nursing home where Ida was still lingering on, knowing no one, refusing to speak, too old to live, Rose listened as Zellie told her about the children, Warren's new job, Lonnie's paper on Soviet Jewry, David's new apartment, and Esther, Esther, Esther, the child still without a secret or a disappointment, though what could it be like for the child, a mother running off so much—it wasn't right. Neither liked to point out the old places, though sometimes, for a minute, they were both silent as they passed a street they both knew, and were remembering. Lewis Avenue was a shantytown once, black as pitch. Now there was a high-rise, a skyscraper, a Hilton hotel, right in Lewiston!—she could only shake her head. Beyond the town it was quieter, all gentile once, a picture postcard: the spare white church on the green lawn, the pond with weeping willows and a graveyard, the stop sign for the geese to cross the road.

When they reached Zellie's house, the child was playing in the sandbox, spending the weekend again since her parents' divorce.

"Look, Ma," Zellie said. "There's Esther!"

Rose knew it was just in case she had forgotten the name. But she had not. She was not that far gone, not yet. "What," she said, "is she all alone?" She opened the door and smiled at the girl, trying to summon the strength to get out of the car. For a while they stared at each other.

"Hello, dolly. Do you know who I am?" she asked, thinking that it must be some natural instinct that made her come up with a grandmother line like that.

"Of course she does, Mother. Esther, you know Ma Rose, don't you, sweetie. Come and give her a big hug." Esther dropped her plastic sand mill and walked over to the car.

"Wait a minute, dolly, I'll get out of the car." Esther watched with scared eyes as Rose hoisted herself around so that her legs hung down. "It's this knee!" she said, surprised that she had forgotten how to talk to children. "It just won't work!" In Miami everyone was old. The doorman had a grandson in college. Even the cockroaches were old.

"Wait, Mother—I'll be right there with the chair." Zellie hurried around to the trunk, pulled out the wheelchair, and quickly unfolded it. Meanwhile, Rose bent down and kissed Esther's soft cheek. On her tiny ears were the diamond earrings Rose herself had worn as a child, the earrings her own mother had given her when she was born. All her sisters had had their ears pierced when they were infants; but then the times were different. Her own daughters only had it done in college. Now she was shocked to see such a little girl with earrings.

"What are you doing, dolly?" she asked.

"Making a pie for the shark."

"Where's the shark?"

"Here. Everywhere. We're in the shark's mouth."

Rose looked around. Although the house was modern and stark, the apple trees were from an old, forgotten farm, heavy already with small green apples. It was not the scene from her balcony, the Atlantic shimmering and vast on three sides, but it was her daughter's home. This was family, and it was all, she knew, that finally mattered. Max had died quite suddenly, but she had been there with him, and he had known she would have the girls. In the night his feet had been cold, and she had spread out the afghan over both of them. Minnie had died in a hospital bed, no one sitting there but Rose. "Don't let them put me with Ida," she said, the day before, and Rose knew what she meant. "Mamma, Mamma, Mamma," she called in the night, and Rose had held her hand, saying "Shh, Minnie, shhh," and waited until morning to call Margie. There was a place, Rose knew, where Minnie was, where her other sisters were waiting for her as well; and her parents were there, and Max. She knew that now. Pearl had dreamed it that night, and Margie too. Flora was there, Pearl said, and Ruthie, and Vera, all of them laughing and laughing when Minnie came in. What were their lives? Not so great, not so much. But together they had always laughed and laughed, holding themselves and running to the bathroom. There was a funeral—Leonard's? Irv's?—when they had all laughed on the front lawn. Stanley had told jokes, and there was nothing anyone could do. Even Irv was there, Pearl said, in that place, waiting with them. No he wasn't, Margie said. My father wasn't there. Yes he was, Pearl said. Pearl was certain.

"Don't be scared, Ma Rose," said Esther. "Just kidding."

"Not with you, honey."

Esther took her hand, and with Zellie pushing they made their way slowly into the house. The first thing Rose saw was her priceless vase in the hall, filled with umbrellas. She touched the rim, where a fisherman still stared after a boat on the horizon. All through the years she had asked herself, Was it coming or was it going? In the living room she saw her blue Turkish rug and the painting she had lived with fifty years. "That's me," Max used to tell the girls, pointing to the wood gatherer walking home through the forest, laden with sticks.

Zellie quickly unpacked her mother's suitcase in the downstairs bedroom, and Rose found herself left alone to take a nap. In the room was her old maple bedroom set, and her sable coat hanging alone in the closet. For a while, lying in the single bed, she thought she was back in the house in Newark, although never once in those years had it ever been so quiet, nor had anyone ever lain down in the middle of the day. There was bread to bring to the baker, meat to deliver, laundry to pick up from the Chinaman. "Chinky chinky Chinaman, eatie eatie rats!"—and the girls had all run off, laughing hysterically; secretly, even still, it made her laugh. And the Italian ladies, picking up after their dogs on the sidewalk, putting it right in their aprons! (For their gardens, someone said.) After school, after the long walk across town two miles rain or shine, there were sweet potatoes warming in the oven, and a few minutes in the kitchen with their mother, leaning over too tired in her chair, sewing a button.

Now the afternoon light filtered into the air, green from the trees, and cool because it was September. In Miami the light was burning hot, and they would never go out during the day in summer. Then, around five o'clock, Max would squeeze orange juice and they would sit together on their balcony, already dressed up for dinner, admiring their view of the ocean. Rose didn't know what time Zellie made dinner, nor what time Sol would come home, nor what time she should sit up and press the buzzer for Zellie to come and help her onto the chair.

They had chosen Miami because it had seemed, thirty years before, when they had first spent a week or two, exotic and warm and friendly enough to Jews. Max in the end had talked about Haifa, now that they had some money, but they knew Miami, and Israel was not their home. Still, every year at the seder, at the end after "Next year in Jerusalem!" he had winked and squeezed her hand under the table. There was a picture somewhere (George, Max's brother, used to have it) of a village someplace in Europe, where they had come from, the Levins —or not the Levins but Esther's family. That, Esther said, was their home; her own mother had painted it, along with the old man in the woods. For years the two had hung side by side; now there was only the old man. The other half, his village, was gone, bombed out during the war, and the only proof was a picture. Rose had asked for it in a letter, offered to pay money—for years it was sitting in a basement. Oh no, Lily had said, it's valuable, we're saving it. But Lily, said Rose, it's in the basement, let's put them together for a while, our side and your side. Oh no, Lily said, it's valuable, Rose, it's George's grandmother as well. So there it sat, in a basement. These days she thought more and more of that missing scene, that village, evocative to her though it had no people in it and was not even her own family. But it was Max's family, his grandmother's work, and it had become hers too; now all of them were gone.

The green-brown of that picture made her smile, coming so vivid in her mind. It was the same as the light outside the window now, which overlooked a field with a stone wall. The light here was so rich and soothing, after all the electric lights, the staying up late for a week to sit *shivah*, so many people in when all she wanted to do was sit quietly somewhere, alone with family. Lena was her friend of fifty years, and yet even Lena was too much. It wasn't family. There had been so many, and she could hardly breathe, no one looking in her eye, seeing death there in her as well. Now she wanted to breathe in more than she actually could, wanted to absorb all the color and the September shade, and the peacefulness of living in the country again, away from concrete. There was too much—the smell of crushed acorns on the driveway, the real blond of the child's hair—and she was glad, now, to be lying quietly. Just when things were desirable, they might begin to slip away.

When she opened her eyes, it was already dark. She jerked her head but couldn't sit up. Then she remembered: push up first with the elbows, then slide to the side. She could smell Zellie's cooking; there was chicken, onions. Recently she had stopped cooking; it had become too much, although Max still had put the eggs and the beater in front of her at the table, pretending she could help. She pushed the little buzzer, and instantly Zellie ran in.

The house was mostly without steps, and she found she could wheel herself anywhere—even, if she chose, outside to the pool. But in the living room she stopped, just in front of the big painting of the woodcutter. Zellie had always liked it best. More than anything else the two girls had fought over it, though it would never be worth much, and in the end Pearl had given in. Rose loved it too, though she was glad to be free of it now; it had hung over her too many years. How old were those real twigs the old man carried! She had often thought she would like to give out everything to the children before she died, so she could feel before it was over not only that the girls were appreciative of her things but that she was free of them. When it was the end she wanted to be as light as air, held down by nothing, not crying for her own mother fifty years too late. Even without Max it would be easier now. She liked the idea of being unshackled, purified. Then there would be no bickering. Already, before Minnie died, Danny had called up Margie in the hospital, and they were fighting, fighting.

Esther came into the room and timidly hugged her hand.

"How are you, dolly?"

"Fine, Ma Rose."

"Do you know who that is in the picture?" Rose asked, and Esther shook her head no. "That's your Poppy Max. That's what he looked like when he walked home through the woods."

Esther looked up to the picture, wide-eyed as though she were frightened of the dark woods, the web of branches. Then she looked at Rose, and Rose wondered if it was right to have lied like that. Children remembered; she certainly knew that much. Turning back to the painting, she reached up to switch on its brass light, which reflected so much on the canvas that the painting itself looked black.

"There, Lonnela, how's that?"

"I'm Esther."

Rose looked at her and pulled her close to her, up against the metal of the chair. "I'm sorry, Esther, I just made a mistake." In her ears were Rose's diamonds. Her hair was the same gold as her mother's, but the eyes staring at her were Rose's eyes, and her face was round like Lonnie's, like Zellie's, like her own.

Rose felt her own earlobes. For years she had worn only clip-on earrings; she was not even sure if her others would go through her ears anymore. "Let's look at my jewelry box," she said, and wheeled herself into the bedroom, Esther pretending to push. Esther sat on the bed, next to the padded box, and took out some necklaces that interested her. She smelled the coral flowers and pulled a string of false pearls through her fingers. Rose found the velvet pouch where she kept her own diamond earrings. She let them slide out into her palm.

Esther stopped and was watching her. "Look," she said, turning her head for Rose to see, "those are like mine." She reached down into another felt pouch. Rose's diamonds were not merely chips; they were the size of Esther's earlobes. If she gave them to the girl, she would have to find something else for Pearl's new infant. Boy or girl, it was expected soon—though perhaps not soon enough, everything coming too late now, taking too much time. The boy would be a father, and already Pearl was anxious for equal treatment. "I know it's not the first one, Ma," she had said, waiting for an answer; but what could Rose have said? Rivalries started like that, and sisters at fifty and sixty were still vengeful because of what happened at five. Her girls were not speaking to each other, had hardly said a word when their father died, though they hugged each other and organized the food. Vera long ago had gone to her grave still jealous because Lottie, two years younger, had won a contest. Sixty years after, there were still words, and worse. Somewhere in the box was an opal she could leave to the other one.

"Would you like to try these on?" she asked, holding one of the earrings by its wire.

Esther nodded, seriously, and stood up from the bed. Rose slipped the hooks through the holes in Esther's delicate ears. "They're heavy!" Esther said, rotating her head to make them swing. Then she went over to the mirror to examine herself. The diamonds, Rose could see, were much too big for such a little girl; she would have to keep them with Zellie. Quickly

Esther took them off, impatient to try on the flowers. Rose was clasping her own naked earlobes when Zellie came in.

"Were you trying to rest, Mother?" Zellie asked, straightening the pillow. "I'll take her away."

"No, we were just trying some things on for size. Would you help me a minute?" She held out her diamond earrings, and Zellie took them, trying to find the spot on her mother's ears.

"Mother," Zellie said after a moment, "they won't go through. The holes have closed."

"Push it through," Rose said.

"I can't," Zellie said, and started to cry. With her arm she brushed away a tear. She tried again but then stopped. "Mother, I'd have to go through the skin."

But Rose insisted, assuring her it didn't hurt very much. Her eyes were closed, and she was seeing colors behind her eyelids she hadn't noticed in a long time.

"Push, Zel, I used to wear them every day." She would leave them to Esther. But for now, while she still had to look cheerful and pretend to care what people thought of her, she would try to wear them again. They were her fortieth anniversary present from Max, whose card, signed as always "Your Loving Husband, Now and Forever," she still had in her drawer. Already they pulled on her earlobes, but she wanted to remember. That she wanted more than anything else.

Zellie sighed, with relief or disgust. The hook finally poked through, pushing out fifteen years of powder and whatever else could collect in an ear. With a tissue and some alcohol she wiped away the dirt. "There!" she said, trying to smile in front of her mother, wiping her eyes again, and right away took up the other one of the pair.

Rose opened her eyes, remembering the weight, and already in the mirror she could see the difference the jewel had made. "There!" she said, turning her head slightly to make it swing.

. . .

BETH WOKE UP feeling nauseated, moaning into her pillow.

"I know what it is," said Cory, turning onto her side to observe. "You're hating yourself again."

"No," Beth said, shaking her head.

"Yes," Cory said, "you can't stand people thinking you're a lesbian, and the whole thing seems disgusting."

"No, no," Beth said.

"Oh dear," Cory said, and rolled onto her own pillow, hiding her face. "How do you think that makes me feel, making love to you? I love you, I love loving you, I love to touch you."

"Cory, it's not that." Beth held Cory's hand, stopping her caress.

"And you think touching me is disgusting. I *feel* disgusting. Every morning I wake up, I'm never sure which it is—if you think it's disgusting or not, if you love me or not."

"I do!" Beth said, pulling Cory's arm around her head. "I can't believe it, but I think I'm really happy with you. It's true, Cory. I don't care anymore."

"Then what is it?"

"Well," Beth said, "how do you think it feels if you're pregnant?"

"I wouldn't know."

Beth couldn't help but agree; still, thinking back on all her long store of discomfort—experienced, imagined, or empathized—she had to admit that she didn't know, either.

"I think," Cory said, "you get a flush, and a happy outlook on the world."

"Cory," Beth said, "you're thinking of cocaine," but really she was pressing herself for some sign of another life.

Cory sat up, watching. "Does this mean you think it's possible?"

"Well, I don't know," Beth said, and moved closer to her, taking her arm one more time. "David and I were fooling around, just as a joke, but it was nothing much."

"Nothing much! What does that mean?"

"You know," Beth said, feeling for the first time the elder, the stronger. Cory's face was all worry. "No great waves breaking upon the shore," Beth said. "No ecstatic waterfall."

Cory looked at her both confused and suspicious, not responding.

"We were just playing around, Cory. We didn't have intercourse or anything. At least, I don't think so. I didn't even have an orgasm. Of course."

Hearing those uncomfortable words of sex, meant more for silence than for speech, Cory jumped as if jolted out of bed, quickly pulling on her clothes. "As far as I know," she said, her face suddenly flushed, "that's not essential."

"Oh, Cory! David didn't either! It wasn't anything! It might be from Glen, anyway. From before."

Relenting, Cory fell back again onto the bed, half-dressed, half-undressed, and climbed gratefully into Beth's own grateful arms.

"Cory," Beth said, "maybe I'll get pregnant and we'll move to Paris together. Wouldn't it be too much, walking down the street with our little French daughter? Monique?"

"Ours?" Cory asked.

"Of course. Oh, David would get her sometimes too. Wouldn't you like that?"

Cory nodded, or else just buried her face deeper into Beth's shoulder. Perhaps, Beth wondered as they clung together, not needing words, she really was pregnant. Suddenly the word, the expression, the state of being made her laugh.

"What?" Cory asked, and Beth shook her head but continued

laughing. Herself pregnant! Even to Beth herself the picture was too funny.

But in laughing so well, alone on her bed when Cory had run out late for work, she found herself pressing her hand to her belly again and, ceasing to laugh, was quickly amazed. For the first time, she could hear that "pregnant" was not merely an idea, an aesthetic change when slim and single had ceased to amuse. Even the sound of it—the round, enlarged vowels, the awkward, abundant consonants—reminded her that what she had laughed at was something amazing, something fortunate and enriching. It was not ridiculous, she decided, jumping up to examine herself, naked, in the mirror; it was lucky, it was probable, it was welcome, and even, now that she thought for a moment, it was expected. She would be beloved, accepted, smiled at by the world. She would be touched by women on the street, protected and adored by men, caressed and indulged by her mother. She was normal; she was fertile; she could create what she had conceived. Even love—and here, wondering to whom she was most bound by love, she looked around the mess of her room, and through the dirty windows, the dirty city, beyond which had to be a better, richer, more understandable life—even love fell short of this. A woman loved her—a woman she loved. Now she could love women; now she could love whom she pleased. What now would she lack? And she thought of David, whom she had loved first, and longest, and who was bound to her now most of all—he was almost herself. And her mother, too, was herself; in the mirror there was a nose she recognized, and familiar eyes, and a round face she had seen as an infant, and a body that already was taking the shape of its destiny: her mother's round shoulders, her same breasts, her long legs. All of these loves she felt coming together as one in the life inside her, the second life that would grow into a separate being, her child, their child together—all of them.

She reached for the phone, cradled it on her neck—but who

to call first? David? Her mother? She hung up, pulled on her bathrobe that had been David's, and ran to find her roommate, Lynn.

"What's so funny?" Lynn asked. She was lying with her head back in a tub full of suds.

"Why don't you guess."

Lighting a cigarette and closing her eyes again, Lynn suggested, "Your mother's coming."

"No," Beth said. "But close. I'm pregnant."

The cigarette dropped into the suds. "Amazing. How did that happen, pray?"

"Oh, come on, Lynn. You can remember all that stuff, can't you?"

"I suppose, though it's foggy. Don't you need a male member of some sort?"

"Yes," Beth said, and more shyly added, "It's David."

"Well, well, well," Lynn said, sliding down again into the tub. "How did that happen? Or should I say *why*?"

"Why?" Beth shrugged her shoulders. "It just sort of did."

"Well," Lynn said, "you can move pianos."

"What do you mean?"

"My mother always moved pianos. Most of the time it worked. Not with me, though. She couldn't shake me. I guess I really wanted to be born—ha!"

"Oh, Lynn," Beth said, ready to find some kind word, some gesture of love for one who was sure that no lesbian was ever breastfed, and who still struggled, in everything she did, in love, in work, for her mother's withheld affection. Once Beth had hated herself as much; now, already, she could help another.

But Lynn stopped her. "I have a good doctor," she said. "Three abortions—I got to know her pretty well. I almost asked her out."

"No thank you," Beth said. "I might keep it."

For the first time Lynn really opened her eyes. "Beth!" she said. "Can you see yourself pregnant?"

Beth simply shrugged her shoulders and said, "Yes, easily. I *am* pregnant. Anyway, I've always known I'd keep it." Impressed with her own words, she drew back. She had spoken impetuously and she knew it—but who could be sure of acting otherwise?

Lynn was staring at her, vaguely aware that some challenge had been made, and met, and was wondering just how much had been truth. "And you have no money," she said. "Oh, well, I guess the daddy's got a bundle. But who's going to be the mother?"

"Lynn, what is that supposed to mean?"

"Just that—who's going to take care of it?"

"Both of us," Beth said, confidently, thinking back with relief on David's rare willingness, or at least his ability. "We might all raise her—Cory and me, and David and Andrew."

"Beth," Lynn said, "why do you need a baby so much? It's not going to change anything."

"I know," Beth said, shrugging despite herself, and sorry already to have spoken so soon. Now they were apart, adversaries somehow across a gulf.

"So," Lynn said, and suddenly rose, like Neptune, dripping and powerful from the tub, "will I be looking for another roommate, or will the whole family just move in here?"

"Oh, I never really thought of that."

"Well, think again. And meanwhile, you better go buy one of those kits. It's easy," Lynn said, wrapping her wet hair into a turban. "They turn blue if you're knocked up."

"Oh no," Beth said, holding her head. "And have the man at the counter leer at me? I can't bear to, Lynn—wouldn't you go buy it for me?"

"Can't—I have to rush off. Go yourself, it's no big deal."

"Sure," said Beth, almost to herself, as she left Lynn to her powders and perfume. "That's what you think." And after dressing, slowly, carefully choosing her clothes as if for an appointment, she made her own way down five flights of stairs, dreading every lonely echo of her steps, but excited as well about that dazzling color blue, the sure sign of a future she could already see.

NOTHING WAS OUT of place in the corner bedroom. When the sun pushed through the curtains, nothing stirred except a thousand particles of dust, swimming up as if a community of little life had been awakened at the bottom of the sea. The channel of light reached across to a chair behind the door, old now but once a coveted seat in a rich living room. The gold print was faded, the high cushion was depleted; but these were the very marks of comfort. Here late-night vigils had been waited out, lighted with one small lamp. Here novels had been read to the end, and letters read and reread in the privacy of late hours. Beneath the chair the light fell upon the carpet so that a dark wedge stretched out behind one of the mahogany legs, as though it were hiding from the light. Nothing was out of place, except perhaps those few irregularities which from long and silent stasis had assumed a sort of propriety: a book leaned casually against the clock; one curtain was higher than the other; the bedspread was creased with a frozen whirlpool where someone had sat and turned, away from the collection of plastic ships on the dresser, in order to look out the window.

But what could have been seen? What change in the little square of trees and sky would have been peculiar or sudden enough to fill up the white frontier of the eyes and cause someone to look? The window beside the bookcase looked out high above the backyard, where the huge folds of green which were trees shimmered and swelled as if they were green waves in a vast ocean. Several times during the day a cloud might have blown into the fragmented blue space between branches and so have muted the light, and then the cloud might have lumbered off or dissolved so that the brightness would pour into the room again as if the ceaseless peaks of green were indeed a sea, and a tide had been held back and then released. If it had been five or six o'clock in the morning and the empty hours had been spent with open though ill-attentive eyes, the blackened and reflective window might have been lanced suddenly by a needle of sunlight; or else, because attention wanders and consciousness is half dreams anyway, the window might have brightened and expanded into an image of the backyard at dawn, as if the dark room were a conjurer, and the window itself a crystal ball.

Most of the time there was no one to watch as the light swept across the room throughout the day, slipping eventually from the confines of the one window by the bookcase, and sliding gently back into the room by an afternoon window above the desk. When the last touch of light had slipped from the curtain, and the shadows like a pool had quivered and settled, the long row of books clarified from the dimness. *Know Your Dalmatian* was visible, and *Cornfield's History of New Jersey*, and two letters of the *Golden Encyclopedia*, as though all of them had slept through a shyness of light and now stared out into space.

But there was nothing to see, now that the light had gone and the room was sunk far below the surface, where objects were immovable and could only have undulated in the depths. The spaces under the chair and under the dresser were indistinguishable from the greater spaces. Underneath the bed were boxes of games and a rolled-up map of Magellan's voyage, and a strong box with a broken lock, filled with childish treasure: a fossilized snail, an English shilling, a photograph of a girl at the beach with something written across the back, though the words might not have been written there, inside the box being quite black. Even the carpet was a dull desert of gray, stretching endlessly from wall to wall. The gloom had rubbed out entirely the patterns etched there, the various swirls and stains and ruffled patches where someone's foot must have brushed it the wrong way. A black spot a little way out from the bed was the only disruption of the monotony. It reflected differently, it was much denser, and it could not be picked up by the vacuum. (Irene, who cleaned there, had seen it once, and bent down to try and scratch it out—it was a crayon, ground into the carpet in an act of vengeance—but when she was on her knees, and felt the smooth wax under her nail, and saw the box of treasure under the bed, she began to cry.) Dull as it was, it picked up the light more than the surrounding carpet, and glowed in a limited way when the afternoon light crept through the window over the desk, spreading like rich liquid through the dust.

All the shadows reappeared, all the contours and contrasts which in the morning had shrouded some objects and thrust others into the light. Some of them filled up the spaces they had left, and others clung like mirror images to the opposite sides of things: the other side of the bed, the other sides of picture frames. Mesmerizing patterns reappeared in the carpet along the sweep of light, byways and flourishes which, if the carpet had been a desert, would have been taken for designs and messages from above. The row of books sank back into shadow now that there was the contrast of light. The curtains which in the morning had hung diaphanous and lively were now opaque and still. Shadows grew longer, shadows behind books, out-of-the-way shadows which no one could have seen.

Quite suddenly there was a shuffle and the rumble of voices, and the door swung open, violent in the stillness as if there had been a terrible natural disaster, though the sound had been almost nothing. Esther was holding on to the doorknob and looking back at another child, her cousin.

"And this was Matthew's room," she said. Then she shut the door and they raced back down the stairs. Underneath the old chair the afternoon light was spreading out the other way, and the shadow reappeared, a dark wedge stretching up toward the window.

"WHERE IS HE?" Pearl asked, looking under her dining-room table, which was piled already with fluted porcelain coffee cups and silver forks and cake plates, and also noodle pudding, coffee cake, even a brisket and apple pies—all the holiday foods friends and relatives had prepared months in advance, in times of joy and plenty, for just such sadder times as these.

"I don't know," Zellie said, also pretending to look around the room. "He's with Esther somewhere. I'm sure they're all right." They could talk to each other, could stand intimately side by side during all the last hours, but they could not look into each other's eyes. For a moment they stood with nothing to say; and looking up, where each would see her mother's eyes looking back in a sister's face, seemed inevitable.

"As long as they were alive," Pearl said, taking some relief in merely talking, "we were always someone's children, someone's daughter. Now," she said, and shrugged, "we're just mothers, wives." She frowned, not to cry.

"And sisters, Pearl," Zellie said.

"Yes, I know, Zel," Pearl said. "Also sisters."

Then Esther and Joshua slid down the stairs, bumping down step by step. "There he is," Pearl said.

"Who?" Zellie turned and saw them.

"The first great-grandson. I wish Mother could have gotten to know him better."

"Oh, well," Zellie said, trying even now to sound cheerful,

and for a moment they were both silent, waiting for the children, before another word could come, good or bad, to make them cry.

"I told you they're okay," Zellie said. "She takes care of him, Pearl."

"All right, Zel. I believed you."

"All right, Pearl."

"Irene!" Pearl called into the kitchen. "Is there coffee yet? I'm dying!"

"It's coming," called Irene from the kitchen. "I think."

"Grandma," said Esther, running over.

"Grandma," said Joshua.

"Excuse me," Pearl said, strangely formal, and, pulling Joshua up into her arms, left Zellie alone in the room with Esther, whose blond hair, curly now, had come loose from its braid. Zellie tried to fix it, but stopped after a moment and stroked Esther's head.

"What would you like to eat, honey?" Zellie asked, picking up a plate. "Do you want some noodle pudding? Have you had any supper?"

Obediently Esther took the plate and made her way to the food, afraid suddenly of the daughter's grief behind her grandmother's struggling smile. But Zellie had already done her crying—at least, she thought, for the day—and she kept her hands on Esther all the while, stroking her hair, kissing her head. It was the others now coming in who would cry, large-eyed and ready to hug her or at least kiss her cheek if she would let them. At each embrace, however, she froze, as if letting go into someone's arms she would melt entirely and there would be nothing left. Or rather it felt already that there was nothing left, that already she was a burnt silhouette of her old, usual self; instead of sensitive, vulnerable, responsive at each approach and possibility, she was dull, brittle, almost nonexistent.

She could stand against the wall now and no one would notice her; they would walk right past. Her mother had had a long life, a good life, a beloved life; and we must say goodbye without calling it a tragedy. For so long she and Pearl had been daughters, had been children of—and now they were not. They were parents, they were wives, they were sisters, but daughters they were no more. They had had many years of that blessing. But no more. Their own mother had had less.

Gloria and Harry came into the room, kissed Esther, kissed Zellie. Harry's face, though lined, was still handsome, and his hair, though pure white, was still full. Without speaking, he held Zellie for a moment. Then, pulling back, he winked. "Who's the little princess?" he asked, picking Esther up in his arms.

"Esther," Esther told him, as he carried her into the living room.

Gloria, newly thin, and smooth-cheeked as if she were young again, unwrapped a brisket, set it on the table. She stood with Zellie, watching him.

"I was so in love with him, you know, Gloria."

Gloria continued smiling.

"I mean," Zellie said, "when I was seven."

"Oh," Gloria said, and laughed. "Everybody was in love with Harry."

"But at your wedding, I mean. You were both so beautiful, walking down the aisle. I thought, that's what I want, to be you, to have Harry. It seemed impossible."

"I'll tell you, Zel, it *was* impossible."

"I wanted to touch you both, hold you both. We were afraid you'd leave us."

They both nodded, remembering.

"That was before my mother died. I guess I might have, otherwise."

"I'm glad you didn't," Zellie said, her eyes full of tears, but it was not about Gloria that she would cry, nor this simple, single memory. As she reached for the tea across the table, she spilled the small pitcher of milk and merely watched as the milk absorbed quickly into a dark stain, spreading beneath the candle. Was there nothing more? she wanted to ask her cousin, who had been so beautiful, so important. Nothing more to say? Nothing more to remember than this moment, fleeting, insubstantial?

"Oh, Zel," Gloria said, wiping away a tear herself. "Now you have something to cry about."

"Let's go in," Zellie said. "I think they want to start."

"They?" Gloria said. "Zel, who's 'they'? You're 'they.' We'll start whenever you want."

Zellie nodded, smiling, but couldn't think what she meant. Anyway, Gloria kissed her, and they made their way into the living room.

Beth was sitting in a corner with Aunt Ruthie, both of them in stiff folding chairs. When Zellie came up to them, Beth offered up her seat and hurried toward David.

"She just said I could live with her if I wanted," Beth said. "And paint in the barn. She kissed me, and told me she'd like someone like me around. Where does she live?"

David thought a moment and remembered. "Near the duck pond," he said.

"You mean here in Lewiston?"

He nodded, and Beth shook her head. "Oh, well," she said. "I guess that's that."

For a while they stood, as if looking around for a place to go. Andrew sat with Lonnie on the sofa, talking, pretending not to watch them.

"She said she doesn't like her grandson much. Maybe she'll leave her fortune to me."

"Maybe," David said, meeting, for an instant, Andrew's glance.

"David," Beth said, taking his arm suddenly, "let's go somewhere."

"Where? They're about to begin."

"I don't know!" she said, and released him, shrugging as if surrendering some unspoken contention. "You know," she said, whispering, "I thought I was pregnant."

"You did!" David said, too loudly. "By who?"

"By you, David." In her squint there was anger hidden, and already the welling up of tears.

"Oh, come on, Beth. What are you talking about? We didn't do anything."

"Thanks a lot."

"I mean—" he said, leading her by the elbow, "—you know what I mean." They made their way through the crowd to the porch, which overlooked the backyard, and beyond it the marsh. "Beth," David said, "come on. I just mean not anything to get pregnant over."

"I guess not," she said, quietly now that she had him, no longer challenging, and sat down on the plastic love seat like his mother's—the other of Rose's old set. "Do you think, though, we ever will?" she asked, and then added, "have a child?"

David looked away, out the windows, over the marsh, at the setting sun, thinking of what to think about. His grandmother was dead; he had stayed away when he might have come home, made a difference, helped her, somehow, to feel better. Now it was too late; but even before now it had seemed too late, all of her long afternoons that could not be filled up. From him there had come no letters, no phone calls, no connection that now was impossible. Why had he hidden, why refrained? He shrugged, turned his head, and sighed as if struggling for an answer. Beth was waiting, as if after a word perhaps they could marry, have children, love whom they wanted to love and still love each other. The questions were too grand, life and death hovering always nearby, touching others but never touching them. Could they follow along the family's path, he wondered, or would their own way, even together, lead them too far ever to return?

"I don't know, Beth," he said, and shrugged. "I just don't know." And as if that were it, the final, crystallized, struggled-for answer, he sat down next to her and, from his own side trying to push both of them evenly, they rocked.

"We better go inside, Beth," he said. "It's time to begin. Anyway, I don't want to leave Andrew alone."

"He's not alone, David," she said, following him inside. "He's sitting with Lonnie." But inside, they could see Andrew had given up his seat to Zellie and now sat in the corner where Beth had been. David hurried over to him.

Aunt Ruthie was watching silently, and for once Andrew too was silent.

"You okay?" David asked.

Rather than answer, Andrew shrugged, several times, staring across the room until David tried to take his hand, which he pulled away just before anyone saw.

"What?" David said quietly, not wanting an answer.

Andrew looked away from him.

"Excuse me, young man," Ruthie said, "but do you have green eyes?"

"Yes," Andrew said, looking down immediately into his lap.

Ruthie peered down to see his eyes, and her own then opened wide, her thin, penciled eyebrows arching high above them. "I'm ninety years old," she said.

"Really!" Andrew said, looking up, trying to smile. "You don't look—" For once he didn't know how to finish.

"Do you know," Ruthie said, "all my life I've read about heroes with green eyes, and I never believed it. Finally I've met a hero with green eyes. Now I believe it."

Andrew shook his head. "I'm not a hero," he said.

"That's not true," David said, tugging at Andrew's arm until the muscles tightened. He let it go.

"All my life," said Aunt Ruthie, still looking Andrew in the eye, and shaking her head. "Now I can believe it."

Stevey was standing behind her, and quickly came forward. "Ruthie," he said, "I have green eyes myself. Haven't you ever noticed? I think my eyes are green, that is—aren't they? Big Josh has green eyes, anyway. Hey, David, tell her—don't you think my eyes are green?"

The rabbi stood up by the piano, a young new assistant rabbi whom no one knew very well, and who was still addressed, even privately, as "Rabbi." The old rabbi, who for so many years had led them all through worship, celebration and grief, had fled quickly to Florida the year before in a flurry of adultery and divorce. Lonnie herself, it was said, might have led the service: she was not yet ordained but had completed her degree; she would be a rabbi herself one of these days, to her family's surprise and unending amusement. Two years in the Peace Corps had made her once again suburban, the heat of the African desert returning her, like others before her, to her deeper roots.

She might have led the service, but she refused, in grief at first, crying at the news, and later in more familial dread— they would only criticize, and mock her the more. So she sat with her mother, holding her hand, supporting where for too long, perhaps, she had been supported, reciting the Hebrew perfectly, with feeling, and all the time shaking her head at the old translations.

" 'We fervently pray,' " said the young man, looking up at the family he didn't know, showing off, Lonnie saw, that he had memorized the words, " 'that the day may come when all men shall invoke Thy name, when corruption and evil shall give way to purity and goodness, when superstition shall no longer enslave the mind, nor idolatry blind the eye, when all who dwell on earth shall know that to Thee alone every knee must bend and every tongue give homage. O may all, created in Thine image, recognize that they are brethren, so that, one in spirit and one in fellowship, they may be forever united before Thee. Then shall Thy kingdom be established on earth and the word of Thine ancient seer be fulfilled: The Lord will reign forever and ever.' "

"This is too much," Lonnie whispered, shaking her head. "It's so old-fashioned, Mother. And sexist."

"It's how they always said it here. Since I'm a girl. It makes me feel better."

"I should have read the Kaddish, at least, myself. The real translation."

"Maybe you should have, then."

" 'Make us to know Thy ways that in our love we may triumph over grief and despair. Calm Thou our troubled spirits that athwart our tears may arch the rainbow of Thine eternal promise. Praised be Thou, O Lord, who comfortest the mourners. Amen.' "

All around, the family said "Amen," and waited a moment, trying not to turn, not to breathe or make a sound or move beyond the silence, as if something more might still come from it—a silence more definite, more profound, more eternal. But soon there was movement. There was sound.

Lonnie turned violently in her seat, still holding her mother's hand. "What's he talking about?" she whispered. " 'Athwart'!"

"I don't know, honey," Zellie said, no longer crying, trying to smile. "But I like 'the rainbow of His eternal promise.' That's nice."

"I guess," Lonnie said, crossing her arms and her legs. " 'Athwart'!" she said, snorting up toward the ceiling. In a few minutes the service was over, and Lonnie hurried toward the food, away from any incipient condescension. But the dining room was crowded as well. Teddy sat with his nephew, playing with the grapes. Mel was slicing turkey, and Stevey piled it on the platter. Lonnie soon found her brothers, huddling with their plates and eating in silence. How long would it go on? How soon could they sneak home?

Margie came up to them, wiping her eye with a napkin, and all three of them turned slightly away before she was upon them, insisting no doubt that they cry with her. But she only pointed to the table. "Try the turkey," she said. "Have you had some? Twenty pounds—it could feed an army! Warren, you'll have some, won't you?"

"Sure," Warren said, nodding affectionately, the only one of them to speak.

Lonnie turned farther and was suddenly among more of her aunts. "I swear it's true," Pearl said, starting to laugh though trying to whisper. "She owns the whole plantation, slave quarters and all. She told me the whole story! They're apartments now, she said, but the whole family lives in the big house— her parents, her oldest kids, and all the sisters' kids."

"Who?" Lonnie asked.

The women were laughing, but Gloria turned to her for a moment. "Irene!" she said, and laughed again, her mouth wide open, a hand on her breast. "She bought a plantation!"

From the living room, Zellie heard them laughing and was sure, turning her head to hear better, that she must be imagining it —that the voices she heard were the women in Pearl's dream, all her dead aunts laughing in a room somewhere at something Flora had said, all of them waiting for their sister. Could it be? She knew exactly what it would sound like, and this was it— these raucous, breathless, almost tearful laughs, the sighs trailing off at the end, of disbelief, of relief from hysteria. But the laughter continued, and Zellie was holding on to a real chair in her sister's living room; this time it had to be real. In the kitchen, the memorial candle was already lighted. She hurried around the corner, then into the dining room. There was Pearl, laughing, Gloria, Margie, and her own children around the table, rather than anyone dead. They were laughing about she didn't know what—it was odd, but it was all right, it was real. It was not anyone dead.

But which of them, she still wondered, pouring herself some tea, would be next?—remembering, as she looked around, that anyone in that room could disappear from them, even herself, could sicken and die and then, looking around again, there would be one less familiar voice, familiar face. "You've got to hold on, Ma," she had said. "There's a lot of people depending on you. "I'm trying!" Rose had said. "I'm trying to hold on." Could there be a world without her mother? Of course there could be, there would be, there already was, as there would be a world without herself. That she could easily imagine. No ghost would remain, no chair would stay empty, no space open up; only a small flame left in the kitchen. Which one would it be? Rose herself might still walk into the room—Zellie felt the possibility, the scene was that ordinary—slowly, cheerfully despite her cane or walker, merely old, struggling but not yet bedridden, not helpless; speaking cheer, whispering curses; as she had finally succumbed. Even Lena Carp, in the end, had not escaped, finally, from that old, well-hidden wrath, Lena who had stood with Rose at Planned Parenthood, who had moved to Florida to be near her, who all those years had bridged with her that gulf between Jew and gentile. "I never trusted her," Rose said. "Where do you think she got all that silver? Solid forks, solid knives, everything silver. You think that didn't come from her neighbors in Europe? The minute they took them away. No wonder she loves the Jews—guilty as hell!" Rose had said all that, and more, only Max escaping her final judgment. But Max, who had lived so long and now would be silent forever, Zellie's father, who had been silent all his life, humming a little tune to keep anger away, and despair—what of him? What of himself had he left behind?

"Who could believe it?" Rose had said, crying out from her single bed for him, though only Zellie was there. "Oh! Oh! Max! How could such a thing happen to a family?" She didn't moan but cried out, complained, frustrated, bitter, and finally silent. While you still have your parents, she had always said, you're not supposed to cry. It wasn't right. But what had happened? Why, Zellie had to wonder, had she shown such bitterness to her daughter, leaving behind the burden of such a question? Zellie wanted to ask, but she was no longer a daughter, she could not, and for the rest of her life, now, the question would be hers to answer.

"David," she said, and as David made his way to her she almost grabbed his arm. "David," she said, putting down her cup of tea. "Come take a walk with me. For a minute." He nodded, and they walked through the empty porch into the backyard. Where Pearl's garden had been was now a brick patio, with a built-in grill and redwood deck chairs.

Pearl was already there, standing alone, a small woman meditating with folded hands. When she saw them, she stood up straight and smiled widely. "Oh, David," she said, "I see where you're looking. But my time for gardens is over, that's all. It was time for a patio—you know what I mean?"

"Yes," David said.

"They still send me the catalogues, though, and every year I'm tempted. I could dig up a spot by the water, I guess. I don't know—maybe next year Stevey'll help. Where are you going, Zel?"

Zellie didn't answer, but David turned and said, "Over to the water. We'll be right back."

"Okay," said Pearl, "I was just asking. I understand." And she waved to them, shaking her head for a moment before turning back.

At the water they stood for a moment silently. The old cattails were overblown, and with each shudder of the reeds a new tuft separated and blew off. David wondered what there could be to say.

"Are you happy with Andrew?" she asked, suddenly.

He looked away from her, over the marsh, where the sun was setting. After a moment he said, "Yes, I am."

"I'm so glad," she said. "I worried so much over you. And now with AIDS—I guess you're very lucky."

"Yes," David said, hesitantly. "I guess I am."

"Do you think you'll always be together?"

He shrugged. "Yes."

"And what about Beth?"

He shrugged again, and again would not look at her. For the first time such a direct, vital question from his mother was too much. He was imagining instead a wedding ceremony, traditional, lavishly attended, in which, surrounded by family beneath the *huppah* and before the holy ark in the temple, he would be holding Andrew's hand, and they would bow their yarmulke-covered heads and be blessed by the community, everyone in new dresses and tuxedos and surrounded up and down with flowers. "We bless these young men," the rabbi would say, "these young lovers, and we celebrate their commitment." The clarinets would race, old melodies from Eastern Europe, and everyone would dance and eat from the buffet and raise their glasses for a toast. And what about Beth? Zellie might whisper, even to the last minute hoping for a reverse. Just as likely, just as unlikely, it would be Beth in the temple holding his hand, her own mother giving the blessing. No matter what they would both be there, Beth and Andrew, if only, as they had threatened, to blow their own brains out, and maybe David's as well, before anyone could take a vow. It was an impossible vision—not only such a marriage, such a blessing, but any certain life like that. Even their friends would mock such conservatism—reaching through travesty, they would say, for some sort of begrudging respect. No, no, David might object, it was just for the presents—the Cuisinart, the candlesticks—but that would be to hide the truth. Which one of them would be up there with him, in faith if not in fact, he didn't know. Any resolution, any larger vision of their lives, he could not imagine. And yet this too had once seemed impossible; this standing here simply with his mother, holding her hand, and looking together, honestly at last, as far as they could see.

He was staring out over the water, and Zellie looked over there as well. "Oh, David!" she said. "Look! Look at all the swans!" On the water, behind the reeds as far as the horizon, a flock of swans had taken refuge from the dusk. In the glint of the current, hundreds were stretching out their necks, dipping deep into the water, stretching and folding their wings in the last light before evening.

"I thought you were afraid of swans," David said.

"I am," she said. "Up close when they're honking at you. But not like this. Look!" she said, and pointed across to the weeping willows. Beneath the long, draping branches two swans were pressing breast to breast, curving their long necks down to rub beaks as well. Again and again the space in between was a heart, a perfect valentine. "Oh, David," Zellie said, touching him lightly on the arm, and holding him there.

When Pearl stepped back inside, Lonnie was leaning across the piano, writing in an old notebook. "What's that?" Pearl said, pointing, out of politeness, from a distance.

"Notes," Lonnie said.

"Notes?" said Pearl. "What kind of notes?"

"About the family. You know, Irene's mansion. Family notes."

"Why are you taking notes?"

"I always have," Lonnie said. "It's good material."

For a moment Pearl looked at her, shaking her head and struggling not to open her lips, not to criticize. In her eyes was a fury Lonnie had often seen but never understood, unaccountably silent, challenging and pleading at the same time, and now accompanied almost with tears, reflective and withheld. "Lonnie," she said at last, smiling but still shaking her head, "you can't write about our family."

Lonnie didn't answer.

"How could you?" Pearl continued. "You don't know what went on. You weren't there."

"Yes I do," she said. "I've heard the stories."

"Stories! You think you've seen all the skeletons in the closet? We only tell the good things, honey. Let me tell you, there was plenty of bad. My mother just told you the good things. She had it plenty hard herself, you know. A hard life. Oh, well! We all did. Zellie's my little sister, you know. I'm speaking for both of us." Her eyes were bright with deep feeling, hoping to be understood.

Lonnie shrugged and walked away into the kitchen. A candle was burning on the ledge by the sink. Irene took out a tray of noodle pudding from the oven. "Hi, Irene," Lonnie said.

"Hi, Lonnie."

"How have you been?"

"Fine," said Irene. "It's a sad time. She was a good woman —she lived a long life, Ms. Levin. How about you?"

"Oh, I've been fine."

"That's good," said Irene. They both nodded, until Lonnie found herself wondering when to stop. Even knowing all about each other as they did—Irene had been her nurse, after all, had bathed her, changed her, even punished her—they were still silenced, trapped, as if their two separate paths were already so far apart that although they still could see each other and wave, perhaps, the distance was too far to speak; any words would be lost. On an island far away Irene had her overgrown plantation, the mansion house filled with unknown children, husbands, poor relations—slaves as well, for all Lonnie knew. There were banana trees down there, nutmeg and cinnamon trees, and palm leaves waved by servants on hot summer days, swinging on the porch. Why wasn't she there now? Lonnie wondered. Why did she continue here cleaning houses? Lonnie would never go there herself; she could never ask. And now she saw what the end of her childhood with Irene had come to: even with another twenty-five years, she would never ask, she would never know.

It was true, she realized, what Pearl had said; even in her own world she could not know what had gone on before. The stories she had heard were only partial renderings. The real past, the real lives that had waited patiently and worked hard and unfolded slowly long before she was around to see them, were lost now, vanished, even to the ones who had lived them, even to the ones still alive. Max and Rose, her own grandparents, had catered at the mansions, ruins now, for dog shows, for the summer balls of the rich and elegant, for the rulers of the country. They had been cheated, by cousins, by sisters— egg cartons only halfway filled, meat undelivered, men at the counter without enough money to pay. It was the times, they said, it was the Depression; it was all so long ago. No one really knew when they were born, Ida, in a fit of vanity, having torn out that page from the family bible. All that was left, as Pearl had said, were slight stories, distorted and sentimental, too sweet or nostalgic for real life. And yet they had been real people, even then. Toward the end, Lonnie could see, flipping through, her notebook was filled with quick notes and descriptions, mere references to anecdotes long forgotten. Dreaming one night that her father had died, Rose's mother had gone back to Russia, she read. Back past all the borders she went, still a young woman, tipping the guards a second time with coins from between her breasts. Indeed he was sick, and soon he died. How did she know? her daughters always asked, answering, a moment later, that she had had a dream. Had she really gone back, or was that too a dream?

Once, Lonnie read, she herself had woken up screaming, as if the Nazis had come into the room to take her away, pushed her into trains, into cattle cars without air. They had taken away other little girls. Was that her own dream? She could not remember.

The rest, she could see—all those stiff pages written years before when, as a teenager, she had fumed alone in her room —were pages filled merely with complaints, criticisms, and grudging descriptions of people who once had seemed unreasonable, uncouth, insensitive. But that could not have been the truth, either. She could hardly even read her writing from that time, the cramped, secretive letters. The real vision of her life, she saw, of her family's life, had to be beyond her, above her, greater than her own knowledge, too big and too lofty and removed, and she would never know it. For better or worse, then, she was stuck firmly among them, her family, close to the ground, and she would do better merely to remember, or perhaps not remember, and trust simply to that. That was the real history, the real life—what she felt and carried with her all the time without trying.

Before Irene could dump out the coffee grinds, Lonnie pushed her notebook deep into the garbage pail and waited until it was safely covered over with the sopping black mess, and dirty napkins, and paper plates.

Outside, it was getting dark. The clouds, distant and glowing a moment before, were now ominous on the horizon. Zellie pulled her sweater closer around her shoulders and looked for a long time at her son. He was still watching the birds, and in profile like that he looked just like his father at thirty—the straight nose, the narrow face. "David," she said, "I wish you had gone to the seder this year. I feel bad that you missed it."

"Well, we made our own, sort of. Is there still a seder in Newark?" he asked. "All these years?"

"Of course!" she said vehemently, feeling that she had proved a point, though she wasn't sure. "Didn't you know that? Just because you haven't been there doesn't mean it hasn't been going on. It's a big family, David."

"I know that, Mom. But you haven't gone much, either."

"Not with Ma Rose sick. I couldn't bear to. But we all went this year. We made ourselves, in case it was her last one. I told you about it, you know. Well, I guess if you don't feel bad, I shouldn't."

"I do, Mom," David said, turning to her but not touching her. "I do. I couldn't have gone with Andrew, though, could I?"

"I don't know," she said.

"Well, anyway," he said, "I'm sorry I missed it."

"Me too," she said, more gently, and, holding him a moment around the waist, remembered not just that last seder but all the seders she had ever gone to, with children, with husbands, and with her parents alone, long before there was either husband or children to come along. Would they continue, she wondered, when she was no longer there?

Even now in the failing light it seemed to be one event, that seder, going on perpetually from year to year, though each time she would come to it only that one day. As she remembered it, a cold rain was always drumming down in huge drops, just as everyone crammed into the big Oldsmobile—Rose and Max, Minnie and Irv, Danny and Margie and Zellie, all in their dress clothes and winter coats. Pearl, once, was coming from New York with Gloria, with Harry, and, Pearl had said, by the way and at the last minute, with a friend of Harry's from the army, a Melvin Green from the Bronx. "What do you think of that, Max?" Rose had asked, pressing her lips together in the front seat, studying her lipstick with the upraised mirror of her compact.

Max had shrugged, but Minnie, from the backseat, laughed and tapped her sister's shoulder. "Oh, Rose!" she said. "You always see *it* in everything! He's just a friend of Harry's! A nice boy."

From the car, every town had looked the same. Traffic lights splintered and reflected in the windshield, and in the single drops clinging to her side window Zellie saw now red, now green, a miniature version of all the lights and darkening sidewalks which, revolving, changing color, seemed always to reflect the same corner, the same trestle, the same parked cars. Squeezed into a corner of the backseat, she pressed her face to the glass, watching people huddle against the cold evening rain, town after town, as if merely hunching their shoulders could protect them from the downpour. From Lewiston they traveled east through all the towns: mansions, slums, Jewish and gentile. An ancient sign—"Welcome to Union"—still hung lopsided across Main Street; here Betty and Dave had lived, here Vera and Moe lived still; here was the park where her parents had courted—here they had rowed in a boat, here he proposed on his knee. They were almost there.

"Max," said Rose, "can you speed it up? It's almost time."

They were stopped at a light, and Max started humming quietly to himself.

"Max," said Rose, but he didn't stop. "Zel," she said, turning around to the backseat, "we're almost there, dolly. What do you think? Are you happy? You'll see Harry again."

"I'll bet she can't wait," said Irv.

"Zellie," Minnie whispered, next to her. "What's the matter, dear?"

"Why doesn't she answer?" asked Irv. "What's she waiting for? Elijah?"

But, turning from curious eyes, Zellie remembered, she could only shrug, lean harder against the window, and stare down that road from light to light through her own reflection, closer and closer toward that place, still far away, where all the family would be waiting.

Where These Hands
Have Been

BARBARA IS HERE for my son again—her grandchild—and to prolong our parting just a bit, as well as to keep Barbara waiting, I have reminded Colin about our trip to the swings and the sandbox, the farewell visit I promised him before he goes away. He takes my hand, looking up at his grandmother to see whether or not she approves. I believe she has never spoken a word against me—in front of him—but children are sensitive plants, bending or shrinking at the slightest touch. Though she is anxious to take him and be gone, she smiles and raises her eyebrows: permission granted.

Begrudgingly she puts down her summer bag and Colin's small suitcase and follows him out to the elevator. We are silent all the way down. At the corner, where I usually let him run across the street to the park, Barbara takes his hand. We could have a conversation about this—my negligence even at street corners, her experience as a mother—but we have had all these conversations before, walking along the street, whispering in my apartment, spelling out or abbreviating words angrily on the phone. "What's a flying F, Daddy?" Colin asked me. "It's just an expression," I said, and drew him a picture. Now, we let the gestures speak for themselves. I let go of Colin's hand when the light changes, and Barbara takes hold on the other side. And so we cross.

In the park, however, Colin sees the Good Humor man and pulls away from his grandmother, running to take his place in the ambiguous line of young New Yorkers. He is smaller than the other unguarded children, but at five he has known the park for five years and stands with a certain propriety.

"You let him do that?" Barbara says, as we move more slowly toward the ice cream truck. "With all the crazy people in this world?"

"Sometimes," I say, and already we are there among them.

Barbara shakes her head, and Colin asks for the rocket kind, a tri-flavored ice in the appropriate shape. "Here," Barbara says, reaching into the pockets of her skirt, but I am younger, and quicker. "One Blast-Off," I say, and give the man my dollar, as Colin greedily unwraps his ice, and miraculously, like a model grandson, carries the paper to the trash.

Barbara is still pushing at the bottoms of her pockets, searching for change. "I would have brought my purse," she says. "You told me no."

"Forget it, Barbara," I tell her, "I've already paid." And I squeeze her arm reassuringly.

Once, it seems to me, I was high up on the scale of Barbara's affections. She knew me from the first as one of her daughter's peculiar but interesting college acquaintances, colorful, educational, and temporary. Those were experimental days, and as Barbara herself was a liberal, open-minded citizen of the enlightened community, she expected her daughter would be as well. Through college and then afterwards, Beth made her way with other men, then women, but then the first, experimental years became our real lives, I lost my hair, and Beth and I found that we were still together. She had moved downtown for a man, and I had moved uptown for the same reason. I was no longer dressing so colorfully—politically, we liked to say—but then I did show up at their summer house with a man, once or twice, and despite a few tears and tense moments, we all seemed to have reached an understanding—more or less.

"I do understand," Barbara told her daughter in those first, innocent years beyond college. "He's your special friend. I think that's very nice." We laughed about that one—"special friend"—for a long time, until Barbara started looking around, when she came to visit, at the mattresses pushed together on the floor. It was true that other men—wonderful men, Barbara said, a Wall Street lawyer, a doctor from Boston—would find me sitting there with a book sometimes when Beth invited them up after dinner. "Is your *friend* coming?" Barbara started asking, when we would meet her for lunch somewhere expensive, or drive up to the Cape. Innocence and euphemism were gone by then, but I hesitate to find another name.

Once, at a wedding, Beth's grandmother pulled me down to the next chair and looked me in the eye. She was Barbara's own mother, and was too old, she said, to be shy.

"I hear you're Beth's *special friend*," she said, nodding approval in advance. I've always responded well to that kind of economy, and told her indeed it was true. "That's nice," she said.

"It's hard," I said, "always having to explain to people."

"What's to explain!" she said, tapping my hand. "Whatever you are, you are. It's nobody's business but your own. You think I don't know what goes on? I'm a modern woman, I've lived a long time."

"Thanks," I said, and sat back in my chair. There was a band playing "Hava Nagila," and I had to speak up. "You know," I said, "most people have a hard time, understanding me and Beth."

"What's to understand?" said Beth's grandmother, whose name was also Rose.

"About me being gay," I said, leaving Beth out of it, and louder than I had the nerve, because of the music. I should mention that people were dancing in a big circle, everyone old and young, except for Rose, who really was too old, and myself.

"So? Gay!" she said, and flipped her hand in a gesture I thought was mockery. "So you should be ashamed? Enjoy yourself, is what I say. You're both young. You think I wouldn't be up there dancing if I could? If you can dance, you dance, if you can't, you can't."

By the time Colin was born, Rose was several years dead, or I would have asked her to explain once more, to everyone.

"What a mess!" Barbara says, wiping Colin's hands violently with a napkin. We are walking along the esplanade, Colin between us, watching the boats cruise by on the East River. A woman, nearly naked, reclining on the deck of a yacht, waves to us, and I wave back.

"Who was that?" Colin asks, staring after her.

"That was a mermaid," I say. "She fell in love and was transformed into a real person."

Barbara gives me a look and strokes Colin's neck. "That, darling, was a very rich lady."

"What happened to her tail?" Colin asks, but the Circle Line is drawing near, its loudspeaker loudly describing us, and the history of this park where the mayor lives. Hundreds of people wave, men and women, and Colin waves back to them.

"Who are they?" I ask, holding him against me at the railing. His dark hair is just washed and smells of Mr. Bubble.

Arching up, he looks into my chin, already patient with my jokes, but cynical. "Mermaids," he says, and goes on waving.

Even from the beginning—that is, while we were still in college—Beth told everyone she wanted to have a child. How much of that was the truth, even now I don't know. But she was afraid to trap herself, she told her mother, avoiding tenser issues, and mothers were still the maids, and there was no man—sometimes excluding myself—to convince her otherwise. The world was unsafe, she continued, polluted, doomed, and there were so many orphans already. For a while she talked about a refugee child, one of the thousands of Asians pouring in.

"You'll be ruined," Barbara said. "You'll have nothing but trouble. They're darling children, like any other, but it's not like your own. All I ever wanted was a grandchild—is that such a terrible thing?"

"Mother," Beth said, "for me it is. I'm just not ready." She would repeat her list of doom, the first bombs already pointing toward New York. "And," she said, "there is no one I'd care to have a child *with*."

"How about that nice man from Brookline," Barbara asked.

"You never met him, Mother."

"I spoke to him on the phone."

"Once. You spoke to him once. And I haven't seen him in a year."

"Any man," said Barbara, "who comes in and sees you with your *friend* is not going to be so happy about it. No wonder you haven't seen him in a year."

"He moved to a kibbutz, Mother. Outside Jerusalem. He wears *tzitzas*. He shaved his head." One long telephone sigh to the contrary, Beth had the last word. "All right?" she said, and her mother said, "All right."

I moved in, I moved out, uptown again near the hospital, and Beth came over sometimes to spend the night. When I met Andrew, it was at one of Beth's parties; anyone could see that times were changing.

"I think I'm dying," she said soon after that, leaning her head on my shoulder one day on the subway. Of her many ways to keep my attention, this was no longer the most effective. "If I am," she said, "I want us to have a child."

"I don't know," I said, pressing my fingertips against her temples. "What would we name it?"

"Alexandra," she said. "Persimmon. Joan."

"Yes," I said, "but suppose it's a boy?"

"It has to be a girl," she said. "To remember me by."

I never appreciated this kind of humor, and tried to speak in a general way. " 'Mrs. Jesús Ramírez,' " I read, " 'No Longer Suffers From Hemorrhoids.' " Soon we were out on the street again, and Beth took my arm. It was winter, and we crossed into the sun.

"Alexander," she said. "Christophe."

Again I objected, because our mothers would object. Chris, Kristina, Christiana—they are all *trayf* as can be.

"Quentin," she said, "Gilbert, Colin."

"You," I said, "are an anti-Semite," trying to make a joke, afraid already that Andrew would get wind of this; but Beth pulled away, into a coffee shop.

We looked at menus, ordered what we always ordered, and then I took her hand. "Okay," I said, "Colin," and her headache seemed better, she seemed to forgive me. I smiled and she half-smiled back, expecting a punch line. So I said, "What if you don't die?"

"Colin!" Barbara shouts, as Colin runs away from us to chase pigeons. He jumps into the middle of them and shouts "Pigeons!" and they fly around him, hesitant to leave their bread. The old woman who has been feeding them sits angrily on her bench, staring not at Colin but at me. "You scared them!" she says, and Colin walks calmly away as if he were innocent.

"Sorry!" I tell her, but she mutters toothlessly and turns

around, waiting for the birds to return. Colin has run ahead to the playground, and Barbara too has hurried on.

"Disgusting birds," she says, as I catch up.

"Are those same little boys there this year?" I ask. "Across the street?"

"The Salters," she says. "They haven't come yet. I assume they're coming."

"And do you think you'll go to Provincetown again, for the fireworks?"

Barbara stops and turns for a moment to look at me, not unkindly. "You know you can come up any time," she says. "You know that."

"I know that," I tell her. "I'll try to get away. But will you call me? Or, I mean, remind Colin to call? In case he forgets?"

"We'll call you tonight," Barbara says, nodding, as if that is the last anxiety I am allowed.

"And Barbara," I say, "is Carol Anne coming?"

"Yes. And she's bringing Hope along this time."

"Oh, really?" I cannot help looking surprised.

"Yes, really. I hope." She looks up, made nervous by her joke.

By now Colin has found his friends in the sandbox—a French boy of four whose father is dead, and two little girls, light-brown twins from Haiti. I know their mothers, and nod first to one, then the other.

"Carlene," I say, "this is Colin's grandma."

She is gently pushing a carriage back and forth, rocking her youngest, but she lights up to Barbara with a big smile and says loudly, "This is your boy?"

"Beth's mother," I say, nodding away her mistake.

"How do you *do*!" she says, and calls to Monique. "Monique, you meet Colin's grandma? This the *mother's* mother!" And Monique comes over to introduce herself, along with two other mothers we know, and also Mrs. Heathington, a nanny. Colin, sensing attention and possible praise, steps out of the sand and runs to us. He stands not by me but by Barbara, surrounded by mothers who all know Colin by name.

"Ain't that a boy!" one of them says, and Mrs. Heathington even strokes Colin's hair.

"You're a lucky grandmother!" she says, her head shaking more than usual.

Barbara bends down suddenly until she is just Colin's height, and hides her face against his neck, hugging him.

Colin was conceived in panic, though I think that is not so unusual. Beth could get pregnant, she was told, now but perhaps not later, and she was scared but not so surprised, I think, having worried so long that like anyone else she was vulnerable to everything terrible. But if life was slapping us in the face, it was also waking us up to our brief, meager power to slap it back, and shape it a little bit to our own designs. Without her asking me I agreed; three times that week, maybe three times the next, and sometime later she was pregnant. We had to laugh at what an ordinary couple we had become. Afterwards we stood naked in the kitchen cooking oatmeal.

"Have I cured you?" she asked with her half-smile.

"No," I said, stirring, and she said, "What a waste." I wanted to ask her the same question, again as a joke, but then just in time I stopped myself.

After a month the doctor said, "Are you aware that you're pregnant?"

At that we had to laugh.

My own mother was shocked, then quickly delighted by the news. But Barbara was overwhelmed. "I don't pretend to understand," she said at first. "But that's all right. You'll get it taken care of. I suppose you think this is funny. It's serious, you know. Your life is not a game. Thank God we live where we do."

Beth told her that she might not have the opportunity again and that she wanted the child.

"Oh, no!" Barbara said definitively, but Beth was thirty years old by then, and calm enough to keep smiling. "Well," Barbara said, "I'm not going to baby-sit for a single mother. Your father and I were baby-sitters long enough."

Before we could argue about it or I could say otherwise, Beth had told her we would get married. I was sitting there with her, on the bed, and didn't object. "Mom, come on," Beth said, sighing into the phone. And, looking at each other, we waited while her mother wept, and then was silent.

"When is Andrew moving out?" Beth asked me, soon afterwards.

"Why do you think he would do that?" I said. Andrew in fact had just raged, cried huge tears, and slammed the door behind him. "Wait!" I had said to him, meaning a year, two years. But he would not wait.

She said, "For God's sake, David, it's only appropriate!"

"No it's not!" I shouted, as a couple getting into their car stood watching. "It's not appropriate! Fuck appropriate! It's not appropriate at all!" And turning, I marched away through the parking lot.

Beth stood with her fists in the air. "Will you have a child with me or not?!" she called, and storming back, also with my fists in the air, I screamed, "Never, never never! I'll never have a child with you!"

"Well," she yelled, "good! Because I'll never have a child with you either!"

I must leave Barbara now sitting with the mothers, while Colin and I go to the bathroom. The building is decrepit and urine-soaked, but every door has been removed and there's a lot of supervision—against vagrants, I suppose, and homosexuals. Inside, a mother is standing with her son, zipping up his pants. "Sorry," she says, standing up guiltily, "We're almost done." When she is gone, we stand at the urinal together, and Colin watches the ever-flushing water while I read the graffiti. Phone numbers are penciled into the cement between the tiles, and dates—Thursdays at four, weekends at noon. Most of them are years old and will still be there, I am sure, when Colin is high enough to read them. For the moment he is finished and observes my greater endurance. "I'll meet you," he says, zipping up all by himself and rushing out. Before I am done, another mother comes in with her boy, glaring at me with my hands on my zipper. "I'm just leaving," I tell her, but she turns suddenly and walks out. With Colin gone I am again the dangerous one, the intruder, the man my grandmother always warned us about. You never know where his hands have been.

Back at the sandbox I sit down by Barbara, on the bench where I always sit. Behind us, children scream beneath the spray of water. From here we can see the sandbox, and the jungle gym, and, through the trees, a game of basketball. Here I have sat with many mothers, and with lovers, boyfriends, and men who were strangers but smiled sometimes if I would nod in the right way, holding my son. The young fathers are beautiful, almost all of them, because with their children they have to touch, and seem to be kind. I too, I know, attract attention. Men and women both stop to talk, handsome joggers, rich bachelor lawyers with their dogs.

"Where's Colin?" I ask, and Barbara turns to me blankly.

"You're kidding," she says. "He was with you, wasn't he?"

"Yes, but he raced back to the sandbox."

"Oh my God!" Barbara says, and stands up too quickly, almost losing her balance. "Didn't you stay with him? Didn't you see where he went?"

By now I am standing up as well, and together we run to

the sandbox, surveying the colorful little army of black and brown and blond. I step in among them, disturbing the sand forts and castles. Mothers stand up in annoyance, wary because I am frantic. "Carlene," I say, jumping out again, "Where's Colin—have you seen him?" She shakes her head and stands up helplessly to help. "You try the swings?"

Barbara and I run to the swings, to the jungle gym, to the fountain, but Colin is none of those screaming children. I wish he were, and stare too long into the water as if he will appear, soaking wet and excited, or crying and furious at some enemy.

Barbara grips my arm. "Where does he go?" she asks, very calmly, but her face is squeezed with fear.

"This is where we go," I say, confused, afraid to admit I am afraid. Blindly I look around again. Those who are gone are gone in a second, without a lingering trace, or an echo.

Barbara turns and walks away, past the fountain, unhesitantly into the men's room. Quickly she returns, stands very close and stares at me—full of anger, I think, even hatred. "What?" I say, frightened, also angry at her anger.

But her eyes are full of tears. She reaches for me and leans heavily, crying against my shoulder. "Oh, no," she says, "oh, no," and her arms, that never held me before, hold me tight.

"Barbara!" I say, "Barbara, wait!" and I run out past the basketball, onto the esplanade. There are joggers, and pigeons, and a parade of baby carriages. There are schoolgirls in uniforms, old people struggling for a step, men I have seen and looked at before, and through them all, in a second of clear space, I see Colin at the railing, looking through the bars.

"Hey there!" I say, from a distance, so he will not be frightened. "Hey there! Colin!" He turns around, waves quickly, and then turns back again. Running up, I grasp his narrow, delicate shoulders and the striped shirt I myself have pulled over his arms. Trusting my touch, he doesn't turn again, but with his legs and feet already safe between my own, he begins to climb up. I want to yell at him, squeeze him, scare him because I have been scared—how can he trust these are my hands, this anxious breath my own? The wind finds my tears; I can only squeeze him. My hands, I think, are too fragile a guard. So I press my arms around him, his slight, warm back against my breathing, my lips against his cheek.

"Stop!" he says, laughing but twisting free. When a yacht floats by, he waves and waves until a man with a drink sees him and smiles, waving back. "See? Mermaids!" he says, struggles from my grasp, and runs away into the shade where Barbara catches him in her arms, sweeping him up.

Once, we thought we could have whatever we imagined from life, everything sweet and enviable despite shaking heads and pointing fingers. Whatever it was we expected, our lives have unfolded differently. This summer Beth is in Venice; last summer she was in Greece. Before that for a long time it was Providence, where if staring at childhood walls and halls was a trial, her mother at least could help take care of Colin; and Colin, before he could walk, had traveled those miles between us too many times to count.

Even now I turn around always expecting a familiar face, a smile of recognition. But the room is empty, or the street is crowded with strangers, or else the eyes that search my own close by are new to me and cannot see where I have turned from. What is worse, they have turned from secrets of their own. Next to me a father calls to his son, *"Amore! Amore!"* expecting he will come. On the grass, just over a fence the height of pigeons, a man lies almost naked on his towel, searching eyes hidden behind the mirror of his dark glasses. I have seen him before; I will see him again. I have lain like that on the grass, and I have stood by the water calling out for love in my own language. I do not know, even now, what will come. But surely, I am both of those men.

• • •

Now Barbara wants to leave right away, but Colin objects this time and cries for the swings. Barbara will not look at me.

"Okay," I tell him, "but just a few pushes. Okay?" Over his grandmother's shoulder he nods his promise, but his eyes, I am sure, have conspired in half a wink.

"Goodbye, sandbox," he says, as we pass the pit of sand. Barbara has put him down at last, but holds his hand firmly in hers. I hold the other. "Goodbye, jungle gym. Goodbye, ice cream man. Goodbye, Carlene."

"Goodbye, sugar!" she calls back. "See you later!"

At the swings I push, while Barbara stands by, arms crossed, looking at her watch sometimes. "Higher," Colin calls, "higher," and though he screams whenever I push him, and though Barbara turns with her critical eye, I oblige with almost all my might. Each time, though, for an instant, I hold that small body in both my hands, and trust that in the nature of things, the faster he goes, the sooner he'll be back in my arms.

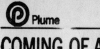 Plume

COMING OF AGE

Plume

NOVELS OF GENIUS AND PASSION